Margaret Bingley was born in Surrey in 1947 and was educated at Sutton High School for Girls. She worked briefly at the BBC and then in publishing. Now married, she live[illegible] [illegible]on and three Cavalie[illegible] [illegible] *Dead* is her sixth no[illegible]

By the same author

Children of the Night
The Devil's Child
Such Good Neighbours
The Waiting Darkness
After Alice Died

MARGARET BINGLEY

The Unquiet Dead

GRAFTON BOOKS
A Division of the Collins Publishing Group

LONDON GLASGOW
TORONTO SYDNEY AUCKLAND

Grafton Books
A Division of the Collins Publishing Group
8 Grafton Street, London W1X 3LA

Published by Grafton Books 1988

First published in Great Britain by
Judy Piatkus (Publishers) Ltd 1987

ISBN 0-586-07460-0

Printed and bound in Great Britain by
Collins, Glasgow

Set in Times

For my Father

Prologue

Kate couldn't remember the woods ever looking so lovely. At last the long, hard spring was over; all around her the bright green leaves and slender, long-stemmed bluebells seemed to share in her relief. Taking a deep breath of the mild, sundrenched air, she smiled with pleasure.

Beside her, sleeping contentedly on his stomach, Thomas lay in his carrycot. Thomas, who had set the seal on her blissful marriage. Of course she and Ray adored their three daughters, but to have a son at last, that was perfection. There were times when she wondered what she had done to deserve so much happiness.

Far away in the distance she could hear the voices of the children, her own daughters and six of their friends from school. It was Fiona's birthday, and she had chosen both the picnic and the location. A tall eight-year-old with a quicksilver mind she was a typical Gemini, forever talking and flitting from one hobby to the next, yet remaining surprisingly constant in her choice of friends.

Kate could remember having numerous 'best' friends at the age of eight, not so her daughters. They had a set of friends that never changed, which was nice. Even nicer was the fact that the children's mothers all got on so well.

Really and truly if a fairy appeared with a magic wand and offered Kate three wishes she wouldn't know what to ask for. She had everything that she could ever want. Her only request would be that nothing should change.

Singing softly to herself she began unpacking the large hamper. The paper plates had pictures of coloured ponies round the rims, replicas of the coloured ponies with matching tails that littered Fiona's bedroom. There were paper serviettes with the same design, and even the plastic cloth spread on the ground had ponies on it.

Kate put the flans and meat rolls in the centre of the cloth, then opened plastic boxes containing various salads. The pats of butter and flasks of cold drinks were in the cool box; she would deal with them last.

Thomas smacked his lips together and stirred slightly. She glanced across at him, and blinked as a sudden flash of light fell across her face. Instinctively she put up a hand to shield her eyes, then gave a surprised smile.

'What are you doing here? I didn't hear you coming.'

No answer.

Again the unsettling flash of light; all at once she saw the glint of a razor-sharp bread knife in the newcomer's hand. She frowned, not yet alarmed.

'Where did you find that? Did I drop it along the path?'

No answer.

'I need it to slice this french bread.'

The knife was turned slightly, but not offered to her.

'It's lucky you found it. Would you like . . .?'

With terrifying speed and deadly accuracy the knife moved, plunging directly into her throat and severing the jugular vein with one easy movement.

Everything happened so quickly that Kate had no time to defend herself, no time to call for help, no time to do anything except stare in astonishment at her assailant before she fell back on to the grass.

The knife was carefully wiped with one of the Little Pony serviettes, then returned to the hamper. After that the murderer walked slowly and calmly away.

In the woods Kate's blood gushed from the gaping wound, running in hideous, scarlet rivers along the folds of the plastic cloth. The only sound to be heard was the splashing of the liquid, but eventually even that ceased and the woods were once again peaceful.

It was still a beautiful day. The leaves were still green and the grass lush. The bluebells remained straight and eye-catching. Thomas continued to sleep peacefully.

The only difference was that twenty-eight-year-old Kate Burgess was no longer there to appreciate the beauty of it all, and four children were now motherless.

Chapter 1

It seemed to Amy that the entire village of Lower Ditton had turned out for the funeral of her beloved sister Kate. As the minister gave his litany of praise for the murdered woman, justified praise for Kate had been one of the most loved people Amy knew, she attempted to distract her mind from the coffin and its contents by glancing round the chapel.

She knew many of the people by sight for she had spent three summer holidays here during the past six years, yet somewhere among them – or so the police suspected – sat Kate's murderer. He, or she, would doubtless have attended in case their absence was noted and commented upon. She wondered how they felt seeing the three pale-faced little girls seated alongside their father in the front pew.

Personally she would not have taken children of eight, six and four to a funeral, but the girls had urged their father to let them come and he – hopelessly adrift without the secure anchor of Kate's love – gave in.

Amy had expected tears or possibly hysterics from the children but so far there had been only this frozen, silent grief. The one outward sign of their distress was the way in which they grasped each other's hands, their small knuckles showing white with strain.

Now the minister had finished, and she heard the soft, discreet hum behind the curtains as the coffin slowly vanished from sight to be swallowed up by the furnace beyond.

It was the girls who kept Amy from collapsing. She could scarcely breathe and the knot of tears in her throat threatened to choke her but she remained dry-eyed. If her nieces could maintain their composure in public then she wasn't going to jeopardize that with a purely selfish display of crying.

Their father was beyond such reasoning. His muffled sobs grew louder and he half-rose from his seat, arms moving in one final, vain attempt to hold back his wife's body; he wanted to keep her with him for one more hour, one more minute, so that he could postpone this final physical parting.

The villagers rose to sing *'Oh God our help in ages past'*, Fiona's voice pure and clear from the opening notes. Ray Burgess continued to sob, making no attempt to join in. Amy looked over the heads of her nieces, trying to catch his eye, but without success. She realized that he had lost all self-control and wondered how he was going to cope on his own.

'*Time like an ever rolling stream, bears all its sons away*,' sang the congregation.

And daughters, thought Amy with horror. Never again would she and Kate laugh over their childhood memories. Never again . . .

'NO!' screamed Ray as he stumbled from the pew. Half-running, half-walking, he lurched towards the front of the chapel and the closed curtains.

'KATE! KATE!'

Most people stopped singing, but one or two carried on, trying for the children's sake to pretend it wasn't happening. The minister attempted to support Ray's sagging body with strong arms, glancing towards the front pew for assistance.

There was only Amy who could help him for the

children were staring round-eyed at their father, while Ray's parents huddled together in shocked bewilderment. She moved carefully past the girls to where Ray and the minister stood and her seven stone, combined with the minister's twelve, proved enough to assist her brother-in-law out of a side door into the shockingly inappropriate brightness of a hot June day.

Gently they lowered him to the ground, Amy leaving a hand comfortingly on his shoulder. She was not Kate, bore no physical resemblance to her sister, but she was her only blood relation and the nearest to his wife that Ray could come apart from his children. He seemed soothed by her touch.

A few minutes later the girls led the mourners out. They had retained their almost unnatural control, but their eyes were blank – that is until they rested on their father and then, for one shocking moment, Amy could have sworn that the three faces twisted fleetingly into glances of gleeful contempt. The change was so brief that afterwards she decided she must have been wrong for she knew them to be gentle, caring little girls.

Back at the family home women busied themselves in Kate's old-fashioned kitchen. Amy had often suggested that her sister should have a new kitchen with built-in hob and fitted cupboards, but Kate preferred the homely comfort of her large Aga and the big, wooden table with its unmatched dining chairs.

Somehow the realization that now there would never be an opportunity for Kate to change her mind seemed ridiculously distressing, and this time Amy was unable to keep back her tears. A fresh-faced woman in her late thirties came over to comfort her.

'It must be a terrible loss,' she sympathized, patting the

younger woman on the shoulder, 'but you must try not to upset the children. They've been marvellous. Mind you, I don't think they realize the finality of it all. Certainly not Sophie or Georgina; Fiona might, being that much older.'

Amy bit her bottom lip. 'I'm sure they all understand,' she gulped. 'That's what makes their courage so unnerving. If I can't cope, then how can . . .'

'Children are incredibly resilient. See that little boy over there?'

Amy glanced in the direction of the woman's pointing finger.

'Yes.'

'Well, only eight months ago he lost *both* his parents in the most dreadful car accident. The family car's brakes failed and it went under the back of a lorry. You can imagine the kind of injuries . . . His mother was literally torn apart. They had to put her remains in a black plastic bag.'

'Please! I don't think . . .'

'Yes, but look at him! Naturally he was devastated at the time, especially since there were no relations to take him in, yet he's adjusted incredibly well.'

Amy studied the small boy carefully. He was eight or nine, she thought, a pleasant, brown-haired, open-faced child with a sprinkling of freckles across his nose. When he caught her looking at him he gave her a quick, shy smile before turning away.

'Who's looking after him?'

'A man called Carlo. He's quite wonderful with children, and when he offered to take Colin in we all agreed it was the best possible solution.'

'What did Carlo's wife think about it?'

'Oh, Carlo isn't married. Mind you, all the eligible

young women round here do their best to rectify the matter, but without success! No, Carlo lives alone.'

'Surely the boy needs a woman's care?'

'Naturally we thought about that, and so *all* the women in the village help both Carlo and Colin. They're positively spoilt!'

'How lovely. I come from a town myself and forget how kind village people are.'

'We all know what it's like in the cities,' the woman agreed.

Privately Amy had doubts about the wisdom of allowinng a childloving bachelor to foster a young boy, but knew better than to voice them.

'Where does this Carlo come from?' she asked, partly to help keep her mind off Kate.

The woman gave her a sideways, measuring glance. 'If you stay here you'll be able to ask him yourself, but he isn't communicative with adults. Now, if you're feeling better I'll go and help Christine with the tea.'

'Yes, of course.'

Alone again Amy sat down in the nearest chair. Her legs felt weak as she remembered Ray's face when he ran towards the disappearing coffin. She looked quickly round the room but there was no sign of him; she wondered where he could be. Just then Sophie came up to her.

'Aunty Amy, Thomas needs changing. Do you know how to change a baby's nappy?'

'Just about. I had plenty of practice when you were little!'

'Good. He's in the small bedroom. Will *you* look after us now that Mummy's dead?'

Amy flushed. 'I don't think so, darling, I've got my photographic business to manage back home, you see.

Besides, Daddy won't want me around the house all the time.'

'*We* want you.'

'That's very sweet of you, Sophie, but let's wait and see, shall we?'

Sophie smiled, showing a gap between her front teeth. 'Yes, we'll wait and see. Fiona thinks you're the best person to take over, so I expect you will. Fiona's usually right.'

'I'm afraid Fiona's influence doesn't extend into the adult world, my love! Now, let's find this baby brother of yours.'

Upstairs the house was pleasantly cool. Amy was just approaching the smallest of the four bedrooms when she was startled to see Fiona and two other children leaving Kate and Ray's room. Fiona didn't look in the least disconcerted by her aunt's appearance, but her friends did.

'What were you doing in there?' asked Amy.

'Making sure that Daddy was all right.'

'I'm sure he doesn't want a stream of children visiting him at a time like this.' Amy's voice was over-harsh but she was upset by her niece's attitude.

'He's asleep. He didn't know.'

'He might have been awake.'

The smaller of Fiona's friends, a dark-haired girl with a wide, full-lipped mouth and broad forehead, shook her head.

'Not after what the doctor gave him. Knock-out drops, he told my father.'

'Did he indeed? And who, may I ask, are you?'

'Gillian. I live next door.'

'Well, Gillian, it isn't very polite to go wandering into adults' bedrooms, as I'm sure you know. Why don't you go back to your own home now? Most people will be leaving soon, and I need Fiona's help getting some lunch.'

'Sure.' The tone was agreeable, the smile wide, and yet . . .

'Off you go then!'

Fiona lifted her chin as though about to argue but seemed instantly to change her mind. Instead, her shoulders drooped.

'I wish Mummy hadn't died,' she said sadly. 'Especially not on *that* day.'

'What day?'

'The day when Daddy had been so cross with her. That's why he keeps crying, because he never had the chance to say sorry.'

Amy was astonished. 'Fiona, I'm sure you're wrong. I never knew your parents to argue over anything.'

'I only said Daddy was *cross*. I didn't say he hit her.'

'HIT HER? What on earth are you talking about?'

'I said he *didn't* hit her.'

'Fiona, have you been talking to anyone else like this?'

'Yes.'

'Who?'

'My friends.'

'Well, if you don't want to cause your father a lot more unhappiness, I suggest that you stop discussing it with anyone at all. Is that clear?'

Fiona looked bewildered. 'What have I said? Why are you so cross? Is it because Mummy's dead?'

'No! That is, yes, in a way. You see, darling, until the police find out who killed your mother everyone is under suspicion, and if you go around talking about Daddy hitting Mummy . . .'

'I said he *didn't* hit her!'

'I know. Unfortunately that implies that there have been times when he did.'

'Does it?'

'To an adult, yes, I'm afraid it does.'

'Oh.'

'So, you understand what I mean when I say . . .'

'Yes, of course. I won't mention Daddy hitting Mummy. It will be a secret. Gillian and Jody won't either; they're my friends.'

'Fiona, you're still doing it! Your daddy never hit your mummy, now did he?'

The three girls fixed bland stares on her. In the room to their left Thomas gave a small cry. Amy suddenly felt hot and horribly uncertain.

'Did he?'

All at once Fiona smiled. 'I'm not allowed to talk about it! Come on, Gillian, you'd better go. Is Colin here?'

'I expect so, I saw Carlo.'

Politely they waited for Amy to move out of their way before walking down the stairs, leaving her shaken and wondering for the first time if Kate and Ray had really been as happy as she had imagined.

Somehow or other Amy got through the rest of the day, assisted by Sara, Jody's mother, who had been Kate's closest friend. She seemed more shocked than anyone by the tragedy.

'I can't believe it,' she reiterated for the tenth time as she dried one of the bone china cups much treasured by Kate. 'She was so kind and friendly. Why would anyone want to murder her?'

'I think the police are equally puzzled. Particularly as they're certain it was someone she knew. Presumably that's because there was no sign of a struggle and no . . . that is, she hadn't been sexually assaulted.'

'I'm beginning to think there's some kind of curse on this village,' continued Sara. 'First of all Jacqueline, then Wendy, and now Kate. The odds against three young women dying inside twelve months in a small village like this must be pretty astronomical, wouldn't you think? It's really scary, like *Ten Little Niggers* or whatever it's called these days.'

Amy felt a prickle of fear touch her skin. 'Who were Jacquline and Wendy?'

'Jacqueline was Colin's mother. His guardian was at the service today with him. Rather a . . .'

'You mean the little boy who lost his parents in a car crash?'

'That's right. Jackie was his mother. Then Wendy was – or possibly still is – the mother of twin boys, Richard and Samuel. They're ten and live three houses up from here. She vanished a year ago next month. The children were at school, Ben – her husband – out at work, and when the boys came home in the late afternoon she wasn't there.'

Amy shivered. 'You mean she just vanished? No note? No secret lover?'

'A *secret* lover would be impossible in a village this size! Besides, Wendy adored Ben and the boys. She would never have gone off like that. We grew up together, I knew her as well as I know myself. Believe me, Wendy would never have left voluntarily.'

'What do the police think?'

'Until this week they were pretty half-hearted about continuing the search for her. They were certain that she'd absconded, like hundreds of other women all over the country who apparently suddenly decide that they can't stand their family any more and go off to make a new life for themselves.'

'And now?'

'Now they're willing to consider the possibility that she, too, was murdered.'

Amy felt cold. It was horrible to know that one of the conventionally grieving faces she had seen today belonged to someone who had most probably killed two young women from his own village. She thought of the killer as a man because no normal woman would deprive families of their wives and mothers, but then neither would any normal man. Nevertheless, in her heart she felt sure the killer was a man.

'Aunty!' The childish voice brought her back to the present.

'Yes, Georgina?'

'May I go and play with Colin before I go to bed, please?'

Amy hesitated. 'I don't think . . .'

'Let her go,' urged Sara. 'Carlo's marvellous with children.'

'So I gather. Well, if you think it will be all right.'

'Much the best thing, I'd say.'

'Off you go then, Georgina. I'll fetch you in an hour.'

'Thank you, Aunty!' shouted her six-year-old niece, going up on tiptoe to plant a kiss on Amy's cheek. Immediately Fiona trailed into the kitchen, sucking a sweet.

'Where's Georgie going?'

'To play with Colin.'

'To *Carlo's*? That's not fair. I want to go too.'

'Oh, Fiona, surely you wouldn't mind helping me just a little bit tonight? Thomas needs bathing and . . .'

'I never wanted a stupid brother anyway!' shouted polite, self-controlled Fiona. 'I *am* going to see Carlo, so there!' She ran away, slamming the back door behind her.

A shaken Amy hoped that wherever Katie was she

couldn't see the speed with which her children were adapting to their loss.

Unnatural. The word lingered disturbingly in her mind, and she knew why. She was used to children, and good with them in her own way. It was a necessary qualification in her line of work, where portraits of children provided her bread and butter. Usually she could quickly get a youngster into a relaxed, happy mood, thereby achieving natural, attractive photographic studies.

Today all of the children she'd encountered had been too controlled, too detached. It was definitely unnatural, and she wondered if they were concealing something from her. She must try to find out, for a vital clue to the identity of Kate's killer might well be locked in the children's minds. If so, it was also possible that they themselves were in considerable danger . . .

At seven o'clock Sara left and Amy went upstairs to check on Thomas. He was awake but happy and, just as she was pondering whether it was safe to leave four-year-old Sophie alone with the baby while she went to collect Fiona and Georgina, her brother-in-law emerged from his bedroom.

He looked grey. His skin had a dead appearance, his brown hair seemed faded and dull, and his dark-ringed eyes were sunken. Even his walk had changed. He shambled like an old man. When he caught sight of Amy he attempted a smile.

'Sorry I've been up here such a long time. The doctor must have knocked me out.'

'He did! Don't worry, I've had plenty of help from the neighbours. I'm glad you're up now, though, because I've got to collect Fiona and Georgie from a friend's house and I didn't like to leave the other two alone with you asleep.'

'Where have they gone?'

'Colin's house.'

Ray's face darkened. 'They spend far too much time with that boy. I keep telling Katie but she won't listen. She thinks . . . thought . . .' His voice cracked.

'I won't be long,' promised Amy, and fled, unable to face his grief yet again when her own was still threatening to overwhelm her.

Sara had told Amy that Colin and Carlo lived at number eleven Bush Close but she hadn't mentioned that the address also housed a health food shop. Amy hesitated outside the front door with its large CLOSED sign in the window, then walked through a small wooden side gate and round the back of the timbered house into a large, sloping garden with plants growing all over the lawn as well as in the flower beds.

She was just admiring this unusual but effective layout when she heard footsteps behind her, and turned to find herself face to face with a man who was undoubtedly Carlo.

He was of average height, five foot eight or nine she guessed, but since she was only five foot two he seemed tall beside her. His hair was jet-black flecked with an occasional streak of grey and grew in crisp curls away from his high forehead.

His eyes were a deep brown, the lashes so long that they curled at the tips. Eyelashes that a woman would kill for reflected Amy. His nose was slender and high-bridged, his cheekbones sharply etched, and in repose his mouth had the almost rosebud shape normally seen only on small babies.

The overall effect was one of aristocratically chiselled perfection, but what made him so heart-stoppingly handsome was his skin. It was golden-brown with a light flush of colour on the cheekbones, and it was flawless. She felt that if she reached out and touched his face it would be like caressing a peach. Never, in all her life, had she seen or imagined such a man could exist outside the pages of a women's romance.

He stood quite still while she studied him, almost as though he expected it, and when she finally realized what she was doing and hastily averted her eyes he stepped forward, holding out his right hand.

'You must be Kate's sister. I am so sorry about her death. She was a lovely person.'

He spoke English well, but just a shade too precisely. Once again Amy wondered where he had come from before his words, spoken in a soft, kind voice, brought tears springing to her eyes.

'Grief is natural,' he added quietly. 'It is a healer.'

'Private grief, yes, but when the children are around I . . .'

'It is good for them to see grief. They need to know that their mother is missed.'

'I hadn't thought of it that way.'

'Few people do.'

She managed to tear her eyes away from him and looked round for the children. There was one thing that puzzled her. She could see why the unmarried girls chased him, but his attraction for children seemed inexplicable. He had a solemn, almost stern set to his features and there was nothing in the least childlike about him. She had expected a Peter Pan figure, not an archetypal Romeo.

'I'll call them,' he said. 'They're inside, in Colin's room.'

Since he didn't invite her into his house she remained on the edge of the lawn, still stunned by the physical beauty of the man. A few moments later he emerged with the children grouped around him. Fiona looked faintly hostile when she saw her aunt, but Georgina ran over to her.

'Aunty Amy! I was telling Carlo that you're here to look after us now that Mummy's gone. She's nice, isn't she, Carlo?'

'Very nice,' he responded solemnly.

'I don't think . . .'

The children and Carlo looked at her questioningly. She hesitated. 'Nothing's been arranged yet,' she said at last. The little group relaxed. Georgina continued to chatter about some game they'd been playing, Fiona wandered slowly over to join her sister and at last the three of them made their way to the gate.

'Thank you so much for having them,' Amy told Carlo. 'I hope they weren't any trouble?'

'In my experience adults are usually more trouble than children.'

Amy was decidedly taken aback for there was no trace of humour in the statement.

'Well, that's one way of looking at it! Goodbye for now.'

'Goodbye.'

Colin smiled his shy smile and whispered something to Fiona, who giggled. After they'd taken a few paces Amy turned back to wave and caught Carlo looking down at Colin. On his face was the most brilliant, hundred-watt smile she had ever seen. The warmth of it seemed quite literally to be bathing the boy in a golden light.

She stood watching them, and then a cloud moved across the sky and the golden glow vanished. The light had been an illusion but not the smile, that had been very real. One day she would like him to smile at her like that, but she suspected that however long she stayed in the village it wouldn't happen. He had made it clear that it was children he preferred, and she believed him.

Giving herself a shake she walked briskly back to Kate's house. She was only here to steer the family through the next few difficult days, until they managed to establish some sort of workable routine for themselves, then she would return to Leicester and her photographic studio.

Just the same, she wished that she knew what her sister had thought of Carlo. Kate's intuition over people was generally very sound; she hadn't been swayed by outward appearances. Yes, Kate's opinion would have been extremely interesting.

Chapter 2

At ten P.M. Amy decided that she couldn't sit opposite Ray in complete silence any longer. They hadn't spoken since the children went to bed, and at least in her own room she could enjoy the luxury of a good cry.

'I'll be going up now, Ray,' she murmured. Immediately he lifted his chin from his chest and looked intently at her.

'Please, don't. Not yet. I must talk to you.'

'There's always tomorrow. We'll both feel better then.'

'No! This is something I need to say tonight, before I try and sleep myself.'

Amy sat down again, remembering Fiona's words about a quarrel.

'What is it?'

He fixed his gaze on a point somewhere beyond her right shoulder and then began to talk quickly, without any pauses, as though terrified of stopping before all the words were out.

'It's my fault that Katie died. But for me she wouldn't have been alone in the woods with only the children for company, she'd have been protected. On Fiona's birthday morning, when the girls were chattering about the picnic, Georgina mentioned Colin's name. I knew very well that Colin hated being separated from his guardian – not surprisingly when you consider what he's been through – and I asked how they'd persuaded him to join them. "Carlo's coming too," Georgina told me. "We *all* wanted Carlo to be invited, he's such fun."

'I was pretty annoyed. I asked Kate what the devil she

thought she was doing trekking off into the woods with a man like Carlo, but she just widened her eyes in astonishment. That was the trouble with her, she imagined everyone to be as straightforward and loyal as she.

'Then she laughed at me, and I lost my temper. I shouted something about no wife of mine going off with a foreign gigolo while I was hard at work, and all at once the happy atmosphere was spoilt.

'Katie went very quiet and said that she'd never intended to upset me, and if that was really how I felt then Carlo would have to stay behind, even if it meant losing Colin, too.

'Fiona started to sulk, but I said it *was* how I felt, and why didn't Kate grow up and think things through before she acted?

'In the end Carlo didn't go, neither did I, and Katie was murdered. But for my stupid jealousy it would never have happened because she'd have had a man there to protect her. What makes it even worse is that we parted on bad terms. When I realize that I'll never get the chance to apologize, I can't bear it. I'd give anything for the chance to tell her just how much I loved her.'

'She knew,' Amy said quickly. 'She used to tell me how lucky she'd been meeting you. She would have understood why you said what you did that day.'

'I don't,' said Ray flatly. 'It was ridiculous. Kate had never shown any interest in Carlo, nor he in her. Everyone round here knows that he likes women, but only single ones. He'd never have caused trouble in a marriage, any more than Kate would have allowed herself to be caught up in some illicit relationship, so why . . .?'

'Did you do it? Because you resent him, I imagine. He's ridiculously handsome, and I'm sure most men must feel the same. Don't build it up out of proportion, Ray. There are so many "if's" in a situation like this.

'*If* it had rained there wouldn't have been a picnic. *If* Fiona had been born on time instead of prematurely then the party wouldn't have been on that particular day. You can go on thinking like that forever, but there's no point. It's over, Ray. Kate's dead, and now it's up to the police to find out who did it, while you and the girls have to learn to come to terms with your new way of life.

'Do you think Kate would have wanted you tearing yourself apart like this? Of course not. She was the last person on earth to bear anyone a grudge. You've got to think positively, Ray, for the girls' sake if not your own.'

'And Thomas . . .' continued Ray, as though she hadn't spoken. 'She was so excited about us having a son, and now she'll never see him grow up.'

At that he burst into loud sobs that shook him from head to toe. Amy waited a few moments, but when they continued she turned and retreated to her own room where she finally allowed herself to cry, struggling blindly with the buttons on her blouse as she tried to undress.

In a way she was relieved to hear about the quarrel from Ray since it explained what Fiona had been talking about. That was what made dealing with children so difficult. You couldn't always trust their reactions because they saw things so differently from adults; they grasped the basic truth of a situation but failed to comprehend the nuances of adult conversation. They sensed what was happening around them, but didn't fully understand.

Although it was very late Colin wasn't asleep. He was standing staring out of his bedroom window. Carlo was beside him, his expression thoughtful.

'The police want to talk to you again tomorrow, Colin.

I think they're hoping you might remember some detail that you missed out before.'

The boy shrugged. 'I can't. There's nothing else to tell. Jody started screaming. I ran over to her and found Fiona's mummy lying across the tablecloth, bleeding. Bleeding a lot. She was quite dead.'

'Yes; the trouble is, they don't have any idea who did it and they're getting desperate.'

'I didn't see anyone. I ran to the village for help and I didn't meet a single person on my way.'

'No.'

'They haven't found Richard and Samuel's mother either, have they?'

'Not yet. The Inspector's hoping she went away voluntarily.'

'What does that mean?'

'Of her own accord.'

'She wasn't very nice, you know. She went with other men.'

'So you told me.'

'She went with Jody's father.'

'With Pete?'

'Yep.'

'I never knew that.'

'She deserved to die really, don't you think?'

'I can understand your reasoning, certainly.'

Colin tilted a surprised face towards his guardian's. 'Surely you agree? You know what that kind of thing leads to.'

'Yes.'

'Of course, Pete was just as wicked.'

'Possibly more so.'

The small boy looked up into the calm, striking features of the one man in the world he truly adored.

'More?'

'Men should be stronger than women, resist temptation. Or, in Pete's case, it was probably more a case of not providing the temptation in the first place. Casual promiscuity wreaks havoc with people's lives.'

All at once the dark eyes were shadowed with memories, memories that still retained the power to hurt. Colin slipped his hand into the man's.

'Don't get upset, Carlo. It will come right in the end.'

'I'm not upset, only remembering. It's time you were in bed.'

'What about school tomorrow?'

'I'll take you after the police have been. The shop can stay closed for once. Come along, let me tuck you in.'

The boy snuggled beneath his blankets. 'Fiona's aunty is pretty, isn't she? Like a doll, all neat and smiling. I wouldn't mind you marrying her, Carlo, then we'd be a proper family.'

'I'll bear that in mind. Good night.'

There was no reply. Colin was already asleep. It was no wonder that people marvelled at the way he had adapted to life with Carlo for he looked like a child without a care in the world.

Perhaps he was. Perhaps his life had never been happier. Who could tell? As Amy had thought earlier that evening, it was difficult to fathom the workings of a child's mind.

The following morning she discovered how chaotic getting three small girls ready for school could be, especially while coping with a crying baby and a father who refused to do anything.

By the time Ray set off for his packaging firm at eight, she was exhausted and depressed.

'Doesn't Daddy ever help in the mornings?' she asked Fiona as she cleaned three pairs of sandals at once.

'Nope! He used to say it was women's work. Mummy didn't mind. Do you?'

'Let's say I don't agree with him. I believe in equality of the sexes, at least in the mornings! Is there anything I've forgotten?'

'Yep!' stated Fiona with immense satisfaction.

'What?'

'Our packed lunches.'

'For all of you?'

'No, Sophie eats the school dinners.'

'Really, Fiona, why didn't you tell me earlier?'

Fiona started to cry.

Amy sighed. 'Sorry, I shouldn't have snapped at you but I'm surprised your father didn't mention it. Do you like jam sandwiches?'

'We aren't allowed jam. The teacher says it makes our fingers sticky.'

'Cheese?'

'Cheese and what?'

'Tomato?'

'I suppose so. Colin brings wholemeal rolls filled with chicken and salad, and lovely crunch bars made with bran and honey. He has . . .'

'Bully for Colin! Not having the advantage of a health shop in the front room I can't quite match Carlo's standard of cuisine.'

'I want paper,' announced Sophie, sitting down on the kitchen floor.

'For school?'

'Uh-huh, for my bottom. I've done some business.'

Amy didn't know whether to laugh or cry. She was struck yet again by the peculiar detachment that Fiona was showing. When Amy had spent the previous summer with Katie and her family, Fiona had been a proper little chatterbox, poking her nose into everyone's business and bustling around hindering Amy in every task. She had changed a great deal, yet somehow it didn't seem like a recent change for Georgina and Sophie weren't put out by her attitude. She wondered what had caused her withdrawal.

'You're meant to do your business in the bathroom,' she said at last, managing to keep her voice light. 'You must have driven your mother mad carrying on like this.'

'She didn't notice,' said Fiona coolly, 'not once she'd got Thomas.'

All three girls fell silent. So that was it, thought Amy, the green-eyed monster had caused the change. Poor Fiona.

'I'm sure that isn't true, darling. Will you sort out the satchels while I clean up your sister?'

'No, and it is true.'

'Fiona! I realize this is a difficult time for you but . . .'

There was a tap at the back door and Sara walked in, holding Jody's hand.

'Everything OK? I thought you might need an extra pair of hands.'

'Don't I just! Am I pleased to see you!'

After that things went smoothly, and by a quarter to nine the three girls were on their way, skipping along the pavement chattering away to Jody without a care in the world. No one could have guessed that their mother had just died, reflected Amy. Not that she wanted them sobbing and clinging all the time, but at the moment they gave no sign of any distress whatsoever. It was quite eerie.

Remembering that Colin, too, had taken his loss with apparent equanimity she felt a sense of unease and decided to find out how the twin boys were coping with their mother's disappearance. She would feel much better if they turned out to be frightened and insecure, because natural childish reactions in the village of Lower Ditton were so far conspicuous only by their absence.

At the time the children were arriving at the school gates, Inspector Barbor climbed out of a police car and walked round to the back of Carlo's house. He liked the man, and the extremely sensible young lad he had living with him. This visit was really one final despairing attempt to get some sort of a clue as to the identity of Kate Burgess's killer. He didn't expect anything to come of it, but there was no harm in one last try.

Ten minutes later he was sitting in the front room above the shop, studying the boy curled up on a bean bag opposite him.

'Colin, what were you playing while Fiona's mother was putting out the picnic food?'

'Stuck-in-the-mud.'

'What's that?'

'I've told you already. I told you about the game on the day it happened.'

'I know, but I didn't quite understand.'

The boy raised his eyebrows while Carlo glanced at the Inspector. He was a good-looking fellow thought Barbor, and wondered if there had been a woman somewhere in his past who was responsible for his apparent lack of interest in matrimony. Barbor's own daughter had been keen on Carlo and he had dated her once or twice, but that was months ago, before he had taken the child in. Since then he had stayed with Colin day and night.

'Two of us were "it" – you know, catchers. Mark and me were on first. We had to chase the others and tig them. When you're tigged you can't move until someone else crawls through your legs and sets you free.'

'Why's it called stuck-in-the-mud, I wonder?'

Colin shrugged.

'And is it a noisy game?'

'Yep, especially with girls playing. They screech and yell a lot when you're catching up with them.'

'If Mrs Burgess had called out to you, do you think you'd have heard?'

'Just an ordinary shout, or a scream?'

'Let's say a scream.'

'Oh, yes.' There was no hesitation. 'We'd have heard a scream.'

'You said that before, Colin, but how can you be positive when the girls were already screaming as they played?'

'A woman's scream is really piercing; it goes right through your head.'

Inspector Barbor gave a small smile. That was what television did to children.

'Have you ever heard a woman scream?' he queried gently.

'Yes, lots of times.'

'On the television?'

'That doesn't count, does it? I mean, television is only pretend.'

'Quite true, so as you say, it doesn't count.'

'I wasn't counting TV.'

'You weren't?'

'No, I was thinking about my Mum. She and Dad were always screaming at each other, and her scream could wake me up. That was an angry scream, of course, but probably a frightened one would be just as loud.'

The Inspector had known Jacqueline and George well, and as far as he knew they'd got on better than most married couples. He was surprised by what he was hearing, but had been in his job long enough to recognize the truth when he heard it.

'Probably louder,' he confirmed.

'Yes, well then we would have heard it. *I* would have heard it.'

'Fine, we must take it that she didn't scream. You're quite sure you didn't see anyone in the woods, Colin?'

'I saw Gillian, Samuel, Jody, Sophie . . .'

'Sure, but apart from the children at the party?'

'No one.'

He was an unusual witness for a child. Often they would try to give the answers they sensed were required; not so Colin. He dealt only with honest facts. A bright youngster, and undoubtedly had the murderer shown himself for even a few seconds the boy would have been able to identify him. Like Amy, Inspector Barbor was sure that the killer was a man. However, he hadn't been spotted, even from a distance, and they had nothing to go on. No footprints, no traces of clothing fibres, no fingerprints, nothing. There was no evidence to show that anyone had been there at all – apart, of course, from the children.

'All right, young man, I'll let you get off to school. Thanks for your help. You'd make a fine policeman when you're old enough.'

'I want to be a vet.'

'I'm sure you'll be an excellent vet, too!'

The boy stood up and held out his hand. 'Goodbye. I'm sorry I couldn't help.'

'Not your fault. Thank you very much, Mr Rivero, for all your co-operation.'

'It was nothing. I, too, wish Colin could have helped you.'

The men walked down the narrow wooden stairs

together, the younger one whistling softly below his breath.

'You've worked wonders with Colin, you must feel extremely proud,' commented the policeman.

'I have done very little. It comes from within him. He has great inner strength.'

'I'm sure he has, but everyone in the village knows the part you've played.'

'Thank you.'

Strange how rarely the man smiled, reflected the Inspector as he was driven away.

Chapter 3

Three weeks had passed since Kate's funeral, yet despite a widespread search and extensive media coverage the police still had no clue as to the identity of the killer. Their investigation hadn't uncovered any secrets in the victim's life. She had been an ordinary, caring wife and mother. There was no hint of another man, none of the long-held grudges that are always possible in small, tight-knit communities. Kate had been popular, but she had died.

The longer her killer remained undetected, the greater the sense of fear in the village. Now Wendy's name was openly linked with her dead friend's. If Kate Burgess could be murdered then so, too, could Wendy have been. Her husband, Dean, started to press the already over-worked police force for results. If Wendy was alive he wanted her found; if dead, then he wanted to see the body. In other words, thought Inspector Barbor, he wanted to know one way or the other, and who could blame him?

The trouble was that again they had nothing to go on. Wendy was a cheerful, fit and friendly young woman with no history of depression or anxiety, so why should she have left her family without a word? There had been some gossip about her friendship with Pete Gregory, but the Inspector was inclined to discard this line of enquiry. From what he'd been told it consisted only of some mild flirting at the village fête and a quick cuddle in the kitchen during a friend's party, probably after a few too many drinks. Not a grand passion, nor even an affair, merely a brief spark of electricity between two attractive young adults that was probably forgotten before the woman vanished.

No, he thought it very likely that Wendy *had* been murdered, and if they found the motive for Kate's death they would probably find it applied to Wendy as well.

At exactly the same time as the Inspector was thinking about Wendy Beckett, Pete Gregory was driving his Volvo through the village on his way to the golf course. He always played at 11.30 on a Saturday morning and enjoyed the weekly exercise.

As he approached the small junction past the health shop he caught sight of his eight-year-od daughter, Jody, standing by the kerb waving frantically at him. From the look on her face it was obvious that she had an urgent message and he felt a pang of fear for Sara as he reversed back to Jody and wound down the window.

'What's the matter? Is Mummy all right?'

'Yes, but . . .' She stopped and put a thumb in her mouth.

'But what?'

'I've found something.'

'Found what? And where? Come on, Jody, hurry up. I'll be late for golf.'

For a moment an expression of secret amusement flickered across her face and he felt an inexplicable chill.

'Is it important?' he pressed.

'Yes, very. It's along there,' and she pointed with her left hand down the footpath to the woods. Immediately he thought of Kate Burgess.

'You shouldn't be in the woods on your own, I told you that.'

'I'm not alone, my friends are with me. Come quickly, Daddy, before someone touches it.'

'Touches what?'

'The shoe!' She sounded impatient at his stupidity. 'We've found a shoe.'

He pulled the car into a lay-by and followed her along the path. If the shoe was a clue, and it seemed likely that it was, then he must first ensure that the children didn't move it, and then send some of them for the police. He quickened his step.

In the centre of the wood, close to the most popular picnic spot, he saw Colin, Richard and Samuel, Fiona, Gillian and Georgina, all huddled together in a small circle.

'Right, let's have a look. You haven't touched it, have you?'

Colin gave him his shy smile. 'No, sir, of course not.'

'Good lad. Mind out of the way, Fiona, I'll just have a peep.'

The circle parted enough to let him in and then enclosed him. He could feel the small bodies pressing against him as he stared down at the tiny plastic shoe. A child's shoe. He didn't know whether to be relieved or disappointed. At least now he'd get his game of golf. He crouched down to pick up the tiny object.

'I don't think this is a clue, Jody. It belongs to a little girl.'

The children pressed closer and he almost toppled on to all fours.

'Steady on there, children!'

'It *is* a clue,' whispered Jody softly.

He glanced up at her. 'No, sweetheart, it isn't. It's a little girl's sandal. Why, it could be yours, Georgina.'

'It is mine,' Georgina said with a smile. At least, he thought she was smiling.

The youngsters were pressing closer now, jostling him,

giggling at their childish game. He felt hot and uncomfortable, also ridiculously vulnerable crouched at their feet, and so started to straighten up.

The pain at the back of his head struck like a thunderbolt. His ears rang and the children's legs spun and tilted crazily for a moment before he pitched forward, then everything went dark.

When he opened his eyes again he felt as though his face was covered by a sticky substance, and tried to lift his hands to feel what it was. He couldn't. His hands were held fast by other hands, tiny hands with incredible strength. Children's hands.

Terrified he forced his eyes to open wider, only to find his vision blurred. His tongue was sticking to the roof of his mouth and it was impossible to draw breath. He opened his mouth to try and take a large gulp of air, but the sticky substance on his face immediately entered his mouth, clinging to his lips and teeth.

His chest was beginning to hurt and he wondered what the hell was happening to him. There was even a constriction round his throat, not a life-threatening one but still a constriction. With a heave he pulled himself into a semi-sitting position, and through an opaque mist saw the strangely distorted faces of all the children looking down on him.

His head felt as though it was going to burst and his heart was racing madly as he tugged yet again to free his hands from their grip. For a second his left hand was released, and he just had time to feel the thin layer of the plastic bag round his face before one of the boys, Richard he thought, grabbed it and forced it back to the earth, sitting upon it to anchor it.

A pulse thudded heavily in Pete's temples and the chest pain grew worse. With terrified eyes he surveyed the implacable circle of children. Some were busy holding him still, the rest were simply watching. Standing, studying him with interest and a strange kind of triumph as he tried to stave off the inevitability of death.

He had no chance. A plastic bag, secured round his neck with a piece of cord, was going to kill him, and as he thrashed despairingly around, fighting with all of his strength to stay alive, he wondered why it was happening. He loved children, he'd always loved them. Not simply his own two but their friends as well. He knew them all. Fiona, Colin, Richard . . .

Their names were spinning crazily in his head. His hands no longer needed to be held for his body was going limp and there wasn't enough strength in his limbs for him to oppose the children.

His mouth opened for one final, despairing gasp and his eyes, rolling wildly in his head, held a look of stunned amazement that remained in them after his body was still and he had ceased to breathe.

'What now?' asked Richard. 'Do we just leave him?'

Colin shook his head. 'Nope! Turn him on to his face for a minute.'

Willing hands shot forward, turning the dead body with swift efficiency. Jody watched with interest and began to eat an apple, taken from the pocket of her dungarees.

'Right, where's the brick I hit him with?'

Fiona, white summer gloves on her hands, gave it to him silently. He was wearing a pair of Carlo's gardening gloves and took it swiftly, glancing around to make sure there were no observers, no unwanted children who didn't belong. Their group was composed entirely of children who understood. Any others would be useless; completely unreliable.

He looked at the back of Pete Gregory's head and saw

the lump where he had first struck him. He swung the brick back carefully and struck again on the same spot. This time the bag caved in, clinging to the torn flesh beneath.

'Right, now put him on his back with the brick underneath.'

Again the children were swift and silent. Colin checked the area with sharp eyes. Everything was in place. They were all in bare feet and weighed little. The grass wasn't excessively trampled upon for a picnic spot.

'OK, let's go. Anything you want to do, Jody? He is your dad.'

They all looked at the little girl with the bright red dungarees and cheerful, smiling face. She stepped up to her father, looked down at him for a few moments, then drew back her tiny feet and kicked him savagely in the ribs. She was an exceptionally small, dainty child for her age, people often commented upon this, but the kick was hard and delivered with calm efficiency.

'Bye-bye,' she crooned. 'Down you go to hell.'

'Down he goes to hell!' echoed all the other children. For a moment they remained staring at the body, their eyes glowing with a strange red light, then in orderly silence they dispersed, returning to a village which had never noticed their absence.

Inspector Barbor and Sergeant Moss left the coroner's court as soon as the verdict was announced, exiting by the back door in order to avoid reporters waiting in the front lobby. It was the third time in the history of Lower Ditton that national newsmen had come to cover a local incident, an honour not appreciated by any of the residents.

'I guess that wraps it up, sir,' remarked the Sergeant.

'Suicide while the balance of his mind was disturbed. Couldn't really have been anything else.'

'No, but I'm not happy about it.'

'In what way?' The Sergeant was surprised. He himself was highly relieved that the traumas of the past months were finally over. Unlike the Inspector he was a local man, and the tension among the villagers had affected him personally.

'I don't know. It's too neat and tidy for my liking. I'm not disputing that Peter Gregory killed himself, there were no signs of any struggle at the scene, but why should he have killed Kate Burgess and Wendy Beckett?'

'He was having an affair with Wendy Beckett.'

'Even if he was, and personally I believe it was more of a flirtation, why kill her? If every married man in the country killed his mistress, the female population would be severely decimated in no time.'

'Perhaps she wanted him to leave his family and go off with her?'

'Unlikely from what we know of her. Still, supposing that's true, why on earth should he kill Kate Burgess?'

The Sergeant hesitated. 'She and his wife were close friends.'

'That's a motive for *murder*?'

'It's the only link there is.'

'Precisely!'

'In my opinion he was simply a nutter.'

'Strange about the lump on the back of his head.'

'He fell on a brick. It was underneath him when the body was found.'

'I know that; but why do you suppose there was a brick lying there? One solitary brick – not several, not even two – just one convenient brick.'

'The brick didn't kill him, sir, so it wasn't exactly convenient.'

'Suppose that he was hit with the brick *before* the plastic bag went over his head. Not in order to kill him, simply to render him unconscious while the plastic bag was put on. If that were the case it *would* be a highly convenient brick.'

'But there were particles of the bag on the brick; if he'd been hit first that wouldn't have happened. Anyway, I thought you weren't disputing the suicide verdict?'

Barbor sighed. 'I know. I only wish he'd left a note, something to explain it all. His wife's completely shattered. According to her he was his normal self, and set off for his regular four-ball at the golf course after promising to take the family to the cinema when he got back.'

'He wasn't likely to tell her he was setting off for the woods to commit suicide because he was a double murderer!'

Their car slid to a halt outside the police station and they climbed slowly out. A flashbulb went off. The Sergeant blinked. Barbor cursed, elbowing his way through the line of press men with a terse 'No comment' as he went. Once inside he sank into the chair behind his desk.

'You're right, Ian,' he continued as though the conversation hadn't been interrupted. 'I've never heard of anyone giving advance notice of their imminent suicide. False threats of committing it, yes; notice of the act, no. It's only that somehow, somewhere, something doesn't quite fit. It's far too neat. If there's one thing I have learnt from my years in this job it's that only on the television and in detective novels does a case finish with such apparent ease, unassisted by any member of the police force. Peter Gregory wasn't even on our list of suspects!'

'Well, sir . . .'

'I know, you wanted him on it. Fine, full marks, Sergeant. Right now I could do with a cup of coffee.'

'Yes, sir.'

Alone at last Sebastian Barbor sighed and put his head in his hands. He couldn't forget the expression on Sara Gregory's face when the news of her husband's suicide was broken to her. She had aged ten years before his eyes, staunchly refuting every suggestion that he had been involved in the two women's murders.

'He didn't have it in him,' she kept reiterating to the Inspector, and he believed her. Deep down he believed her. But if he was right then there would be another murder. If he was wrong the murders would stop. Only time would tell.

He was relieved that she had two children who still needed her, otherwise she looked the type to follow her husband's example. He remembered the children, a boy of fourteen and a girl of eight, nice kids. They'd stood protectively at their mother's side, and masked their own grief with incredible self-control.

The children of Lower Ditton were, he suddenly realized, remarkably capable and resilient. Praiseworthy certainly, but he hoped that if anything were to happen to him his daughters would show some outward sign of their grief. The trouble with such self-control as these children were displaying was that after a time you began to wonder if they had any feelings at all.

In fact, some of his present disquiet stemmed not so much from the lack of evidence in connection with Peter Gregory's death as from general unease in connection with the children. He gave himself a mental shake. The children were nothing to do with him. They hadn't committed any crime, they probably didn't fully understand what was going on. No, he was involved only with upholding the law, and the children of Lower Ditton were far too disciplined to break it. It was one of the few places he knew where even petty pilfering from the small sweet shop was unknown, although he had been told that this hadn't always been the case.

He had to forget the children and concentrate on their parents, and he intended to continue doing so for the next few weeks until he was absolutely certain that the generally accepted theory was correct, and that the women of the village had nothing more to fear.

Chapter 4

Amy had now been looking after Ray and his family for three months. It had proved impossible to find anyone willing to look after the baby and the girls for the whole of their summer holidays and so she had agreed to stay on.

Whilst the house and everyday domestic chores kept her busy she badly missed her own work and kept urging her brother-in-law to advertise for full-time help. He would nod and mumble an agreement but so far nothing had happened, and as long as she continued to keep things running smoothly she suspected that it never would.

The summer was warm but damp, and as a result the children were underfoot more than usual. She was therefore able to study them carefully without their knowledge. As time passed she decided that the detached, almost contemptuous attitude Fiona had displayed after Kate's death must have been some form of reaction for she had now returned to being the agreeable, helpful child of the previous year.

At least with so many youngsters around Amy could keep her photographic hand in, and she shot reel after reel of film which she carefully stored away to have developed in Cheltenham. All of them were taken when the children were off guard, playing together or talking in the serious, absorbed manner of children who are growing old enough to enjoy discussions.

Counting her nieces there was a group of ten children,

six girls and four boys, who went around together. Their ages varied from Sophie who was four to the ten-year-old twins, but despite this they all got on exceptionally well.

After Peter's suicide, Sara Gregory had become a recluse. She rarely left her house, and according to Jody frequently didn't bother to get dressed at all.

The villagers felt sorry for her but – in the light of her husband's suspected crimes – they left her alone. The general feeling was that she and her two children should move away, for there seemed little future for her in the village.

Jody coped exceedingly well. She remained bright and cheerful, although Amy noticed that her clothes were frequently dirty and her hair uncombed. Amy did try to keep friendly with Sara but the woman didn't want to talk to her and made it clear. Finally, after finding Sara drunk at ten o'clock one Thursday morning, Amy confined herself to keeping a careful watch over Jody.

Despite her strong sense of family duty and her desire to ensure that Kate's children weren't neglected, it was doubtful if Amy would have stayed for so long if she hadn't had another incentive: Carlo Rivero.

Colin was the leader of the group of children, and they all spent a great deal of time in Carlo's garden or the house behind the shop. As a result Amy came into frequent contact with the boy's guardian, and it wasn't long before she realized that her stomach had developed a will of its own and began turning over and churning with excited anticipation when he was around.

She took extra care with her appearance. At first Kate's death had drained her of any frivolous interest in her appearance but now she made a regular fortnightly visit to a salon where she had her waist-length hair trimmed and blow-dried so that the chestnut curls were always shining and neat.

Naturally she had worn fairly sombre outfits after Kate was murdered but now she felt free to revert to her more usual, colourful style, and knew from the admiring glances of many of the men that she was right to do so. The only man who didn't seem to notice was Carlo.

One cool Saturday afternoon she went to his shop to collect Georgina, who had been invited to a class-mate's party. Georgina didn't want to go, stating that the girl wasn't 'one of us', but Amy had insisted. Now, hurrying to fetch her and sensing a minor struggle ahead, she felt the beginnings of a headache in the knotted muscles at the back of her neck. It was only since Kate died that she had suffered like this, but she had come to dread the pain and the occasional vomiting that could accompany it.

The children weren't in the garden and finding the back door locked she went back to the front and the shop entrance. Carlo was inside, standing with his back to her, talking quietly to Jody who had hold of his hands and was looking up at him with blind adoration. Amy had the horrible suspicion that she too would look equally adoringly at him if he ever held her hands, and she was not a child but a mature divorcee of twenty-six. It was shaming but she knew that physical attraction is impervious to logic.

'Carlo!'

He spun round, an expression of guarded distrust on his face until he saw who it was. Then he gave a small smile, but not the sort that he gave the children.

'Amy, how nice to see you. You look so young and fresh in that dress I find it difficult to believe that you've already been married!'

'Well, I have!' she laughed, wondering at the back of

her mind who had told him but immensely flattered that he had troubled to ask.

'What can I do for you?' he continued.

'I've come for Georgina. She's due at Justine's party.'

Carlo's smile faded. 'She doesn't want to go.'

'I know that, but it will do her good.'

'Why?'

'She spends all her time with the same children. I think she should mix more.'

'Georgina knows who her friends are, and Justine isn't one of them. She will be very unhappy at such a party.'

He was looking at her earnestly as he talked, and if her head hadn't been aching so badly she would have taken keen pleasure in the hint of admiration in his deep brown eyes.

'I'm sorry, Carlo, but I've accepted for her.'

'In that case . . .'

'Oh!' She gave a gasp of pain as coloured lights flashed before her.

'What's wrong?'

'My head! I keep getting attacks of migraine these days, and this one is particularly bad.'

He moved round from behind the counter and helped her to a chair.

'Sit down here and I'll bring you a cup of herbal tea. It's very good for migraine.'

Amy felt as though she'd be sick if she drank anything, but the pain was so intense she didn't have the strength to argue. When the cup was put in her hands she found the tea's scent not unpleasant and drank the contents in one go.

'Now rest there for a little time,' murmured Carlo, touching her lightly on the shoulder as he passed. Her flesh tingled at the contact and her mouth felt dry.

The infusion certainly eased the pain, but it also seemed to have heightened her senses for when she was finally able to stand up again she could still feel where he had touched her, and as he began to suggest that she took one feverfew leaf a day in an effort to stave off further attacks all she heard was the soft liquid tone of his voice and the attractive precision of his grammar.

Eventually she remembered why she was there. 'Could you fetch Georgina for me?' she asked. 'I don't want her to be late.'

Both Carlo and Jody, who was standing behind the counter with him, looked at her strangely.

'You've been resting for an hour,' he told her.

'An hour?'

'It is now four o'clock. The party must surely be under way?'

'It can't be four o'clock!'

'You have been resting on the chair. The tea relaxes you, encourages sleep.'

'But I didn't fall asleep, I only waited a few minutes.'

He shrugged elegantly. 'You have a watch?'

'Yes, look, it's only . . .' Her voice tailed off as she saw her watch showing ten minutes past four.

'They say that time flies in pleasant company!' Again the small smile, the one he offered to adults.

'I'm lucky you're not a white slave trader! I have to admit that my headache is quite gone.'

'Good, then your visit was worthwhile.'

'It's a pity about Georgina's party, though. I don't want her to feel that she can always have her own way.'

The change that came over Carlo's face was astonishing. The smile vanished instantaneously. All at once his eyes were cold; he stared unwaveringly at her and she was aware of the sudden coolness between them.

'You mean you'd make her go to a party where she didn't have a single friend, and celebrate the birthday of a girl she didn't even like, simply to exert your superior authority, without any regard for the child's feelings? I'm disappointed in you, Mrs Kendall.'

Astonishment and temper, mixed in equal parts, flooded over her. She stared back at him, knowing that she was in the right but harbouring an insane desire to win a return to their former friendly relationship.

'That wasn't quite what I meant,' she said pleasantly.

'Indeed? It was the impression I received.'

'Then I must have expressed myself badly.'

'Possibly.'

He refused to give an inch. She was surprised at the force of his feelings, amazed to find him capable of such blatant rudeness.

'On the other hand, you're not really an expert on child care, Mr Rivero. You don't have any of your own, do you?'

He smiled, but not pleasantly. 'In that respect we are on equal terms, I believe.'

There was nothing more to be said. With a brief nod Amy left the shop, and all the way back to Ray's house she went over and over the scene in her mind, wishing that it could have ended differently. What a strange man he was, plainly identifying far more easily with children than with adults, whilst remaining a mature, intelligent person who communicated with youngsters on a far more adult level than most people. She wondered what his own childhood had been like. It was always possible that the key to his behaviour lay somewhere there and she wondered how she could find out about it.

Back in the shop it was very quiet. Jody continued bagging up dried apricots while Carlo checked through his herbal remedies and noted down stock requirements. They didn't speak much until their jobs were finished, then Jody looked at the man questioningly.

'Don't you like Mrs Kendall? We thought you did.'

'I do. I find her most attractive. She has a curiously untouched quality about her, an almost childlike purity. Yes, I find her attractive.'

'But you sounded cross.'

'I get cross when people disappoint me.'

'She isn't a bad person. Even Colin thinks she's good.'

'I'm sure he's right. However, it's best to state my position on certain points clearly before I get to know her better.'

'Why aren't there many good grown-ups in the world, Carlo?'

'Why can't fish talk? Who knows! It's one of life's mysteries. Call the others while I get the lemonade out.'

Jody stood on tiptoe and kissed his cheek as he bent down to place a jar of liquorice beneath the counter. 'You'll never hurt us, will you, Carlo?'

'No, little one, I'll never hurt you.'

'Are you lost, like us?'

He gave her a quick appraising glance. 'No, but I understand.'

'It's not very nice being . . .'

Lightly he laid the fingers of his right hand across her lips.

'Hush! It's better not to speak of it.'

'I forgot.'

'Why don't you wear your red dungarees tomorrow, Jody? Those green ones are very dirty.'

'Mummy hasn't washed any others. She keeps forgetting – I think it's because of the drink. It isn't nice the way she goes round these days, all untidy and cross. She's being bad, isn't she, Carlo?'

He turned round to look at her, and the sun shone through the doorway behind him, sending a glow over the child's face as he smiled at her.

'Yes, Jody, she's being very bad indeed.'

'Will you tell the others?'

'Yes, but I don't think we'd better do anything just yet. Don't worry; I'll take care of you.'

'What about my brother, Keith?'

'Does he understand?'

'No, he's just . . . ordinary.'

'Then he mustn't be told.'

'But we'll protect him too, won't we?'

'Of course.'

As Carlo went away to the kitchen Jody clapped her hands together and skipped round the shop. Her eyes glinted with a feverish excitement, her features sharpening and becoming fox-like. All at once her face looked pinched, the cheeks sunken, and with her uncombed hair and dirty dungarees she looked a completely different child from the placid, cherubic Jody that Amy loved to photograph. The change was quite astonishing; fortunately there was no camera there to record the metamorphosis.

At nine-thirty that evening, Amy recounted the tale of her attempt to get Georgina to Justine's party, and Carlo's support of the little girl's lack of intrest.

'It isn't good for her to have her own way over everything, Ray. Ever since Kate died the girls have been constantly indulged. I'm as much to blame as anyone, but I really think it's time for things to get back to normal. Spoilt children grow up into perfectly detestable adults.'

'If she wasn't going to enjoy it she was better off with her friends.'

His tone was final: there wasn't any point in arguing with him.

'Talking of friends, it's time I went home again, Ray. Have you advertised for help in the house yet?'

'No, but I promise that I will. I do wish you'd stay on. We'll miss you, Amy. The children are very fond of you.'

They're not, thought Amy, they're only pleased to have someone around to take care of them. Little Sophie quite likes me, and the baby has got used to me, but Fiona and Georgina aren't a bit interested in me as a person.

'I'll interview the candidates if you like,' she offered. Ray nodded reluctantly.

'But you will hurry?' she reiterated.

'Of course.'

She didn't believe him, and decided that if nothing happened within a week then she would pay for the advertisement herself.

The next day the weather remained dry and Ray took the opportunity to tidy up his neglected garden – previously managed by Kate – while Amy put Thomas out in his pram before starting to wash the living-room curtains.

All three girls were playing with their friends at the twins' house, and when Carlo stepped into the kitchen after tapping lightly on the back door Amy assumed that he thought Colin was with her.

'They're all at Richard and Samuel's,' she told him.

'I know. It was you I wanted to see.'

Feeling herself blushing she quickly turned away to dry her hands on the kitchen towel. By the time she faced him again she had her emotions under control, but wished that she was wearing something more attractive than cut-off denim shorts and an old T-shirt.

'If it's about the headaches I remembered to chew some feverfew this morning.'

'Good. Actually, I wondered whether you'd like to come into Condersford this evening to see a film.'

To say that she was astonished was an understatement. After their argument she had been sure he'd lost even his previous marginal interest in her. Now he was inviting her out, and she felt as excited as a fifteen year old.

'That sounds lovely, Carlo! I haven't been to the pictures for over a year. At home I'm too wrapped up in photography, and here I'm constantly behind with the housework. Obviously my organizational skill is on the low side!'

'We could have a meal afterwards if you like.'

'Even better! What film are they showing?'

'*Witness*.'

'Harrison Ford?'

'The same.'

'I've got a soft spot for him; you've certainly guessed my taste in film stars.'

'Not really, Fiona told me, although the only film I could find at first was *Star Wars*, and I wasn't sure you were quite that keen.'

Amy laughed and his dark eyes danced with amusement. He looked very young when he smiled; young and charming, with none of the brooding air that sometimes surrounded him.

'What time does it start?'

'I'll collect you at seven, that gives us plenty of time.'

'The girls aren't in bed by then.'

'Their father will have to cope, won't he? I'm sure Ray knows how to wash and undress his own children.'

'You're probably right but he hasn't given any sign of it so far.'

'All the more reason for you to come. See you tonight, Amy.'

'Yes, and thank you.'

He shrugged his shoulders slightly in a gesture that indicated it was nothing at all, then strolled casually away, stopping to exchange a few words with Ray as he left.

'What did Kate think of Carlo?' Amy asked Ray when she came downstairs early that evening wearing a cream silk dress with a full skirt and tight bodice.

'Carlo? She liked him of course. Everyone likes Carlo!'

'I know. Didn't she say anything more, though? I mean, did she think him handsome or amusing? I'd like to know. I trust – or rather trusted – her judgement a lot.'

Ray looked doubtfully at her. 'He's only asked you to the pictures, Amy. I don't want to sound like a killjoy but quite a lot of girls have lost their hearts to Carlo after one or two casual dates, then they cry their eyes out when he doesn't ask them again. He isn't the marrying kind.'

'Nor am I! So Katie didn't give you any idea of what she thought?'

'I remember her saying that she suspected he was very private, and how she felt that no one here really understood him. Apart from that she only ever remarked on how handsome he was. That's what made me jealous, if you recall.'

'Of course!'

'You know, at first I suspected *him* of murdering Kate. He could have followed them to the woods.'

'But you told me that if he'd been there she might not have died. You can't have it both ways!'

'That was just my guilt complex. No, deep down I was suspicious.'

'But Carlo's so gentle and quiet.'

'Agreed, but we don't know much about him, do we?

Where does he come from? Why is he so patient with the children? What does he do in his spare time? If *he'd* killed himself I'd have been far less surprised than I was by Peter's death. I can't for the life of me imagine why Peter should have murdered Katie.'

'It looks as though he did. Most parents must trust Carlo, otherwise they wouldn't let their children spend so much time there.'

'That's because he became something of a local hero about a year ago – after that it was a triumph to boast that your child had been to see him! Bloody ridiculous because it didn't change him. All it showed was that he was fearless. Either fearless or brainless, I'm not sure which.'

It was unlike Ray to sound so peevish.

'What kind of hero?' enquired an intrigued Amy.

'The usual kind.'

'I meant, what did he do?'

'I can hear his car. You'll be able to ask him yourself. Have a good evening. Here's a key so that I don't have to stay up. The doctor's sleeping pills make me permanently tired these days.'

'Thanks, Ray. See you tomorrow.'

With a marvellous feeling of freedom she stepped quickly from the house, tense with excited anticipation.

Carlo was wearing green linen slacks, a short-sleeved white cotton shirt and had a long, cream sweater draped round his shoulders. The entire outfit was simple, casual and undeniably expensive.

His hair was combed in a more orderly fashion than usual, the curls springing back from his forehead and trimmed neatly around his ears. When he guided her by her arm to the passenger side of the car she found that she was trembling slightly with nerves, and hoped that he couldn't detect the tremor.

'Colin's very envious of me tonight,' he said, glancing at her out of the corner of his eyes as he drove swiftly and efficiently through the village and out on to the main road. 'He thinks you're very pretty.'

'Tell him he's got excellent taste!'

Carlo laughed. 'He also tells me that your nieces say how well you look after them.'

'That's nice to hear. Sometimes I feel that Fiona in particular finds me rather a trial!'

'Children know when an adult truly cares for them, however irritating the result.'

'I feel rather inadequate most of the time. Kate was a natural mother with endless patience – mine isn't quite so open-ended. When I'm tired I start to nag. I hate hearing myself, so it must be far worse for the children!'

'Kate wasn't perfect,' he said slowly. 'I think that . . .'

'What?'

'It doesn't matter. I don't want to talk about your sister tonight. Let's talk about you.'

And talk about Amy they did. The film was good, but Harrison Ford lost some of his appeal for Amy that night because her emotions were occupied with Carlo who was, after all, flesh and blood.

By the time they'd eaten it was nearly midnight, and Carlo had gleaned virtually every scrap of information available on Amy's life. She had told him about her work and the photos she'd taken of the village children. He had heard about her failed marriage, and the traumatic death of her parents when she was fourteen. She had even told him about Ray's doubts over Peter Gregory's guilt in respect of the village murders. He was the perfect listener.

When he dropped her off outside Ray's house and leant

across to kiss her lightly on the lips she realized that not once in the evening had he spoken of himself. She knew no more about him than before their date, whilst he knew everything there was to know about her.

Stil over-stimulated by the excitement of the evening she found it impossible to fall asleep until dawn, and she kept recalling the gleam of laughter in his eyes when she made a joke, or the habit that he had of running his fingers up through his hair in a gesture of mock irritation when things went wrong. It would be very easy to fall in love with him, but she doubted if he would reciprocate such intensity of emotion. He reminded her of a cat; sleek, handsome, and fiercely independent.

After tea the following day the children met in Ray's garden, staying at the far end of the lawn, among the rose bushes and shrubbery, where they sat in a small circle leaning towards each other.

Amy took some photos through her bedroom window using a telephoto lense, then settled down to the ironing. Idly she wondered what they found to talk about at such length. She would have been very surprised if she had been able to hear.

'What did Carlo say?' Mark asked. He was a tall ten-year-old with a mop of over-long strawberry blond hair; a handsome and well-behaved child even by the high standard of Lower Ditton.

'He said she was "Hokay"!'

They all laughed at the perfect imitation.

'Is she really OK?' enquired nine-year-old Helen. 'I mean, would she be *nice* to children, if she ever had any?'

Colin shrugged. 'Suppose so. Carlo ought to know. He's going to take her out again. I like her.'

'She's always fair,' put in Fiona. 'A bit of a nagger sometimes, but always fair, isn't she, Georgie?'

'Yep, I don't think *she* likes Thomas best. She's the same with all of us.'

'People change,' said Jody gloomily. 'Look at my Mum and Dad. We used to think they were nice. Mum's awful now Dad's dead. I'm beginning to think we should have killed *her*.'

'There's plenty of time for that,' said Colin casually. 'After all, if she keeps on drinking she doesn't deserve to live; but who'd take care of you and Keith, Jody?'

'Carlo!' beamed Jody.

'He's busy with me. We don't want any more children.' Colin was adamant on that point.

'Amy then. She used to be friendly with Mum. Would Amy take us in, Fiona?'

'Even if she would, my Dad wouldn't. He's a pain too these days. Still, we've got to wait, haven't we, Colin?'

'Yes. The next adult will have to come from one of you other kids. Any suggestions?'

Hands shot up all round the circle.

'Joanne, who do you want it to be? Your mum or your dad?'

'My dad, definitely my dad.'

The others looked enquiringly at her.

'He's a prize pig,' she continued. 'I'm tired of waiting. I want it to be his turn next.'

As she talked her blue eyes lost their tranquil look and gleamed fanatically, giving her a maturity beyond her years. Her face narrowed, the mouth drawing tightly down at the corners.

Colin nodded. 'Right, next on your list, Jonathan Harris.'

'Jonathan Harris!' echoed all the children, and then they joined hands.

'How will he die?' asked nine-year-old Gillian, her

dimples showing up as she smiled in anticipation. Adults found Gillian Cross's dimples extemely cute.

Colin was thoughtful.

'By poison,' he said at last. 'We haven't done a poison before.'

'By poison!' they chortled in unison.

'Death to Jonathan Harris!' cried Colin quietly.

'Death to Jonathan Harris!' they endorsed.

'Girls!' called Amy, walking slowly down towards them. 'Don't forget to pick me some gooseberries before lunch, will you?'

'We'll all help, Mrs Kendall,' put in Colin.

'What kind children you are. Thank you so much.'

'Our pleasure.'

As soon as she was out of earshot they began to giggle.

'What kind children we are!' mimicked Richard and Samuel.

'So helpful!' chuckled little Sophie.

They leant inwards, their heads close together, and on every face there was the same look of fanaticism. In fact, they didn't look like children at all.

Chapter 5

A few days later Fiona came upon Amy writing to Helena, her Girl Friday at the photographic studio.

'You're not going home, Aunty, are you?' she asked anxiously.

Amy smiled. 'Not right this minute, but I can't stay here forever.'

'Why not?'

'Because I have work to do, my love. Besides, once your father finds someone to help around the house, I won't be needed.'

Fiona fiddled with a strand of hair.

'You will. Carlo likes you. He'll be sad if you go.'

'I don't think so. He's got plenty of other ladies for company.'

'But you're special.'

'That's nice to know!'

'It's true. You see, you're kind.'

'Even when I grumble at you?'

'We don't count grumbling.'

'We?'

Fiona paused. 'Me, Georgie and Sophie,' she said at last.

'Lots of people are kind, Fiona. Why, one day your daddy might find a kind lady he'd like to marry. That would be even better than having me living here, wouldn't it?'

'No.'

'It would.'

'Mmmm. Why don't you come to Colin's house with us today? Carlo said we could put the tent up and play camping.'

'I'll come later, when you're properly organized. There, that's the letter done.'

'Shall I post it for you on my way to Colin's?'

Amy gave her niece a quick hug. 'That's very kind of you. I'll be along to see the camp later.'

'OK. Georgie! Sophie! Come on, it's time to go.'

They clattered out of the back door leaving Amy alone, except for Thomas who was sleeping peacefully in his pram outside the kitchen window. He was a placid baby and exceptionally easy to look after.

Once clear of the house Fiona ripped open the envelope, quickly running her eyes over the three pages of neat, precise writing.

'She says how well we're adapting and how much she'll miss us,' she informed her sisters. 'She also asks this Helena to let her know if there's too much work piling up. Well, if there is, tough luck,' and with a quick movement she tore the pages in two and stuffed them inside a nearby litter bin.

'You're late!' accused Colin when they ran into his garden. 'We've had to put the tent up on our own. At least, Samuel and Richard are here but they keep messing around. What kept you?'

Fiona told him and his frown vanished. 'Well done. We probably don't *need* to do anything, I'm sure Carlo can manage on his own, but a little help won't do any harm.'

'She's coming to look at our camp later.'

'Good!' Colin sounded delighted.

'How's Joanne's father?'

'Still alive,' he stated flatly, then caught Fiona's eye and giggled. 'But not for long!'

'No,' she agreed happily. 'Not for long!'

By the time Amy arrived there were several children in the garden, ranging from four-year-old Felicity to the ten-year-old twins. They moved purposefully around, setting up the barbecue and counting sausages and beefburgers. Amy wondered why the girls couldn't be as self-sufficient at home, where even a request for assistance with the drying up always met with indignant wails.

Colin saw her first. He ran over, a quick smile lighting up his face. She was very fond of the young boy. He impressed her with his courage and cheerfulness.

'Carlo's inside, Mrs Kendall. He isn't going to come out until everything's ready, then he'll do the cooking. Are you staying to eat?'

'No one told me it was a barbecue, but I'd love to. As long as I can bring Thomas.'

His face went blank. 'Thomas?'

'Fiona's baby brother!'

'Oh!'

'He won't be any bother. He's a very good baby.'

'He would be. Fiona's mummy made a dreadful fuss of him when he was born.'

'Mothers make a fuss of all babies when they're born,' she laughed. Colin's face changed. He tightened his mouth and held his hands stiffly by his sides.

'That isn't true. It simply isn't true.'

'Why do you say that?' she asked gently. His eyes clouded over and to her amazement he began to whimper deep in his throat.

'Why not me?' he cried, staring blankly through her. 'Let me come too. Don't leave me here on my own. I don't like . . .'

'Colin! What is it?' She put her hands on his rigid shoulders. At once he screamed, backing away from her in such haste that he tripped and fell. She bent over him, but he buried his head beneath his arms and continued to whimper.

Shocked, she looked about her. All the children had stopped work and were watching the scene in silence. None of them moved. Their eyes darted from the whimpering child to the frozen adult and every face was blank. Then, horribly, their eyes began to glow red within their sockets, as though fuclled by an inner fire. Amy's skin prickled with fear. She felt repulsed and terrified. All at once the cheerful barbecue had changed. It was like a bad dream where the action is unrelated to what has gone before.

While she stared the children gradually began moving towards her. They moved slowly and carefully, their steps small but purposeful. There was no recognition in any of their eyes, only this strange red gleam. They advanced like a small private army, and she knew instinctively that she was the enemy.

'Carlo!' she screamed. The children stopped in their tracks, turning their heads towards the patio doors.

'CARLO!' She prayed that he was within earshot.

'Amy! How lovely, you're just in time for . . .' He took one look at her frightened face before his eyes swept round the garden, coming to rest on Colin.

He crossed the grass, crouched down to the boy and placed his hands lightly on the protected head and shoulders.

'It's all right,' he murmured. 'You're safe, remember? Come on, let me pick you up.' With slow careful movements he gathered the child into his arms, lifting him gently to his feet while keeping him enclosed within the protection of his arms.

'You're safe,' he repeated gently. 'Don't cry, it's all over. Everything's all right.'

From the moment Carlo put his hands on the boy the whimpers stopped. By the time Carlo had finished soothing him, Colin was standing straight again, turning a pale face towards Amy whose legs were shaky with shock.

'What happened?' the boy asked her.

'I don't know, Colin. I was talking about . . .'

'You fell down,' interrupted Carlo, giving Amy a warning glance. 'You're OK now, aren't you?'

The colour was returning to the child's face. 'Yep! I'm hokay!'

The children all giggled. Then slowly, one by one, they returned to their chores. Once again their faces were bright and eager, their eyes normal. They were simply a happy group of youngsters enjoying a barbecue on a summer's day. But what had they become for those few brief moments? wondered Amy, and moistened dry lips with her tongue.

'Off you go, young man,' laughed Carlo, tapping Colin lightly on his bottom. He sped away, leaving the adults alone.

'What did happen?' asked Amy. 'One minute he . . .'

'It's shock. It doesn't happen so often now, but the doctor says it's reaction to his parents' death.'

'But he was saying . . .'

'He says all sorts of things,' put in Carlo smoothly. 'Don't worry. It's frightening the first time you see it, but it never lasts long. The important thing is not to make too much of it.'

'I don't think you realize what happened. He was saying that he didn't want to be left on his own.'

'Quite. He can't face up to being orphaned. Is that so very surprising?'

'Of course not. But the other children were odd. They seemed . . .'

'Yes?' His gaze was quizzical, the eyebrows raised in good-humoured disbelief. She knew he wanted her to let the matter drop, but he hadn't been there, hadn't seen their terrible gleaming eyes.

'Menacing,' she concluded. 'They were all coming towards me and . . .'

'My goodness, such imagination! You've had a nasty shock. It isn't pleasant to watch Colin when he gets like that. Because he's normally so brave and well-adjusted it makes his anguish all the harder to bear. However, time's the great healer. We must give him time. Time and love, they're what he needs.'

'But . . .'

His eyebrows were still raised but his eyes had lost their humorous light and looked almost bleak as he stared at her.

'But what, Amy?'

I could lose him here and now, she realized. If I continue trying to explain what happened he's going to mark me down as a hysterical female and dismiss me from his mind forever.

She didn't want that to happen. She liked seeing his face soften with admiration when she appeared. She enjoyed his carefree attitude towards children, the sense of fun he had retained in contrast to so many adults. Not only that, she was drawn to him physically. There was a sensuality about him that she felt certain would make him a marvellously considerate and sensitive lover. She knew what she had to do.

'Nothing!' she laughed. 'As you say, it was a bit of a shock, that's all. I think I need a drink.' He smiled boyishly, his eyes crinkling up at the corners, and butterflies fluttered around inside her stomach; light, insistent stirrings of desire.

'Now *that* I can believe! Come inside, and I'll pour us a sherry.'

Once they were drinking the pale dry liquid she ventured one further question. 'Did Colin have a baby brother or sister, Carlo?'

'No, he was an only child, which made his parents' death all the more terrible. It left him completely alone in the world.'

'Does he like babies?'

'I don't suppose he gives them much thought! Why all this talk about babies? Are they on your mind at the moment!'

'Yes, but only because I'm responsible for Thomas!'

'I tend to forget little Thomas.'

'I ought to go and get him if I'm staying for lunch.'

'Then fetch him at once. You're our guest of honour; you can't possibly eat elsewhere!'

When she returned, carrying the baby in a sling round her neck, the children crowded round, exclaiming over his tiny fingers and the wrinkled frown on his forehead.

'He's like a little old man!' laughed Colin, putting a finger into the baby's hand. Thomas tightened his grip and held the older boy imprisoned. Colin gave a gentle smile, whereupon Thomas opened his blue eyes and gave a slightly cross-eyed smile in return.

'He likes you!' laughed Fiona. Amy decided not to mention the effect of wind on a small baby. It was reassuring to see Colin apparently content in the presence of a baby, and her earlier fears seemed quite ridiculous. Carlo had been right. She obviously suffered from an over-active imagination.

* * *

Three days after the barbecue the children returned to school. The girls didn't mind, and when Amy collected them at three-fifteen she found Fiona and her close friend Joanne with their arms round each other's waist, waiting cheerfully at the school gates.

'Where are the other two, Fiona? You're supposed to wait for them'

'Joanne's mummy is with them. Joanne's sister, Deborah, started today and she can't do up her own sandals.'

'I see. Did you both enjoy your first day back?'

They nodded, glanced at each other, then giggled. Amy remembered similar behaviour of her own infuriating her mother, and realized why. She refrained from asking them what was amusing, knowing full well that she wouldn't be told.

A few minutes later Joanne's mother, Harriet, arrived. She held a small girl in her arms while Georgina and Sophie clung to her long cotton skirt. She looked hot and flustered until she saw Amy, then she gave a relieved smile.

'How lovely! I thought it was my turn to bring them *all* today, and I've got a terrible headache. I simply didn't feel up to it.'

'Didn't Kate always collect?'

'No, she and I had a rota, but being Kate she naturally did far more collecting than me. Are you as amenable?'

'Definitely not!'

As they moved away from the gate the children ran on ahead. Harriet, a grey-eyed brunette of medium height, glanced curiously at Amy.

'I hear that you've ensnared our most eligible bachelor! It isn't surprising really, you're easily the best-looking girl in the village.'

Amy blushed. 'I wish either of those statements were true!'

'But they are. We women are quite green with envy, but only in the nicest possible way. As for Carlo, you must take it from me that he's definitely smitten. He's never taken such an interest in the same girl for so long before. If I wasn't happily married I'd hate you for that! He's really something, isn't he? Those soft brown eyes and that devastating profile! Mind you, he's wasted in a village like Lower Ditton. God knows why he stays.'

'He really doesn't see me that often, Harriet. I do like him, though, and I often wonder what he's doing here. He is foreign, I take it?'

'We all assume so, but he doesn't talk about himself. You'll have to ask him next time you're out together. Make it a casual query – he can clam up very quickly if he thinks anyone's prying.'

'Don't I know it! I've tried subtle questions. All that's left is a straight "Tell-me-about-your-family-or-I-leave" ultimatum. The trouble is, I don't want to leave!'

Harriet looked slightly uncomfortable. 'Amy, please don't take this the wrong way, but be careful. It's true Carlo's handsome and exceptionally appealing but he has been known to lose his temper, and when that happens – well, you'd better make yourself scarce before the crockery starts flying!'

'I don't believe it, Carlo throwing plates?'

Ahead of them the girls met up with Colin and the twins. They all began chattering, heads close together.

'Actually it was a kitchen knife, and thrown at your brother-in-law. I'm amazed he hasn't told you.'

'Carlo threw a knife at Ray? When? Why? What had . . .?'

'Sshh! Here's Colin.'

'Harriet, you can't stop now.'

'I'll tell you another day, I don't want Colin to hear. Anyway I'm sure *you're* quite safe with him. I wouldn't have mentioned it but Kate told me . . .'

'Hello, Mrs Kendall. Carlo asked me to say he'd be a little late tonight. He's behind with the stock-taking.'

'Thank you, Colin.'

The boy smiled. 'My pleasure. How are you, Mrs Harris?'

'Fine thanks. School all right?'

'Yep. How's Mr Harris?'

'Still in bed. He can't seem to shake off this stomach bug.'

'He ought to try one of Carlo's herbal teas. Peppermint's good for stomach upsets. Shall I bring you some?'

'If Carlo thinks it would help, then I'd be most grateful.'

With a final smile, Colin ran off again.

'He's such a willing boy,' remarked Harriet, 'but that's only since he went to live with Carlo. He was a perfect little swine to his parents. Poor Jackie never knew a moment's peace. If he wasn't howling and screaming round the place then he was out wrecking the garden. It makes you wonder about the role of parents in child development, doesn't it?'

'Yes,' murmured Amy, but she wasn't really listening. Her thoughts were already on the evening that lay ahead.

That night she and Carlo spent two hours at a nearby pub, which served excellent bar snacks and the best real ale for miles around. When they left Carlo took hold of Amy's hand and led her slowly down a lane towards a small, wooded copse.

She had already sensed that in some way this was going to be a special evening. Now, with her hand clasped firmly in his, she realized that she was going to have to decide whether or not she wanted them to become lovers.

Once in the copse he put his arm casually round her waist and walked on without speaking, humming quietly beneath his breath. After a short time he stopped, glanced around them and then drew her to the ground. For a moment Amy felt uneasy as she remembered Kate and realized how foolish she'd been to wander off alone with a relative stranger. His grip tightened momentarily, then her hand was released and the fear passed.

She spread her full skirt carefully out beneath her. Carlo lay on his side, nibbling thoughtfully at the thumbnail of his left hand.

'You shouldn't do that!' she laughed gently, putting out a hand to remove his thumb.

'I know, but I'm too old to change now!'

'I haven't noticed you doing it before.'

'It's only when I'm nervous.'

She couldn't think of any reply.

'You're very beautiful,' he said softly, reaching out to cup her face in his hands. 'Like a porcelain doll.'

'I'm not in the least doll-like. I have some highly irritating habits.'

'Me too!'

'Carlo, why are you nervous?'

He ran the fingers of his left hand through his hair with an exasperated air. 'Because I don't want to spoil things, I suppose. Because I want to do this right. I would hate to . . . offend you, Amy.'

'You won't offend me.'

For the first time since they met he seemed lost. His calm air of command had deserted him, leaving a boyish vulnerability which touched her as nothing had ever done before.

He moved nearer, brushing some imaginary specks of grass from his jeans. 'This is difficult for me because I am not used to such a situation. Most of the girls I've taken out I've known for years – they're rather young and easily pleased with some kisses and endearments at the end of an evening.'

'Only kisses?'

'For me this is not funny.'

'I'm sorry, I didn't mean . . .'

'Naturally sometimes there has been more than kisses. I am not a child, I am a man. But always, always, Amy, it has been of no great matter. When it is not important then naturally it goes well. Now, when I care so much, I am afraid that perhaps I will not make it good for you.'

She tried to see the expression in his eyes, but it was too dark. His face was a blurred outline, undefined and unreadable.

'I'm quite sure it will be good for us, Carlo,' she whispered. Her assurance seemed to be enough. At once he was beside her, his hands caressing her neck and shoulders before moving to her long chestnut hair.

She had been right about him: he was a sensualist, a man who took pleasure in touching, kissing, holding and savouring all the small sensations that led inevitably to the final, surging moment of passion when she was oblivious to everything but the waves of pleasure that he gave her.

Finally she heard him groan and he shuddered above her, dark and mysterious by moonlight. A man with no face, no past and no future, she thought suddenly. She didn't know why such a notion should force its way into her mind, but all at once she shivered, once again nervous of the man who had brought her to this isolated place and then made love to her with an intensity of purpose that was both glorious and terrifying. He felt her movement and quickly wrapped her in his arms.

'You're cold! I should have realized. Come, I will help you dress.'

'It's all right. I'm not cold – just a little bit surprised, I suppose.'

'Surprised?'

'It was very good, Carlo. It's never been so good for me before.'

'No? Then I am happy.'

He sounded happy, but at the same time he was making an emotional withdrawal which she wanted to stop. She longed for the closeness that there had been before their love-making, sensing that if she was to find out more about him it was only at times like this that he would be willing to talk.

He was busy dressing now, his movements quick and deft. Putting out a hand she touched him on the arm. Surprised, he twisted round, his expression almost defensive. It was only when she smiled that he relaxed enough to settle down beside her, still buttoning his shirt.

'Where do you come from, Carlo?'

'A small village called Lower Ditton!'

'I mean originally. You're not English, are you?'

He turned his head so that he was staring into the distance. 'No, I am not completely English. Does that matter?'

'Of course not! I just want to know more about you.'

His hands moved together nervously, as though he were washing them, and his whole body was tense.

'It is not always easy to talk about oneself. There are things in my past that I prefer not to remember.'

'OK. I won't ask again. Sorry.'

'It is I who should be sorry, but perhaps in time . . .'

'Yes.'

'We do have time, I hope? You are not planning to run away back to your city home?'

'I don't think so.'

He relaxed again. His hands were still for a moment then he reached out to ruffle her hair. 'I am very lucky to find you, Amy.'

'I agree!'

They both laughed. The awkward moment had passed and they strolled back to where Carlo had parked the car. He drove home more slowly than usual, occasionally reacing out a hand to touch her leg.

'My mother is Spanish,' he said abruptly as they swung into the village.'

'She's still alive?'

'I imagine so. We do not keep in touch.'

'And your father?'

'I never knew him. I had plenty of uncles, however, to provide me with a "role model" as the child experts so quaintly say.'

'No brothers or sisters?'

He seemed to hesitate. 'No,' he said at last. 'She could not love me, why would she want more?'

His pain was revealed by the very neutrality of his voice, Amy longed to comfort him, to reach out and tell him that she was there and that she would love him if he gave her the chance. Being wise, however, she said nothing.

'Here you are, safely home. Would Ray let you out again on Saturday night? You could come to supper with Colin and me.'

'Ray doesn't have any say over my movements once the girls are in bed! I'd love to come.'

'Good. Sleep well. It was special for me too tonight; very special.'

She kissed him on the cheek and slid out of the car. He watched her walk down the front path, then turn and wave beneath the porch light. He raised his hand in return before driving home, wondering how it was that women could be so different one from another. And not only women, men too. It was only children who were constant. Constant until they realized what the adult world was like, and what it could do to them.

He was falling in love with Amy, but he knew that he didn't understand her.

He understood only the children, and the children understood him. That was the beauty of Lower Ditton. That was why he had come there to live and why he would never leave. He had been drawn to the village and there he would stay; because of the children, and the knowledge he shared with them.

Chapter 6

Amy sat on her bed studying the photographs with mounting confusion. She was so absorbed in what lay before her that at first she didn't hear the tap on the back door. It was only Harriet calling her name that jerked her back to reality, for whatever else the photographs showed it most certainly wasn't reality.

She hurried downstairs. 'Harriet! I asked after Jonathan this morning, but you know what children are like. Fiona didn't really know how he was.'

Harriet looked pale, wore no makeup and her hair was badly in need of attention. With a jolt Amy realized that Jonathan must be far worse than she'd imagined; nothing else would account for Harriet's appearance. She was normally extremely fastidious.

'The doctor's just been. He wants Jonathan to go into hospital for some tests. Amy, I'm at my wit's end! He can't keep any food down and he's literally wasting away. It doesn't make any sense. There's no fever, no signs of anything definite, but he's in constant pain and vomiting virtually non-stop.'

'Then hospital's the best place for him. You never know, one day of tests and they might locate the problem straight away. Within two days he'll be back home and on the mend. You wait and see.'

'He looks as though he's dying,' whispered Harriet.

Amy shivered. 'Don't be silly! If he were dying the doctor would be taking it far more seriously.'

'*Haven't you been listening?*' Harriet shouted. 'He *is* taking it seriously. Jonathan's going into hospital.'

'That doesn't mean he's dying! Look, I know it's horrible when people are ill and no one knows why, but it's probably only a virus. He's a strong well-built man. How could he possibly die of a stomach upset?'

'I don't know! I don't know anything except that he's desperately ill and nothing seems to help. I'm frightened, Amy. What's going on in this village?'

With a sharp intake of breath Amy remembered the photographs upstairs, then told herself not to be such a fool. They were peculiar, it was true, but that was all. Certainly they had nothing to do with Jonathan Harris's illness.

'Going on? How do you mean, Harriet?'

'I mean why are so many people dying? Jacqueline and George; Kate; Pete and Wendy. Five people out of one small village. Then there was . . .'

'Who?'

Harriet was immediately on the defensive. 'No one else.'

'You were going to say someone else.'

'I wasn't. How could I? There hasn't been anyone else.'

'But . . .'

'I should know for Christ's sake! I live here, remember? You don't, not yet.'

'Not yet?'

The woman gave her a look that was a mixture of envy and distaste. 'I imagine that a certain someone might persuade you to put down roots in Lower Ditton if marriage were offered.'

'I imagine he might,' Amy confessed honestly.

'You certainly didn't let your sister's death slow you down, did you? Carlo's been pursued before, but only by village girls, of course. You've the advantage of city glamour.'

Amy flushed. 'I haven't been pursuing Carlo, but even if I had I don't see how it affects you. As for Kate, I'm quite sure she wouldn't want me to mourn her forever.'

'A few weeks wouldn't have been excessive, but you didn't wait that long, did you?'

Amy felt her temper rising. 'I don't see how all this is going to help Jonathan.'

Harriet edged towards the back door. 'No. No, you're right; it isn't. I'm sorry, I'm being ridiculous. Forget what I said. After all, it isn't any of my business. I'd better get back to Jonathan. I need to sort out some pyjamas for the hospital. I had hoped . . .'

'What?'

'Would you collect Joanne for me this afternoon?'

All Amy wanted now was for her to leave. 'Of course,' she agreed quickly, but Harriet lingered.

'Have you noticed anything strange about the children lately?' she asked, her voice strained.

Amy's laugh sounded false to them both. Harriet looked at her in surprise while Amy tried to force the memory of those photographs to the back of her mind.

'No. At least, not Kate's three. Why do you ask?'

'It doesn't matter, we'll talk about it another time. It's just that this morning Joanne came down to breakfast, asked for a boiled egg and *then* enquired whether or not her father was still alive! It was so cold-blooded, not a bit like the Joanne of old, but she has changed lately, and not for the better.' Harriet finally left, leaving behind a very disquieted Amy.

Shortly before lunch she decided to walk through the village and call on Sara Gregory who had, after all, been a close friend of Kate's. Amy felt that she owed it to her sister to try and help Jody's mother a little. Perhaps if she had more visitors she would rely less on drink for consolation.

Passing Carlo's shop she was suddenly struck with a horrible thought and, quickly revising her plans, hurried in to see him. There were two middle-aged women inside who gave her knowing smiles before stepping to one side and allowing her to duck beneath the counter. She went through to the small dispensary where he made up some of his own liniments and cough mixtures.

Almost immediately he followed, his smile of welcome making her tingle with pleasure despite her fears.

'To what do I owe this pleasure? You're not unwell, I hope?'

'Never better! No, it's just that Jonathan Harris is apparently terribly ill and I remembered Colin had promised to take him some of your peppermint tea. Did he?'

'Not to my knowledge. Does it matter? It couldn't have harmed him, you know.'

'Are you sure? He's got much worse suddenly, and if it ties in with drinking something from your shop . . .'

Reaching out, he smoothed back a curl from her forehead. 'You're worried about my reputation? That's very sweet of you, but I assure you it's quite unnecessary. In the first place peppermint tea is merely soothing – it might help indigestion but nothing more serious – therefore its failure to cure Jonathan would hardly be surprising. Secondly, since I didn't even send him any because Colin forgot to ask me there is absolutely nothing to worry about, but I appreciate your concern.'

'It couldn't have harmed him?'

'Not as much as the drugs his doctor has undoubtedly been pouring down his throat!'

'I see.'

He frowned. 'You are still worried, I can see it. What's wrong?'

'I wondered if Joanne has ever mentioned her father's illness to you.'

'Yes, she has. All the children discuss their families from time to time.'

'This morning she asked Harriet if her father was still alive!'

'She wanted reassurance, which is surely to be expected?'

'No, dammit, that wasn't the way Harriet told the story! She made it sound as though Joanne didn't care.'

'Harriet is a somewhat hysterical type of woman who would undoubtedly put the worst possible construction on anything her daughter said at a time like this. She is besotted with her husband to the exclusion of everything else, including her two children. Now, if you'll excuse me, I have work to do.'

Aghast, Amy stared at him. His eyes were flashing and his mouth was set in a tight line. He both looked and sounded extremely angry.

'Carlo, don't you ever wonder if perhaps just occasionally the children of this village might be in the wrong? Must you always take their side?'

He pushed her roughly out of his way. 'I have to go. I will see you around, Amy.'

'See me around?'

She was talking to an empty room for Carlo had returned to the shop and she was entirely alone. It was as though they had never been lovers, never given each other such glorious pleasure. She could have been a stranger to him. He, in such a mood, was certainly a stranger to her.

Even more disturbed now than when she left the house,

she pushed Thomas up the hill, then round the tight curve in the road and along the path to Sara's house. Her knock was answered immediately by Jody's mother but although it was mid-day she was still in her housecoat, holding a glass of red wine in her left hand. She had difficulty focusing on Amy, but once recognition dawned was quick to ask her in.

'Excuse the mess,' she muttered, stepping across a pile of dirty washing and accidentally kicking over the dog's water bowl. 'Since Pete died I don't seem to have got myself together.'

'Don't worry about it. I only wanted to see if there was anything I could do to help.'

'Turn the clock back, you mean?'

'No, of course not. I wondered if you'd like to come and give me a hand with Thomas one morning? I'm not used to babies and . . .'

'I'd probably drop him! Let's be honest, Amy, I'm half-cut most of the time. I never go out; I never see anyone; I slop around in filth and wonder how the hell it all happened.'

'Sara, I . . .'

'Amy, you're a nice person, just as Kate was a nice person. Be careful you don't end up like her. I don't believe Pete killed her. That's a load of rubbish. The police must be out of their tiny little minds to believe he did. God, look at these dirty mugs! Can you see a clean one anywhere? If so make yourself a coffee.'

'It's all right, I . . .'

'Aren't I good enough for you any more? Don't you want a coffee in my house? Do I shock you?'

'Of course not.'

'Well, I should. I shock myself. I'm a disgusting slob. Jody's right, I'd be better off dead.'

Amy felt her skin prickle. 'Jody said that?'

'Says, Amy, Jody *says* that. All the time. Day after day. It's her morning litany. She's probably right: sometime I'll get round to doing something about it. God, she's changed. She looks a nice kid, doesn't she? Pretty in a neat way, with such calm eyes. Don't be fooled, Amy, she's got a very hard streak in her. Children are strange. You bring them up, do what you believe to be right, and then they go and change on you.'

'Change?'

Sara re-filled her glass. 'Sure, Jody's changed. Even Pete saw that before he . . . When he was alive. She used to be soft as butter, cried over Walt Disney films, wanted to be a nurse, loved sitting on our laps. Then, all at once, pouff – vanish old Jody, enter new, super-sophisticated version complete with armour plating. Excuse me, I think I'm going to be sick.'

She rushed from the room while Amy sat completely still on the kitchen stool, trying to make sense of all that she had seen and heard during the course of the day.

After a few minutes Sara returned, pale but looking more herself. She filled the electric kettle and plugged it in. 'I'll join you, might sober me up. What was I saying?'

'That Jody's changed.'

'That's right. Probably they all do around her age, I just wasn't ready. I'd lost track of the time and kept thinking of her as a little girl.'

'She *is* a little girl; she's only eight.'

'They grow up fast these days. God, I miss Pete!' She began to cry silently. Amy quickly made the coffee and handed her a mug. Sara cupped her hands round it and hung her head until she had regained control.

'Jody tells me you're going out with Carlo.'

Amy pulled a face. 'I was, but somehow I think that I

blotted my copybook with him this morning. Oh no! That's Thomas crying. Look, I must dash, but I meant what I said. Please come down to see me tomorrow morning. I'd like some company.'

'I'll try. Amy, watch yourself with Carlo.'

'It's a bit late for that!'

'I didn't mean sexually, I meant . . .'

'Yes?'

'I don't know, I'm probably being stupid but I've always thought that he was a little odd. Oh, the children think the sun shines out of him, and he's done wonders for young Colin, but he isn't the same with adults. He can be very touchy. Besides, I used to think that he was the one who . . .' She giggled. 'Bother! Lost my train of thought. Have a drink for the road!'

She reached for the bottle and Amy let herself silently out of the house. She guessed what Sara had been going to say because Ray had said the same, but he was biased and Sara an alcoholic. Carlo would never have killed Kate. He had no reason to kill her. Pete had done it; the police wouldn't have closed the file unless they were certain of the facts. No, hard as it might be for Sara to come to terms with, there was no doubt that Pete had been leading a double life.

None of which, she thought as she hurried Thomas home, explained the photographs lying on her bed at this very moment.

An hour later, with Thomas fed and sleeping, she reluctantly climbed the stairs to study them again. She had been looking forward to seeing the many off guard studies of the children she had taken and had hoped to have one or two really good ones of her nieces to enlarge and frame for Ray. The way they had turned out she didn't even feel like showing them to him.

They were still on her bed, and they hadn't altered. Time and a better light through the window didn't put a different perspective on them. They were all just as strange as she had originally feared. It wasn't that they were bad pictures – Fiona in particular had photographed well. No, what was wrong with them was that the faces that stared out from the photos weren't the faces that she saw every day.

Caught unawares, the children's features had changed. Every one of them had a bony, poverty-stricken look. Their cheekbones were too sharply defined, the cheeks hollow. Then there were the eyes. Sophie had lovely eyes, large and gentle; she was the epitome of a cuddly four year old. In the photos her eyes were narrowed, glinting with a sharpness that indicated a premature disillusionment with the world more normally found in street-wise children from the slums. Also, every child's eyes were red, as though the pictures had been taken with a cheap flash gun, and every face bore the stamp of poverty and harsh living that Amy associated with the past, photos from the days when children were forced up chimneys and down coal mines. If each picture were to be sepia-tinted then the illusion would be complete. Only their clothes would set the children of Lower Ditton apart from their miserable contemporaries of the past.

The twins were still identical, but they looked thinner and more frail than in reality. A small smudge on Richard's cheek even looked like a bruise, and the way in which he and Samuel huddled together was pitiful. It was as though they were seeking comfort from each other in a hostile environment.

Picture after picture told the same story. When these children, the group that her nieces played with, were unaware of any adult presence they apparently – unless she was losing her mind – physically changed in appearance. Not one child remained the same, but it was in Colin that the greatest difference was apparent.

His face became that of a wizened little old man, his shy smile a twisted sneer at the world, and his obvious position as leader of the children was no longer a tribute to his cheerful, inventive mind but instead looked to be due to the air of blazing ferocity and intensity which emanated from him. There was no charm, no air of hesitancy about him when he was with his peer group, only a frightening energy that held his followers in thrall.

All at once the telephone rang. With a startled cry Amy sprung up, scattering the photos all around her. Quickly she gathered them together, and then impulsively hid them beneath her mattress before hurrying to answer it.

It was Harriet. A remarkably calm, self-possessed Harriet who informed Amy in a flat, expressionless voice that Jonathan had died ten minutes earlier in the hospital. She asked Amy to give Joanne her tea and then hung up. There had not been any miracle. No quick diagnosis and speedy recovery. Harriet had been right and Amy wrong. Now Jonathan was dead, and as yet no one knew why.

When the time came for her to collect the children from school she felt increasingly nervous. This wasn't only because she had to collect the unsuspecting Joanne but also because she feared that the faces of the children might appear the same as in the photos, forcing her to question her previous images of them. It would be terrible to discover that she had seen not what was actually before her eyes but merely her own romanticized vision of how she wished things to appear. If this were true it would destroy her belief in her own judgement of adults, too, including Carlo.

Fortunately for her peace of mind Fiona and her sisters

looked exactly as they always had. Amy hugged Sophie extra tightly as the little girl smiled up at her with a soft, reassuringly childlike expression. Joanne was about to walk by when Amy released her niece and caught the older girl by the arm. To her surprise the child flinched away as though burnt, fear flashing across her face for one brief second before she composed her features into their normally cheerful expression. But it had been there, that moment of distress.

'Joanne, your mother asked me to collect you today. You can have tea with us as well.'

'Lovely! Isn't daddy well still?'

'No, he's . . . I'm afraid he's worse, darling. He's gone into hospital.'

'Hospital? Will they be able to make him well?' Amy was relieved to hear the anxiety in Joanne's voice. It made nonsense of Harriet's earlier claims about her daughter.

'They'll do their best, Joanne, but he is very ill.' It was the furthest she dared go in preparing the child. Joanne looked her directly in the eye.

'He's already dead, isn't he?'

'It really isn't my place to . . .'

'He is. I know he is. Poor Mummy. Is she very upset?'

'What's happened?' interrupted Fiona. 'Is your father worse?'

'He's dead,' said Joanne in a chillingly matter-of-fact tone. 'He looked pretty bad last night. I'm to have my tea with you.'

'Great! Georgie, Sophie, Mr Harris is dead so Joanne's having tea with us.'

'Yippee!' shouted Georgina, and the girls skipped off up the road, leaving a stunned Amy clinging tightly to the handle of Thomas's pram.

All around her mothers and their children jostled and pushed, chattering, laughing and complaining as they made their way home. Richard and Samuel were the last out of school, and because she had been standing in shocked disbelief for so long Amy saw their father drive up in a tearing hurry.

It was the first time she had seen the missing Wendy's husband. He was a short, well-built man in his early thirties. It was obvious from his harassed expression and continual glances at his watch that collecting the boys was an inconvenient and time-consuming task. On a sudden impulse Amy went over to him.

The twins were already in the back of the car. They smiled politely at her; two nice, well-scrubbed boys with impeccable manners.

'Mr Beckett, I'm Amy Kendall – Kate's sister. I was wondering if it would help you if I brought the boys home from school each day. I have to come for my nieces.'

His relief couldn't be hidden. 'If you honestly don't mind it would be marvellous. I run my own business and although the boys are old enough to come to my office on their own, I suppose I'm over-protective now that Wendy's gone. I feel doubly responsible, you see.'

'I do see, and I'd be exactly the same. The boys will be perfectly safe with me, I promise.'

'Yes, we will,' put in Richard. 'Mrs Kendall's very nice; she's a friend of Carlo's.'

Amy felt a blush rising to stain her cheeks but Dean Beckett simply regarded her with renewed interest. 'Of course! In that case my mind is completely set at rest! Incidentally, have you any idea how poor Jonathan is?'

Amy bit her bottom lip and he read the message in her eyes. 'Oh, God!' he whispered, and then he was gone, driving the car at breakneck speed as though to escape from this latest news of death.

Once home Joanne and Fiona settled down to schoolwork while the younger girls played in the garden. Amy laid the table and began to prepare a shepherd's pie. Now and again Fiona giggled, and Joanne would whisper a response, the words unintelligible.

She made no further reference to her father. She ate a good tea, finished her homework without complaint and finally rushed away with Fiona to find some of their gang. Amy's head was aching. She felt that if she didn't soon talk to another intelligent adult she woud go mad.

At six o'clock Ray arrived home and she gave him the news. He went white round the mouth then retreated to his bedroom, saying that he didn't want anything to eat. She was still alone.

At seven o'clock, just as she had Thomas's bath ready, Harriet tapped on the back door. Her eyes were red-rimmed and her face totally without colour.

'I'm so sorry,' murmured Amy.

'There's to be a post mortem,' Harriet blurted out. 'The police say it's necessary.'

'I suppose it would be, and you must want to know why he died.'

'The doctors say they know already. The post mortem is for confirmation only.'

'Have they told you what it was?'

Harriet's face twisted bitterly. 'Yes, they've made their position extremely clear. You see, according to them Jonathan was poisoned.'

Amy shook her head. 'No! That can't be true. It doesn't make any sense. Who'd want to poison Jonathan?'

Harriet tried to hold back the tears. 'No one, no one at all, but don't you realize what this means, Amy?'

'That he had an enemy?' she asked stupidly.

'No! Who looked after him? Who nursed him all the time? Administered the medicine Dr Clift prescribed? Who cleaned up after him when he vomited? Disinfected all the bowls, took away any possible clues?'

'Well, apart from you . . .'

'*There was no one apart from me!*' Harriet screamed. 'Now do you understand? The police think that *I* murdered Jonathan.'

'Hello, Mummy,' Joanne said softly. 'I'm so sorry about Daddy dying but in a way perhaps it's for the best.'

The adults stared at the child.

'The best?' repeated Amy incredulously.

'Why, yes. Now Mummy and Daddy won't keep quarrelling all the time. It will be a happy home once again. Don't you think it will be nice to have peace, Mummy?'

Harriet stared at her daughter with loathing. 'Keep away from me,' she hissed. 'You're insane, saying things like that. Insane and unfeeling. Keep away! I don't want you near me, do you understand?'

'Harriet, she didn't mean . . .'

'But she did!' cried Harriet. 'That's the terrible thing – she means everything she says. What's happened to you, Joanne? You've changed so much. What's gone wrong? You were always such a loving child, and now . . .'

'I'll take her home,' said Joanne quietly. 'She doesn't know what she's saying.'

Yes, she does, thought Amy. She knows very well what she's saying. So did Sara. Both Harriet and Sara are saying the same thing. They're telling me that their children have changed, and I believe them because of the photos. I can see what their parents can only sense.

Even as she thought it she realized that the photos must remain a secret. The children mustn't know. She would keep them concealed until she found someone she could confide in. Someone who would listen to her, understand what she was trying to say.

She wished that she hadn't annoyed Carlo earlier in the day, for he would have been ideal. He knew Amy, possibly even loved her, and wouldn't doubt the sincerity of her fears. But, more importantly, he knew and understood the children. If anyone could help it would surely be Carlo. He must understand what was happening.

Chapter 7

That night Amy was sewing a button back on Fiona's school cardigan when she heard a light tap at the back door.

'You go, Ray,' she said casually. 'It's probably someone about Jonathan's funeral.'

'It's all funerals these days,' he grumbled. 'I'm beginning to think I ought to move before it's my turn.'

She heard him talking in the kitchen for a few minutes before he returned, frowning.

'For you.'

'Who is it?'

'Carlo.'

Glancing at his face Amy wished she'd gone in the first place. Carlo was standing by the kitchen table, hands thrust into the pockets of his jeans, his head lowered like a small boy who knows he's in the wrong.

'Yes?' Amy was pleased at how cool she managed to sound.

'I have come to say . . . that is, I was not quite myself this morning. I think perhaps I have offended you. If so I am naturally extremely sorry.'

'Fine. Thank you for telling me.'

His head lifted and he raised his eyebrows slightly. 'You *are* offended?'

'Yes, I am. You were rude and abrupt: I'd imagined that we were friends, you made it clear that we're not.'

'But of course we are!'

'Only when my opinions coincide with yours. I'm afraid

that's too one-sided for me. I like an equal relationship. If you want a "yes" woman, you're not going to find her in me.'

He removed his hands from his pockets and started to chew absent-mindedly at the nail on his left thumb. He looked so miserable and bewildered that she wanted to reach out and touch him, say that she accepted his apology and nothing had changed, but she was too honest and independent to give up on a matter that was important to her.

'"Yes women", as you put it, are not particularly to my liking.' His statement was tentative, a first gesture of reconciliation.

'Look, Carlo, we don't really know each other very well, do we?'

'No, but . . .'

'And perhaps we've both built up false images of each other. The point is that if you're going to take offence and walk out on me every time I fail to come up to your expectations, I shall be a nervous wreck in no time. I can only be myself; I'm no good at dissembling.'

Immediately he smiled. Not his ordinary smile but the full, heart-stopping one that was normally reserved for the children. Her stomach turned over while she tried furiously to resist his charm.

'That is very clear!' he laughed.

'I suppose that's something.'

He reached out and put a hand on her arm. 'I would like to repeat my invitation to you to have supper at home with me one night. Do you still want to come?'

She did, very much indeed, but she kept her expression non-committal.

'You won't leave me alone at the table if I say something you don't care for?'

'Certainly not. I will be the host; it would be very rude.'

'If you weren't the host you might? Is that what you mean?'

He laughed. 'No, you're twisting my words!'

Reluctantly she smiled. 'Then I'll be pleased to come.'

'Tomorrow, about eight?'

'Fine. I've taken some photos of the children that I'd like you to see.'

'I look forward to it, and from now on I will behave myself!'

'You've obviously charmed your way out of trouble all your life. Your poor mother couldn't have stood a chance!'

'My mother was totally immune, as were my uncles. I did not enjoy my childhood.' Before she could think of any reply he turned away, as though regretting the confidence.

'See you tomorrow,' she called, then stood looking thoughtfully after him as he walked away from the house. She wondered if what she had heard explained his devotion to children. Some time, when she knew him better – as she hoped that she would – she would try to find out more about his past.

'Are you going steady with that man?' snapped Ray as she went back to the living-room. She flushed.

'This isn't the fifties, Ray. Mature adults have "meaningful relationships", they don't "go steady" any more.'

'Never mind what it's called – are you seeing that Pied Piper on a serious basis?'

'Pied Piper?'

'Children were enchanted by the Pied Piper of Hamelin, weren't they? Followed him out of their village and off to their death.'

'Meaning?'

'That the children in this village are equally besotted with our foreign friend.'

'I like Carlo, Ray. I like him a lot,' she said firmly.

He stood up, walking restlessly around the room while he spoke. 'I know it isn't any of my business who you see . . .'

'True!'

'And I appreciate all you've done for us, but I do think that perhaps it's gone on too long. I have to get myself organized, and while you're here I'm never going to bother. What I'm really saying is . . .'

'That I can go. Preferably quickly, before I become too involved with the local enchanter.'

'Bluntly, yes.'

'Thank you, Ray. How long have I got before I have to move out? A day? A week?'

'Amy, please! You've been telling me the self-same thing often enough. You should be pleased.'

She stared at him, resentful of the speed with which he was acting.

'This is for your own good,' he assured her.

'Bullshit!'

'Believe me, Carlo isn't the right man for you. You've already had one disastrous marriage . . .'

'Thank you!'

'Oh, I can see the attraction. He's good-looking in a film-star way, and he's got loads of charm, or so all the women say, but you're too sensible to fall for that, Amy. Underneath the smiles and the quaint way of talking there's a completely different sort of person. I know what I'm saying because . . .'

'He threw a knife at you.'

'How on earth . . .?'

'I do mix with other people in the village. That sort of

thing is bound to come up in conversation! What I want to know is, why?'

Ray shook his head. 'I wish I knew. That's what worries me. It was at a small dinner party that Kate held for our last wedding anniversary. We ate early so that the children could share in some of the excitement. After the meal was over the women were in the kitchen and we men were talking about sport and what good losers the British are . . .'

'Riveting stuff!'

'If you'll let me finish . . .'

'Sorry.'

'After a bit I went to light a cigarette. I was meant to have given up, but as an anniversary treat I decided to allow myself one. Just as I reached for my lighter young Georgina started on about smoking being a dirty, nasty habit, and bad for my heart. All the propaganda they hand out to small children these days!'

'Quite right too.'

'That isn't the point. When I told her, very amiably, to remember who was the head of the household and mind her manners, she started screaming her head off. She shrieked and wailed, then ran over to your Carlo and clung on to his arm, begging him not to let me have my bloody cigarette.

'I was pretty annoyed, I can tell you. I grabbed hold of her by her waist and dragged her off him. I was just about to give her a slap on the leg when this cheese knife came flying through the air. It missed me by about half an inch, no more.'

'A cheese knife?'

'Yes.'

Amy laughed. 'Hardly intended to maim you for life!'

'He had no damn right to throw any sort of knife at me!

He was in *my* house, eating *my* food, drinking *my* wine and encouraging *my* children to misbehave. He didn't apologize either. He had the nerve to tell Georgie to go to bed, then mumbled something about an early night and left. It was incredible. He's obviously unhinged.'

'I admit it's peculiar. What did Kate say?'

'Kate made all sorts of ridiculous excuses about him not being the same since . . .' He stopped suddenly, flushing with embarrassment. 'Let's say she was anxious to smooth the affair over.'

'Not the same since what?' asked an intrigued Amy.

'It doesn't matter. It isn't something we talk about in the village. I shouldn't have mentioned it.'

'Has he been in some kind of trouble? Child abuse? Drug-pushing?'

'Drop it, Amy. No, he hasn't been in trouble, quite the opposite, but I can't say anything more. Please, take my word for it and give him up. I don't suppose I really need to worry, though. You must be longing to return to your studio!' He smiled encouragingly at her.

'Not particularly. I like the slower pace of life here.'

He ignored her comment. 'Talking of photos, have you had your films developed yet?'

'No.'

'Pity, I'm looking forward to seeing them. I could do with a good one of the girls.'

'They might not come out very well. I was testing a new camera,' she lied.

'Still, bound to be a couple that are OK.'

'Maybe, I'm off to bed now. Oh, yes, and I'm out to dinner tomorrow night so you can begin "coping" when you get home from work. If all goes well I'll leave in a couple of days. I'd prefer to travel back at the weekend, providing I'm not imposing on your hospitality too long, of course?'

'Amy, please, I didn't want to upset you.'

'You haven't, Ray. I'm somewhat disappointed that you have so little faith in my judgement but . . .'

'He'll let you down, but don't take my word for it.'

'I certainly won't!'

'Ask Ruth Bentley about him. She'll tell you how unreliable he is. She fully expected to marry Carlo a year ago. See her, find out what he's really like before you commit yourself.'

'I have no intention of committing myself to anything right now, and as for Ruth Bentley – whoever she may be – I wouldn't dream of asking some stranger for details of her private life.'

'She'd be pleased to have company. When he jilted her she drove away from his house in a hurry and had an accident. She's paralysed from the neck down. Go and ask her about your charming suitor.'

'If that's true, how come no one else has mentioned her? Most women seem to think he's quite a nice man, and that's an understatement!'

'You women are all the same, taken in by the packaging. There's another thing as well.'

'Really? Perhaps he's a transvestite? Or started life as a woman? Some small detail that's escaped my notice so far.'

'You've always been intelligent, Amy, don't act stupidly now, when it really matters. Whatever you may think about other women or flying cheese knives, surely you've noticed the change in my girls?'

'Yes, I also realize that they've lost their mother. A change is to be expected.'

'It began before that. The girls have changed. So have

their friends. What's more, every child who's changed in this village belongs to the group that hangs round Carlo's house. Ask people; I can't be the only person to see it.'

'Perhaps he's feeding them a secret potion! Honestly, Ray, you should hear yourself. I'm going to bed.'

She fell asleep immediately, but her dreams were filled with thin, haunted children who clung to her, nipping at her flesh with long, broken nails and pursuing her down dark corridors which had no end. She was glad when morning came.

Inspector Barbor studied the report in front of him for the eighth time that evening and shook his head.

'I don't believe it, Sergeant. There's been a mistake.'

'You don't think he was poisoned, sir?'

'If the pathologist says he was poisoned then he was poisoned, I *have* to accept it. What I do not accept is that his wife was responsible. I've interviewed her three times now and I'd stake every penny I possess on her innocence. She's as stunned and uncomprehending as we are.'

'Women are highly accomplished liars,' said the Sergeant morosely.

'Not this accomplished! If only I could make sense of it. I wasn't happy about Peter Gregory's suicide, but I'm even less happy about this mess. There's no motive, no intelligence and no discretion behind this murder. Somehow I'd credit Mrs Harris with enough common sense to commit a far better murder than this one if she wanted her husband out of the way.'

'Which means we have to look for someone else, sir.'

'But there isn't anyone else! Unless you think the doctor did it?'

'I think the wife did it.'

'So will the jury. So will the judge. And so, more importantly, will the villagers.'

'Pity the poor kids. The children here are having a pretty rough time one way and another. It all started to go wrong when . . .'

'Yes?'

'Nothing. It's something the villagers aren't too proud of.'

'Perhaps I ought to know about it.'

'It isn't connected with anything criminal.'

'I'd like to know. The children around here interest me. You say they've had a rough time lately and imply that you know why. If you know, then the children know. Perhaps . . .' He stopped. 'No, that's ridiculous. Even so, I'd like to hear what it is.'

'It's only that a year or so ago there was a bad fire up at the far end of the village.'

'I remember something about that. The local fire engine was out on a false call at the time, wasn't it?'

'That's right. You know what idiots some teenagers can be, making hoax calls and then laughing fit to bust when they see the engine tearing off for nothing. They reckon that's what happened that night.'

'Some people lost their lives, didn't they?'

'Yes, about four or five I think it was. It was one of those battered wives refuge places that caught fire. They seem to be in fashion at the moment. The place was ridiculously over-crowded. Naturally they didn't all get out.'

'Is that it?'

'I told you it wasn't relevant. It simply occurred to me that ever since then other children have been dogged with bad luck. That Colin Masters boy, Jody Gregory, Richard and Samuel Beckett, they've all lost one or both parents.'

'So?'

'So nothing; it just seems like some kind of retribution.'

'Retribution for what?'

'To be perfectly honest, none of the villagers wanted the refuge there in the first place. It brought a lot of undesirables into the community. Not ony the wives and children, though God knows they were a rough lot, but also the husbands. They used to come banging on the doors at night, trying to drag their wives and kids back home, presumably so that they could knock them about again.'

'And the village resented this?'

'Yes. It was suggested at the inquest that someone local had started the fire on purpose, but I don't believe that. It was probably one of the husbands, full of drink and fury.'

'Very colourful, Sergeant, and far more comfortable for your conscience.'

'Sir?'

'To blame an outsider.'

'Understandable though.'

'Quite.'

'As I said, it isn't relevant at all. I just realized that . . .'

'That the village has been a trifle accident-prone ever since?'

'Correct.'

'Leaving that aside for now, would you have known that both yew berries and bryony were poisonous?'

'No, sir.'

'Even more to the point, would Mrs Harris have known?'

'She could have looked it up, or asked Carlo.'

'Did *he* prescribe anything for Mr Harris? I know what

some people are like about traditional medicine these days.'

'I checked. The boy, Colin, suggested to Mrs Harris that Carlo should send her husband some peppermint tea, but never got round to asking his guardian.'

'Carlo didn't give any advice to Mrs Harris about home cures?'

'No, sir. He doesn't practise any form of medicine, only provides some popular herbal remedies that are coming back into fashion. I don't think he's that taken with them himself; he's simply a good businessman who knows his market.'

'But the boy did mention peppermint tea?'

'Yes, to Mrs Harris.'

'He's a bright lad. He found Kate Burgess's body, didn't he? I think I'd like another chat with him. Nothing formal, only a casual conversation. Any idea how I could bump into him?'

'He cuts through that alleyway to the shop after school every day. That would be at about three-forty.'

'I think I'll try and meet him there tomorrow. There's something going on in this place that we're missing. Perhaps young Colin will help point us in the right direction.'

'I'm sure he'll do his best. He's one of the politest lads I know.'

'Yes, a rather unusual boy I thought. Well, that's for the future. Right now we'd better go and pick up Mrs Harris. The warrant's been agreed, we're to charge her with murder.'

'Hard to see how she hoped to avoid it under the circumstances.'

'Exactly, and that's what bothers me. Get a policewoman to come along. She might easily become hysterical.'

The Inspector was correct. People from five or six houses away heard her screams, and when Christine and David Cross – nine-year-old Gillian's parents – collected Joanne and Deborah to take them home until their grandparents could be contacted, they were quite prepared for hysterics from the children too. Deborah cried a lot, but Joanne was amazingly composed.

'Do they still hang murderers?' she asked softly as she was tucked up in the spare room with Deborah asleep beside her.

'Of course not!' whispered a shocked Christine. 'Besides, I'm sure Mummy will be back home soon.'

'I hope so. It was a happy home again with Daddy gone. If she isn't, will I go and live with Carlo?'

'No! Your grandparents will look after you. Now get some rest. If you don't feel like school tomorrow you can stay here with me.'

Joanne smiled. 'Thank you but I'd rather go to school. All my friends are there.'

'How sensible of you. Good night, Joanne.'

'Good night, Mrs Cross.'

'She's very strange,' commented Christine, repeating the conversation to her husband. He put his arms round her and gave her a quick squeeze.

'She's only eight; far too young to understand. It's probably like a television programme to her. She thinks that tomorrow it will all be over. Poor kid, it's only just beginning.'

Of course he was wrong. It had really begun a long time before.

Interlude

Thomas had been a placid, contented baby ever since Amy arrived at Lower Ditton. He rarely cried, smiled at visitors and gave less trouble than any baby she'd seen. Despite this his sisters didn't like him. It wasn't that they teased him, or complained about him, that would have been easy to deal with; no, to Amy's distress they simply ignored him. When he gurgled at them they looked away; when Amy had him out in the pram they never once looked in or dangled a toy. They tried to pretend he didn't exist.

Then, at tea-time on the day Amy was going to Carlo's for dinner, everything changed. She was buttering bread for sandwiches when she heard Thomas start to cry. Not quiety but loudly; irate screams of fury that sent her flying up to his room.

The girls were already there, crowded in the doorway, gazing at their brother kicking and screaming in his cot, his face flushed with temper.

'Did any of you touch him?' shouted Amy, dashing to pick him up. Three heads were shaken, but their eyes were alert. For the first time Thomas interested them.

Amy picked him up. He wasn't wet, he wasn't dirty and he wasn't due to be fed, but something had upset him and his tiny fists flailed in the air.

'Sshh!' she soothed, rocking him in her arms. Normally he loved to be cuddled, but not this time. He went stiff and a finger nail caught one side of her face, leaving a long weal speckled with blood. 'Ouch!' Startled, she dumped him back in his cot. He stopped crying and stared up at her, his eyes furious.

Amy dabbed at her cheek and then bent over the cot. The malevolence in his previously placid features startled her. She blinked, and for a brief moment the baby's eyes glowed redly out at her, just as the children's eyes gleamed red in the photos.

Her scalp prickled and she twisted to look at her nieces. They were moving quietly into the room, their gaze fixed on Thomas. Her own presence was ignored as they crowded round the cot, their hands softly patting his face and stroking his shoulders.

'Isn't he sweet?' crooned Fiona.

'Lovely baby!' cried Georgina.

'Baby like us!' shouted little Sophie.

Thomas was calm now. He looked up at his sisters and his arms reached out towards them. Normally they would have turned away, but not this time. All three of them responded, so that finally the girls stood in a semi-circle round the cot and there they remained, all four children linked together in some strange ritual of bonding that was beyond Amy's comprehension.

With a stifled exclamation she left them alone; fearful when she should have been happy, but knowing instinctively that she was right to feel fear.

Thomas was exactly four months old.

Chapter 8

It was obvious that Carlo and Colin had gone to a lot of trouble preparing for Amy's visit. The dining-room smelt of polish, and both were dressed up for the occasion. Colin had abandoned his jeans in favour of green cords and a brown patch-pocket shirt, while Carlo was in a dark lounge suit with white shirt and deep red tie.

At the last moment she had decided to leave her photographs at home. This was partly because she knew that Colin would be with them for a considerable part of the evening, and partly to avoid any possible disagreement with Carlo. If he remembered to ask after them she would pretend that they had slipped her mind.

'We've got stuffed courgettes,' enthused Colin. 'They're my most favourite food. Then we've got roast beef with Yorkshire pudding, and after that . . .'

'Leave in some element of surprise!' laughed Carlo. Amy smiled at the excited child.

'It all sounds delicious. Did you help with the cooking?'

'No, but I watched carefully!'

'I was pleased to get out of the house tonight,' she confessed, sipping her dry Martini. 'Ray has decided to start coping alone, but the beginning wasn't highly auspicious. The bathroom has more water on the floor than in the bath and Thomas is rolling round on his changing mat naked from the waist down because his father can't manage the safety-pins!'

Carlo gave her a questioning glance. 'You're not leaving him, are you?'

'It looks like it. I'm not needed any more.'

'You can't go!' said Colin indignantly. 'Carlo and I need you. Why is Fiona's daddy being mean?'

'He isn't being mean, Colin. He feels that while I'm there he isn't going to make any effort to cope, and he's probably right.'

'You won't leave the village, will you?' pressed Colin. Amy caught Carlo's warning look and put an arm round the boy.

'Not if I can help it!'

'Oh, good. Mr Burgess would be most unpopular if he made you go away.'

She laughed at his solemn tone. 'I'm flattered to think people would even notice.'

'The children would.'

'I don't know that many children.'

'I mean our gang,' he said impatiently. 'You know, there are eleven of us. We're all bonded together, until death us do part.'

'What qualifications are needed to join this exclusive club?' The boy looked puzzled.

'How do you choose your members?' explained Carlo. Colin gave him a surprised glance.

'*You* know.'

'Yes, I know, but Mrs Kendall doesn't.'

'It's a bit difficult to explain, but we're all . . . we think the same about things. We understand one another.'

'Even the little ones?'

'Not exactly, but the little ones . . .'

'Come on,' said Carlo impatiently. 'Time to eat.'

Amy was sorry that he'd interrupted. She very much wanted to know the secrets of the eleven children who couldn't be photographed properly. However, if Carlo knew then he was determined to keep the knowledge to himself. Colin took the hint because once they were at the table he started talking about football and fishing and made no further reference to his friends.

Once the boy was in bed Amy started to clear the dishes, but Carlo stopped her. 'They'll keep. Let's not waste time on dirty plates!'

Over coffee Amy told him about Ray's real reason for asking her to go, but implied that he was worried about the way she was neglecting her work rather than revealing his intense dislike of Carlo. Her subterfuge didn't work.

'It's me he hates,' he said crisply. 'I have always known this. Never mind, you can stay here.'

'I couln't possibly! What would people say?'

'Who cares? I will tell them that Colin needed a woman around the house and that you are helping rehabilitate him.'

'They won't believe that. Colin is perfectly well-adjusted, he certainly doesn't need a woman in his life.'

'I need one in mine.'

'Yes, a fact they'll all appreciate! I can just hear the sniggers now. No, thank you, Carlo. I wouldn't feel right.'

He moved along the settee and kissed her lightly on the forehead. 'Too much talk is bad for us. I would rather love you.'

She had expected to feel inhibited by the unseen presence of the child above them, but with Carlo there was very little opportunity to think of anything apart from the exquisite sensations that he skilfully elicited from her. At one point she cried out, certain that she could not stand such pleasure, but she was wrong. Finally it was over. She lay exhausted on the deep pile carpet staring up at her lover with a mixture of pride and gratitude.

'You certainly don't make leaving easy!' she murmured, pulling his head down to her shoulder.

'You can still talk of leaving? What must I do to keep you with me?'

'I can't spend my entire life here just waiting for moments of passion! Unfortunately there are other things to be done.'

'Nothing more important!'

'There's the small matter of earning a living.'

'You're like Kate, you do not need to work. Your parents left you both money, is that not so?'

'That's true, although I can't think why Kate told you. I, however, invested most of mine in a photographic studio, and I certainly can't live off the interest on what's left.'

He gave her one final kiss and then sat up, running his fingers through his hair in an attempt to smooth down the wiry curls.

'In which case we will get married,' he announced casually. 'It is quick, I know, but why wait? It would have happened eventually, let us precipitate matters a little.'

Amy blinked in surprise and began to pull on her cotton dress. 'Married? Is that a proposal?'

'No, I will make a proper proposal when I am sure you won't turn me down!'

'Carlo, we really don't know each other properly.'

He scowled. 'Do you always make love to men you hardly know? Is this the way it is done in the towns? Surely our physical commitment is – how do you say? – the icing on the cake? You could not have made love to me if you did not have feelings of a serious kind, could you?'

There were spots of red on his cheekbones, an undoubted flush of anger and, she feared, disenchantment.

'I don't go hopping from one man's bed to another's,

no; but honestly, Carlo, I hadn't considered marriage. Oh, I'd dreamed that perhaps one day we might, but that's all it was, a dream. I'm not sure that I'd be a good wife to you. I certainly wasn't very satisfactory the first time round! Besides, haven't you ever slept with a woman without intending marriage?'

He looked away from her so that she could only see the sharp planes of his face and the tight, straight line of his lips.

'That is quite different.'

'Why?'

'For men it is not the same.'

'How would you know? Don't tell me you're a closet chauvinist?'

'Are you a closet feminist?'

'No, I'm an open feminist. Not one of the "I'm better than a man any day of the week" variety, but I happen to believe in equal opportunities and a common set of standards.'

He gave an exclamation of disgust. 'Ridiculous!'

'Carlo, please! I'll be honest with you. Yes, I find you incredibly attractive, great company and a fantastic lover. But, and it's a big but, you can also be moody, unpredictable and are such a private person that I couldn't possibly consider marrying you until I knew a great deal more about your earlier life. If you really love me and want to marry me, surely you want to tell me all about yourself?'

'Why? It is what I am now that counts. I am amazed that every time we are getting on well you have to spoil things. For you the past was happy. You can talk of it and I learn only about your childhood and your wonderful family. From this I realize why you are open and loving. It is nice to hear these things.

'It was not the same for me. There would be no pleasure

in such a conversation. It would make you sad and spoil the good times, which are now. I do not wish to discuss my past. It was not pleasant.'

Amy sighed. Plainly she wasn't going to get anywhere at this particular moment, if ever, and it seemed wise to change the direction of the conversation without altering the fact that she would not commit herself to marriage yet, however much her emotions urged acceptance.

'All right, if that's how you feel then obviously I won't pry. It doesn't stop you talking about your years here, does it?'

'Persistent, Amy! No, it doesn't, although I would rather we made love again.'

'Stop it! I mean that, Carlo. Tell me about Ruth Bentley.'

She heard about deafening silences, but this was her first experience of one. Carlo's face changed radically. She could feel him withdrawing emotionally from her, his features closing, his eyes losing their softness and warmth. At the same time he withdrew physically, standing up and walking over to the window so that he could stare out at the garden. All she could see was the back of his head. He was motionless except for his hands; they moved constantly at his sides, the fingers flexing non-stop as though cramped and aching. She wished that she'd kept silent.

'Carlo, I'm sorry. If you don't . . .'

'Why apologize? You are right; it is something you should know.'

'I'm ruining tonight, aren't I? I didn't want to, it's only that I'm confused. Part of me wants to stay here with you, but another part wants to leave and get away from . . .'

'From what?

'All the deaths.'

'Deaths?'

'Yes, my sister's; Wendy's; Pete Gregory's and Jonathan Harris's. That's rather a lot in the space of a few weeks.'

'Wendy may be alive.'

'I doubt it. Also, there's Harriet.'

'She isn't dead!'

Amy wished that he would turn and look at her. 'I know she isn't, but she's been arrested.'

'She shouldn't have killed her husband.'

'I don't believe she did.'

'You have information to prove this?' he queried sarcastically.

'No, but I saw her when he was at his worst. She was devastated.'

'Women are born actresses.'

'In that case I'm surprised you want to marry one.'

He made a sound of annoyance before turning towards her with a look of resignation.

'Let's not quarrel. You asked about Ruth Bentley; well, I will tell you all you want to know. She was a teacher at the village school here. A lively girl, not as beautiful as you, but pretty and cheerful. The children liked her and she was always good company.

'At that time I lived alone; Colin's parents were still alive. She would spend weekends here with me and after a time we became lovers. I did not feel for her as I do for you, but I liked her a great deal and thought that she was kind.

'Last year there was a fire here in the village. A refuge for battered wives was set alight, some people think by a villager, others by a drunken husband, it is not that important. Whoever started it was either evil or completely lacking in intelligence for there was no way that everyone could get out.

'I knew several of the children. They used to come to my shop and talk to me, then steal a snack bar or some dried apricots from the tub by the counter. I did not mind; I understood them.

'When I saw the flames from my front room window I went there at once. The fire engines had been called but did not come. Amy, you could hear the women and chidren screaming from the opposite end of the main street – I will never forget those sounds. Some of us tried to help the people inside. We got one or two out but most died. They burnt to death, Amy, while we stood in the cool night air and listened to them dying.'

'How many died?' she whispered.

Carlo shrugged. 'Many, I do not know the exact number. After a long time the screaming stopped and almost immediately a fire engine arrived. I did not stay to watch them, there was no point. Those children, who had lived their short lives in fear and pain, died in terror and agony. There is no justice.

'When I got back Ruth was waiting for me. I told her what had happened. I was shocked and distressed. I cried for the children. She tried to comfort me, told me that I had done all I could and that I must not try to take on the suffering of the entire world.'

'She was right, Carlo.'

'Yes, in that she was right. Unfortunately she didn't leave it there. She started to say that the women and children were probably partly to blame. She explained that some women like to be abused, that they encourage it and then run screaming to the police. In that, too, she may have been right. However, after that she made the most shocking statement imaginable.

'She said that if it was a villager who had started the fire she was sure that he – or she – hadn't intended such horror, but was probably tired of the way the children went round causing trouble.

'She cited examples of the children's crimes. Throwing stones at cars, swearing at younger children, fighting at the least provocation. I tried to tell her that this was because of the lives they had led. It was all that they understood.

'Ruth became cross. She said that if I had to teach the little monsters I wouldn't be so sympathetic towards them, and informed me that she had already written a letter of complaint to the head of the board of governors requesting that the refuge be closed down because the children were unteachable and a bad influence on our own youngsters.'

'But . . .'

'There is no "but". I knew at once that I could never marry such a woman. She was pretty and gentle but she had no compassion, no understanding of the importance of a child's early years, or the damage that lack of love then can do. She would never have been a good mother to our children. Her outlook was entirely coloured by her profession.

'The next day we went out for a meal and I told her that it was over. I also explained why. She did not understand. I hadn't expected her to. She was a woman of limited vision and I had only just discovered it in time.

'We came back here and she wanted to make love. I couldn't. By then I truly knew her and it was physically impossible. I apologized and suggested that she left. She was crying, but not hysterical. On her way home she collided with a drunken driver and was paralysed. Naturally I am sorry, but it was not my fault.

'I am sorry if I sound harsh but I, too, can only be myself. Children need protection. You understand this – I have watched you with your nieces, you are wonderful with them. Colin too worships you. There is nothing brittle or shallow about you, Amy. You will be a marvellous mother to any children you may have in the future, whether by me or some other man.

'I love you and I want to marry you, but that is all. I cannot offer you a great deal materially, and I know that at times I am moody and difficult. However, for you I would try to be less difficult! More than that I cannot promise.'

Amy couldn't respond because she was crying. She was crying partly for the children who had died, but also for Carlo whose past was obviously such a nightmare of neglect or abuse that it had left him wary of all adults but trusting and compassionate with every child, however difficult or wilful.

As she moved into his arms and he soothed her with murmured endearments and gentle, rhythmic movements of his hands on her body, she knew that she would never leave him. She had been stupid to fight against the intensity of her feelings for him, and considered herself incredibly fortunate to have gained his love and trust.

She did not realize the danger that involvement with such a complex and committed man would involve. She recognized his humanity and love for children and imagined it extended into most areas of his life. She could not see, for it was deeply hidden and carefully concealed, the twisted hate that was the second legacy of the nightmare that had been his childhood.

All eleven of them were there, sitting in a silent circle on the floor of Dean Beckett's garage, waiting to hear what their leader had to say.

'They're going to get married!' he announced, after allowing a suitable pause for the tension to build up.

'Hurrah!' they chorused.

'Quite soon, Carlo told me. Before Christmas, because he wants her living with us over the Christmas holidays. Aren't I lucky?'

Ten heads nodded, and ten pairs of eyes held a yearning expression which was inexplicable considering that they all came from happy homes with at least one loving parent of their own, whilst Colin had no blood relatives at all. Even so, it was plain that they envied him, and he gloried in it.

Fiona didn't like all the attention to be on Colin. She gave Gillian a sharp dig in the ribs with her elbow. 'Amy isn't as perfect as everyone thinks,' she whispered. Colin looked at her coldly.

'You're jealous, Fiona; jealous because you won't have her living in your house any more. Well, it serves your horrible father right. He's the one who tried to push her out.'

'I don't care. She's taken photos of us, did you know?'

'Why shouldn't she? I'd like to see them.'

'No, you wouldn't.'

'Would.'

She slipped a hand into the pocket of her smart blue pinafore dress and drew out a four-inch square snapshot. This she dangled high above her head, waving it around so that no one could see properly.

'Come and take it – if you dare!'

With a bellow of rage Colin launched himself across the circle and butted Fiona in the solar plexus with almost animal ferocity; then, ignoring her laboured breathing and gasps of pain, he snatched the photo from her grasp and held it to his chest.

No other child moved. No girl went to Fiona's assistance. No boy attempted to see what it was Colin held. Every one of them remained seated, their eyes flickering back and forth, some fearful, some glinting with excitement.

Colin bent his head and examined the print cautiously. He stared for a few seconds, then held it up to the light and stared again. Finally he threw it to the floor in disgust.

'It's only an ordinary picture! There's nothing special about it.' Fiona rubbed at her eyes, trying to breathe without wincing and flashing a look of hatred at Colin.

'Look again, smarty-pants!'

He looked again.

'OK. It's one of all of us, taken when we were meeting at your place. Why the fuss? I'm glad she takes pictures. I can have photos of myself all round my room once she's married Carlo!'

'Dummy! Don't you see it isn't *us*?'

'It is. There's Jody, Gillian, Mark, Joanne . . . Oh!'

'Now do you see what I mean?'

He frowned. 'I don't understand what's happened. How could a camera change our faces? And look at our eyes!'

Joanne grabbed it from his hand. 'Let me look.' She giggled. 'It isn't very good of you, Fiona. You're all thin and scraggy! So's Jody! Where am I?'

'You're there,' said Colin quietly. 'We're all there – in a way.'

Now everyone wanted to look and the photo was passed round the circle, leaving in its wake a trail of astonished, uncomprehending faces.

'Has she said anything?' asked Colin at last.

'Nope, but she will; anyone would.'

'Perhaps she'll show it to Carlo. I wonder what he'll say?'

'If she shows Carlo,' said Richard, always the more assertive of the twins, 'then we don't have to worry. It's if she chooses someone else that we're in trouble.'

Colin looked doubtful. 'Even Carlo might be a bit surprised.'

'No, he won't. He's lost, too, but in a different way from us.'

'Is he?' asked Georgina. 'I didn't know grown-ups could be lost.'

'Inside he isn't a grown-up, stupid!' retorted Colin. 'I thought we *all* knew that.'

'I didn't.'

'I'll try and find out some more about the pictures,' Colin continued. 'Check that she doesn't go round asking awkward questions, OK?'

They nodded agreement. He never broke his word, and however fond he might be of Amy they knew that should she threaten them in any way Colin would make sure she was silenced, and silenced quickly.

'Right,' he sounded highly relieved, 'if that's all settled we'd better move on to the next item on the agenda. Jody, what's your mother like at the moment?'

Jody quickly began to tell them, and the circle of faces turned towards her, features changing in the uncertain light from the garage window. Very quickly they took on the appearance of the photo currently in Colin's hip pocket. A group of tough, under-fed neglected children, mature beyond their years with eyes that glowed red with hatred.

Two separate sets of identities, and not a single child present knew which one was the mask.

Chapter 9

It had been a long school day for Colin. He particularly hated Wednesday afternoons with double swimming. Despite his terror of the water he had learnt to swim, but nothing could ever make him enjoy it. Every week he spent the first two days dreading it and the last two unwinding from the fear before it all began again the following Monday.

It was therefore with extra enthusiasm that he rushed down the narrow alleyway for home, cutting through to Carlo's shop and, because his head was down, he didn't see the approaching adult until too late. With a startled cry he ran straight into Inspector Barbor, nearly knocking him to the ground.

'I'm so sorry, sir!' he apologized, picking up his school cap. 'Are you all right?'

The Inspector gave a rueful smile. 'Just about. Actually, I was hoping to bump into you!'

'Oh?' Colin smiled brightly at the man. 'Why's that?'

'I'm hoping you might be able to help me. You're a smart lad and obviously keep your eyes and ears open. Is there somewhere we could have a chat?'

'At the shop?'

'Excellent.'

'It's through the gate here. Mind the rose, it's trailing everywhere. Carlo isn't keen on gardening.'

'Perhaps Mrs Kendall will be.'

'Perhaps,' agreed Colin, but his face was cautious and

he saved his smiles for the moments when the Inspector could see him.

Soon they were sitting in a large bed-sitting room situated directly over the shop. The Inspector was drinking peppermint tea – which he had specially requested – and Colin a milkshake. Carlo had left them alone, returning to the shop as soon as possible. It was plain that he had other things on his mind. Probably, thought the Inspector, his forthcoming wedding.

'Nice tea this,' he commented casually.

'Yes, it's good for indigestion. Carlo buys it from the warehouse. He does make up some herbal teas himself, but not that one.'

'Has it ever helped you?'

'Helped me?' Colin looked puzzled.

'When you've had a stomach upset.'

'If I get a stomach upset, Carlo starves me for twenty-four hours. He says that's the best cure for stomach bugs!'

'But you have fluids, surely?'

'Boiled water usually. Burnt toast is good for wind, if that's what's bothering you.'

Barbor smiled. 'I'm fine, but I'll remember the tip.'

'The charcoal acts as an absorbent.'

'Really?'

'Yes, really.' For a moment it almost seemed as though the boy were smiling mockingly at the Inspector, but of course he wasn't. He always smiled. He was a cheerful child.

'I believe you suggested this tea for Mr Harris, Colin.'

'Did I?'

'Mrs Harris says you did.'

'Then I must have done. Why should she tell a lie?'

'I can't imagine.'

Colin looked thoughtful for a moment. 'Yes! I

remember, I did. On the way home from school, a day or so before Mr Harris died. She was with Mrs Kendall, telling her all about Mr Harris's pains, and I said Carlo recommended peppermint tea.'

'What did she say?'

'She wasn't very interested. Well, she was, but not in the peppermint.'

'What do you mean?'

'She didn't want the peppermint, but she started asking all about herbal teas. How Carlo made them; what ingredients he used; that sort of thing.'

'I see.'

'I explained that you have to be very careful. I mean, some plants – like foxglove – can make a medicine that's good for your heart but if you make the preparation too strong it kills you. You have to know what you're doing. Carlo's always on about that.'

'And that's the example you gave her – foxgloves?'

'Yes, and I mentioned berries, too. When Mrs Leyton's baby was small she wanted to make her own rose-hip syrup. She came to Carlo for the recipe, and guess what?'

'What?'

'She'd collected yew berries!'

'Is that bad?' queried the Inspector.

'Lethal! They're poisonous; the poor baby would have died if she'd used them. Carlo told her off.'

'And you told Mrs Harris this story?'

'Yes; not because I thought she'd try making Mr Harris rose-hip syrup, but as a sort of example of the mistakes people make.'

'Quite. Did anyone else hear you telling her?'

'Mrs Kendall might have done, but she was busy with Thomas.'

This wasn't at all what Inspector Barbor had hoped to

hear. However, it was extremely damaging evidence, and he had no choice but to note it down. It looked as though he had been wrong in his assessment of Harriet Harris. In some ways he felt mean tricking the boy into making such a statement, but Colin was so precise and confident that he wanted to take full advantage of the apparently informal interview. Police stations and court rooms could inhibit children. It was at times like this that the most reliable information was usually obtained.

'I've enjoyed my tea, beneficial or not! Let's forget Mrs Harris for a moment, shall we? I'd like to see what you remember about the picnic in the woods on the day Mrs Burgess died.'

'Carlo doesn't want me to talk about it any more. He says it's over and I must try to forget.'

'I can understand that, but . . .'

'I'll have to call him,' said Colin firmly. The Inspector cursed beneath his breath. When Carlo Rivero returned he gave the policeman a hard stare.

'What is this, Inspector? An interrogation?'

'Of course not, sir. The fact of the matter is, young Colin here is a very reliable witness and I'm just clarifying one or two small points with him.'

'About Kate Burgess? Surely that's over and done with?'

'Officially yes, but . . .'

'The boy's had enough.'

Barbor gave in. He stood up, allowing himself a small sigh to indicate his disappointment. The man in front of him remained unmoved.

'One thing, Colin,' he added, almost as an afterthought.

'Yes?'

'What did you think of Mr Gregory?'

The response was instant. 'I didn't like him.'

'Why was that?'

'He was always smiling and joking with other women, but he made Mrs Gregory very unhappy – I don't really know why. Perhaps it was something to do with that.'

'She seems very upset now he's dead,' commented Barbor, slightly shocked by how much children learnt from watching the adults around them.

'I guess so. Maybe she sort of enjoyed him making her unhappy. Perhaps it's like a toothache. She misses the pain now it's gone!'

The Inspector stared at the lad, took in the wide-apart eyes, the sprinkle of freckles and the cheerful, upturned mouth. A normal, healthy nine-year-old boy who somehow saw and understood far too much for his age.

His guardian seemed to think so as well for there was a frown creasing Carlo Rivero's usually smooth face and he shook his head at the policeman without Colin noticing. With a smile the Inspector patted the boy's shoulder.

'Possibly you're right, young man. Thanks for the chat, and look where you're going next time you start rushing home. Good afternoon, Mr Rivero.'

Carlo stuck his hands in his trouser pockets and nodded. As soon as he'd shown the Inspector out he returned to the upstairs room where Colin stood in the middle of the floor.

'What was all that about?'

'I ran into him in the alleyway.'

'Fancy that!'

'Does he think . . .?'

'What?'

'That *I'm* the one who killed Mr Gregory.'

'Don't be stupid: no one killed Pete Gregory, he committed suicide, remember?'

'There have been so many deaths I get muddled. I'd like to lie down now, my head's hurting.'

'Sure.'

So many deaths, thought Carlo to himself. Yes, there had been a lot. After a little further thought he resolved to make sure that the Inspector stayed away from Colin in the future. It couldn't do any harm to be careful, just in case.

Amy was trying on her pastel-blue wedding dress when the girls knocked at her bedroom door.

'Wait a minute, please,' she called. The dress was perfect, and it was to remain hidden away until next Saturday when she and Carlo became man and wife.

'We can't wait,' retorted Fiona. 'There's a bike scramble in the woods this morning. We're off now.'

'*Wait!* You are not to play in those woods. Both your father and I have told you . . .'

'It's all right,' Georgina placated her. 'Everyone will be there. Richard, Samuel, Mark, Gillian . . .'

'I really don't think that . . .'

'Bye!' yelled Fiona, and they clattered down the stairs and out through the garage, collecting their bikes on the way. Amy went to the window on the stairs in order to watch them leave. She was relieved to note that Sophie hadn't taken her bicycle; obviously her role was purely that of spectator. She knew that she should have been firmer, forbidden them to go, but now that they would soon be on their own – for Ray showed no inclination to find a housekeeper – there was little point. Very soon they would do precisely what they wanted all the time.

'Dad,' said ten-year-old Mark to his father, 'is it OK if I take my bike this morning? The gang are having a scramble.'

'Where?' asked Lionel West, his attention mainly on the sporting pages of the paper. He was wondering why anyone bothered to educate their children when you could become a millionaire by spending your formative years hanging round snooker halls.

'Probably in the woods.'

'The woods?' Rosie West was more alert than her husband, and totally disinterested in all sport. 'I don't think that's a very sensible place to go.'

'Where else can we hold it? You wouldn't want it in the back garden, would you?'

'Don't be rude, Mark. You've got far too cheeky lately. Lionel, surely the woods aren't safe for the children?'

'Why not?' asked her husband irritably. He had just discovered that a cricketer could also become a film star, and his own work as a bank manager seemed hideously mundane.

'You know perfectly well why. Remember Kate?'

He sighed and threw the paper to the floor. 'That's over. They caught the man . . .'

'They did not!' said Rosie quickly.

'Very well, the man killed himself – does it matter? Either way the woods are now as safe as they ever were, and that's where the children have played since they were old enough to leave the back garden. You can't keep that boy tied to your apron strings forever. It's a pity you aren't as anxious to keep me by your side.'

Rosie knew what was coming next; an argument about her lack of enthusiasm for the physical side of their marriage. Lionel was as bad at making love as he was at playing the sports he so much admired, but she had never dared to tell him and disinterest was her only answer. They had quarrelled about it for years, and she didn't want to start up again in front of Mark.

'All right, go then; but be careful.'

'Thanks, Mum.' He left the house and collected his bike.

'Carlo, is it OK if I go to the woods for a bike scramble this morning?'

Carlo was busy working out whether or not he could afford to have a house built for the three of them on a vacant site near the end of the village that was going cheaply. He was tired of living above and behind the shop.

'Sure,' he said casually. 'Take care of the little ones.'

'Will do.'

Colin, with far less trouble than his friends, collected his bike and set off in the direction of the woods.

All over the village the eleven children were going through the same ritual. Only Joanne was refused permission. Her grandparents, who were caring for her and her sister while their mother was in police custody, were afraid to take the risk of letting her out of their sight.

She pleaded, cried, sulked, threw a temper tantrum, and finally swore fluently at the elderly couple. Immediately they sent her to her bedroom for the morning. She stamped theatrically up the stairs, slammed her door, put a chair against it then climbed niftily out of the window on to the garage roof. Joanne had no intention of missing the fun.

She too set off on her bike in the direciton of the woods.

They all met on the outskirts of the woods, where the stone path turned into a dirt track. Carefully they wheeled their machines deep into the trees, laid them down and then set off for their real destination. They had plenty of time; it was, as yet, only nine-thirty.

Chapter 10

Jody let them into the house with the front door key that she now wore round her neck all the time. Her mother had given it to her after one unfortunate afternoon when she was too drunk to let her daughter in after school.

Moving swiftly and silently they entered the hall. Their voices were a low whisper that was quite beyond the hearing of Sara Gregory, already on her third glass of scotch that morning. The first she knew of their arrival was the moment when Jody stood in the doorway of the kitchen, her eyes flicking round the room, taking in the filth and squalor that was now an integral part of her home.

Sara blinked in surprise. 'I thought you were . . . you know, out.'

'I was. Now I'm back.'

'I've got a bit of a headache. Play quietly, won't you?'

'Sure. I've brought the gang with me, is that OK?'

Sara frowned, unable to recall exactly how many were in her daughter's gang of friends. It didn't matter much. They were quiet enough. Why, she hadn't even heard them come in.

'That's nice, sugar, have a . . .' She lost the thread of her conversation, sat down on a kitchen chair and gulped her drink. If only Pete were here, he'd help her sort herself out.

'Jody!' she shouted, the idea taking root.

'Yes, Mum?'

'Ask your father to get up and give me a hand. It is Saturday, after all.'

Jody sighed but refrained from telling the truth. There was no longer any need.

'I will.'

'You're a good girl, Jody.'

'Drunk as a skunk!' proclaimed her daughter to the waiting children. Sophie giggled.

'We'll go on up,' said Colin, leading his followers up the dusty stairs to the landing where they stood in a silent group, waiting.

Jody knew that once drunk her mother had no sense of time. She barely waited a minute before running back to the kitchen. 'Mum, Dad isn't well. Can you come and look?'

Sara frowned. She knew that there was something wrong; that what her daughter was saying couldn't be right. She knew, too, that Jody was looking at her in the contemptuous manner which had become a fixture of late. Unfortunately her alcohol-dulled brain couldn't work out the flaw in Jody's statement.

Sara wanted Pete's company. She was lost without him at her side, and so, wanting to believe what she heard, she obeyed, desperately hoping to find him once again in their double bed. Half-way there she stopped, her mind clearing for a second. 'Your father's dead!' she said in bewilderment. 'Why did you say he was ill?'

'Dead?' Now Jody's expression had softened. Her eyes were innocent and luminous, more like the Jody of old. 'Mummy, he isn't. You haven't been drinking again, have you? He doesn't like that.'

Sara shook her head, trying to make sense of it all. Yes, she had been drinking, but surely that was because Pete was dead. She didn't remember drinking when he was alive. Alcohol had never caused trouble between them. Jody was taunting her, mocking the fact that her mother could no longer function as a mother should. Infuriated, Sara followed her daughter up to the landing. She would give her a good slap when she caught up with her. The girl was out of control.

At the top of the stairs she paused to get her breath back. Once she had been able to run up them without any trouble; once, before all the unpleasantness began.

Slowly she turned towards Jody's bedroom and never even saw the small figures that flitted from behind the closed bathroom door to stand at the top of the flight of stairs.

'Jody! Let me in! I'm tired of your insolence and . . .'

'Good morning, Mrs Gregory,' said Colin politely, stepping out of Jody's room. She stared in surprise.

'You haven't been very good today, have you?' he continued pleasantly.

'I don't know what you're talking about. Get out of my way.'

'I'm afraid you'll have to be punished,' he continued smoothly. 'We don't like doing this, but it's for your own good.'

'YOUR OWN GOOD,' shouted a chorus of voices.

Sara spun round. The entire landing was full of children. They came from every room, all blank-faced yet emanating disapproval. She knew them, or thought that she did, but apart from Colin's their names escaped her.

'Get out of my house!' she said loudly, her voice strident, the words slurred.

'This is going to be a serious lesson,' remarked Colin sadly. 'You don't know how to behave any more.'

'YOU'RE BAD! VERY BAD!' shouted the rest of them.

Despite the protection of alcohol Sara was beginning to

feel frightened. She tried to push past the group of girls who were standing in front of her bedroom but they refused to give way. One of them stuck out a foot so that she tripped, ending up sprawled on the landing carpet.

'Get up!' shouted a girl's voice, then a pair of hands grasped her hair, tugging viciously at it until she lifted herself on to all fours to minimize the pain. Her heart was pounding uncomfortably as she sensed the venom surrounding her.

'Disobedient little bastard,' yelled a boy's voice.

'Teach her a lesson,' whispered Jody excitedly. 'Go on, teach her a lesson she won't forget.'

Sara couldn't believe it was happening. She struggled to get free, but so many children were holding on to her arms and legs that it was impossible. She was half-drunk, her reactions were slow and her control minimal. She wondered what the lesson would be.

Chattering and whispering, hands pinched and poked her as some of the bigger children dragged her towards the bathroom. At one moment she nearly wrenched herself clear, but then a child jumped on her back and squashed her face down on to the carpet. When she lifted her head she could feel a small trickle of blood from her nose. After that she was too frightened to struggle any more.

'Turn on the taps,' commanded Colin. 'She's filthy. She needs a bath. A hot bath.'

There was the sound of water being run and she was aware of steam filling the room. Then they began to strip her. She fought them as much as she could, but when she opened her mouth to scream a tiny little girl poured more whisky down her throat, making her even more feeble and terrified.

Sara couldn't imagine where the children's strength

came from. She heard them jeering at her body once all her clothes were off, and she expected them to pour water over her as some kind of bizarre punishment for neglecting Jody, for she didn't truly believe that a group of children could lift her bodily into the bath.

They did, and the bath was scalding hot.

Her scream echoed round the silent house, a shrill, pain-ridden sound that would have chilled the blood of anyone near enough to hear. Anyone except the children.

Desperately she began to pull herself out, but they pushed at her with their sharp, bony little fingers, forcing her back into the burning water.

She knew that small blisters must be forming on the backs of her legs and her buttocks, and dreaded the moment when they turned her over. To her relief that moment never came. Instead the plug was pulled out and the water drained away. She trembled and shivered with shock, too stunned to leave the bath itself. She started to cry.

Another boy, taller and with a fresh complexion, stepped forward and hit her a stinging blow round the head. 'Shut up!' he commanded. 'We don't want the neighbours to hear.'

In the ordeal that followed Sara's mind became mercifully detached. She was beaten and abused in ways that defied belief, yet felt herself to be merely a spectator. Nevertheless, it was real; the pain could not be totally suspended, and eventually she slipped into unconsciousness. Thwarted, the children left the room.

When she came round and discovered that she was alone the relief was exquisite. With trembling hands she tried to free herself from the blindfold tied round her head, but blistered flesh on her left palm made it almost impossible. She shook her head from side to side, ignoring the pain in her temples, desperate at least to loosen the gag that was half-choking her.

Eventually, after what seemed like hours of struggle, she managed to pull the blindfold off her eyes. Blinking, she tried to focus her blurred vision on some object to tell her where she was.

It was the bathroom. No one was there. The bath was empty, and only the sodden carpet told her that it had really happened.

Pain was everywhere, but she crawled towards the doorway, unaware of the trail of blood she was leaving behind her. There was a telephone in her bedroom. All she had to do was reach that.

Panting and whimpering, she made it out of the doorway and on to the deserted landing. There she was forced to wait a moment to catch her breath. 'Come on!' she urged herself aloud. 'You can make it.'

The bedroom door swung open, and a wide-eyed Jody looked out. 'Why, Mummy! What *are* you doing there?'

Sara was completely bewildered. Surely Jody knew. She had been there; had helped them to torture her. It had been true. Her body showed that.

'I . . .'

'You were meant to stay in the bathroom,' continued her daughter sweetly. 'Won't you ever learn how to behave? We told you that you weren't to come in any other rooms, remember?'

'Leave me alone!' whimpered Sara.

'But you've been naughty again. You'll have to be punished.'

Doors on all sides of Sara opened wide. 'YOU'LL HAVE TO BE PUNISHED!' shouted the children. All of them. All of her daughter's friends. She had known them since they were babies. Watched them grow, had them to her house for tea, baby-sat for their parents. They were nice children; good playmates for Jody. She and Pete had always said how lucky they were that Jody has such nice friends.

'Why?' she croaked. 'What's made you like this?'

When they began pushing and pulling at her again all her injuries screamed in protest, and Sara screamed too, but this time they didn't gag her for they were nearly finished. Instead they manhandled her to the top of the stairs, forced her into a semi-upright position, rocked her violently to and fro for a few minutes and then pushed with all their might.

With one terrible, final cry of desolation Sara fell, landing with a sickening thud at the foot of the stairs. Eleven pairs of eyes stared at her. Eleven pairs of hands began to clap lightly together.

'Down she goes to hell!' crooned Jody.

'Down she goes to hell!' they responded. Then, the ritual completed, they began to disperse. They left the house stealthily in ones and twos, well aware of the danger if they were seen.

They were not. Very few people came along the lane to Sara's house any more, and her neighbours were out. The children had known this.

By eleven they were safely back in the woods. Without any discussion they picked up their bikes and began to mark out a course for the scramble. As the older boys selected the best place for hills and hollows, the older girls scattered handfuls of dust and leaves over the hidden machines. Then they told the little ones to roll around in the coarse grass, making sure that there were plenty of stains on their clothes. They all knew what they would be expected to look like after even one hour of scrambling.

Their attention to detail was meticulous, which was very fortunate. At eleven-fifteen Carlo wandered along the woodside path to see how the scramble was going. He saw the bigger boys crouched over their handlebars, the bikes covered in grime, and noticed the state of the little ones with an amused smile. He always liked to see children enjoying themselves.

After a few minutes he left and continued on his errand. He had been foolish to worry. The children were perfectly happy.

Chapter 11

Before the murder of Sara Gregory the various tragedies in the village of Lower Ditton had touched upon the lives of only approximately twenty out of the six hundred strong population. After her death it was different.

This was a murder of outstanding sexual and physical ferocity, even in the abuse-hardened nineteen-eighties. It was reported that a young policewoman had been physically sick in the hallway where Sara's body was discovered, and Inspector Barbor's grim features and shell-shocked eyes spoke volumes when he was interviewed for national television.

'This man has to be found,' he told the reporter. 'Until that time no woman is safe.'

He wasn't found, and therefore every woman lived in fear of her life. Husbands formed themselves into vigilante groups, patrolling the streets at dusk and stopping visitors to the previously quiet and peaceful village.

The police broke up such unofficial groups, reminding them that they were not entitled to take the law into their own hands. They said this, but every one of them understood the emotions in the men's hearts and felt secret sympathy for their actions.

At first Inspector Barbor was certain that the man would be caught speedily. Any stranger to such a tight-knit community would have been spotted during some stage of his crime. All it needed was the right trigger to elicit a vital clue from one of the villagers. If his assumption was right then they never did find the required trigger.

In the midst of the enquiry Amy and Carlo were married quietly in the Registry Office of Condersford, with only a handful of friends to watch. Ray had finally come round to the idea of the wedding, and his three girls were bridesmaids while he carried a fretful Thomas in his arms. They would all miss Amy. He knew that now, and regretted his attempt to send her away. But for that she might very well have remained single. He suspected that by his precipitate actions he had brought about the one thing he'd feared, and vowed not to repeat the mistake when his daughters began courting.

After a ten-day honeymoon in the Isles of Scilly, Carlo and Amy returned to the house over the shop, both of them glowing with an almost visible aura of happiness. Colin looked – if possible – more content than before, and work was quickly begun on a new house for them at the top of the High Street.

Jody and her brother, Keith, did not stay on in the house where their mother's body had been found. Their unmarried aunt, Sara's younger sister, came to live in the village and bought a small, terraced cottage in a quiet turning just off the main street. She was an attractive, lively young woman of twenty-eight who had previously been a children's nanny and a kindergarten assistant. She was kind and the children loved her. In this she was fortunate.

Harriet Harris appeared before the local magistrate's court and pleaded not guilty to the murder of her husband. After much consultation and legal arguing it was decided that a fair trial in her own area would not be possible. Her case was moved further away, to Cheltenham, with a resultant delay of three months.

Joanne Harris began to tire of her grandparents and their fussy ways. They could cope with her sister, Deborah, but found Joanne difficult and exhausting. They talked at length together and decided that they were too old for the responsibility that had been thrust upon them, but they were good people and didn't know what else they could do except stay where they were and hope her behaviour would improve.

A month after Harriet's trial was postponed for the second time, Joanne's grandparents discovered her cutting out articles from local newspapers, articles in which her mother was described luridly as 'the quiet woman no one really knew', and 'the wife with a secret', despite the fact that before the law she was still innocent. Her grandfather promptly had a stroke. It left him paralysed down his left side and incapable of speech.

Once again the neighbours rallied round; just as they had rallied round poor Colin and the unfortunate Burgess children. They supplied the children with meals and weekend visits. They called regularly on the elderly grandmother and assisted her with the arduous daily routine that care of such an invalid demanded.

Finally the exhausted old woman agreed thankfully with Mr and Mrs Rivero's suggestion that Joanne should stay with them for a few weeks unti her grandfather's health improved. At last Joanne was happy. Deborah stayed where she was. She liked both her grandparents and disliked Colin. Her grandmother didn't mind; Deborah was never any bother.

Slowly the initial optimism of the police began to fade. There were no clues. No one had seen anything. There were no fingerprints, no footprints, no concealed weapons. The madman was either very cunning or incredibly fortunate. The Inspector knew that unless he struck again there was now very little chance of his being caught, and he strongly suspected that someone in the village was leading a double life. The outsider theory simply didn't hold up.

One evening in early December he was sitting in his office with the Sergeant, sifting through piles of papers, one of which just might offer up that one vital scrap of information. It was doubtful, but had to be done.

'We did check on the alibis we were given for that Saturday morning, Sergeant, didn't we?' he enquired idly.

'Yes, sir. They weren't all cast iron, but then they rarely are outside of books!'

'What about Carlo Rivero?'

The Sergeant raised his head in surprise. 'Carlo, sir?'

'Yes, dammit! Carlo, the paragon among children.'

'Let's see . . . His alibi was water-tight.'

'Interesting! How come?'

'He works in the shop on Saturday mornings. He was seen there throughout the entire time, except when he took ten minutes off to check that the children were OK in the woods.'

'Ah!'

'But even then he was seen, by old Mrs Bales. She had just bought a lot of dried fruit from the shop and he was carrying it home for her. She accompanied him to the edge of the footpath and waited while he checked on Colin. He was never out of her sight.'

'Oh!' The Inspector couldn't quite conceal his disappointment.

'Why pick on him? Just because of his phoney accent?'

'Phoney?'

'Well, I doubt if he's ever set foot in Spain but his broken English leads people to think otherwise. I like him, but I can't see why he won't speak properly.'

'Probably finds it adds to his attraction for the opposite sex! No, it has nothing to do with his accent – phoney or not – I'm simply not quite easy about him. Also, I don't think he has a very high opinion of the police.'

The Sergeant refrained from pointing out that neither did most of the villagers any more. They wanted results and the police weren't delivering them.

'Right, let's start at the beginning again and see what we come up with. Now, her daughter Jody left the house at what time?'

'Nine-thirty A.M.'

'And went straight off to this bike scramble?'

'Correct.'

On and on they went, unpleasantly aware of the six-man team from New Scotland Yard who were arriving the very next morning, and who would be examining their efforts under a microscope. There must be nothing left to chance.

At three A.M. they finished, no further forward. Sara Gregory had been killed by person or persons unknown, and it was likely to stay that way.

Wearily they made their way home, horribly aware of their dismal showing in the eyes of the villagers. Many people had watched with thinly concealed derision as they went about their business, and more than once quite audible comments about local men letting the side down had floated out of houses and followed them down front paths.

Only the village children remained the same. Cheerful as ever they would smile and wave at the Inspector whenever they saw him. He envied them their powers of recovery. Envied them, and yet felt a vague sense of unease that the tragedies had touched them so little.

During his darkest moments he began to wonder if

their senses had been blunted by fictitious television serials and all too real, but still violent, television news. Something had certainly affected them, for they were incredibly carefree and friendly considering the disasters of the last few months.

He found their attitude as disquieting in its own way as the look in Carlo Rivero's eyes when they talked together. Strange, but there was a similarity that he couldn't define, couldn't pin down.

He also knew that whatever was the matter with Mr Rivero, his wife was a wonderful woman. He had never met such an attractive, good-hearted, lively female. Yes, he envied Carlo his wife. She was an extraordinary person, willingly to take on yet another child before she had been given an opportunity to have a family of her own.

He must talk to her one day. She was virtually an outsider. She hadn't lived in the village long. There was always the chance that she had seen or heard something which could help him. He jotted her name down on his notepad and went home with a slightly lighter heart.

Superintendent Parker from New Scotland Yard was a tall, thin man with a mass of long, fair hair and a tight mouth that never smiled. He was also an excellent detective, quite unused to failure. However, after six weeks in Lower Ditton he reluctantly had to admit to being completely baffled.

Sara Gregory's house had been examined with a fine tooth comb, athough it was his private opinion that the local force were bound to have ruined any clues during their initial search.

No illicit love-letters had been uncovered; there was no suggestion of any relationships at all for the dead woman.

This was hardly surprising, her husband had only been dead a few weeks. Just the same, it had been known; but not, it appeared, in the case of Sara Gregory.

Whilst motiveless, sex-crazed attacks by psychopaths were becoming almost commonplace across the country it was unusual for one to occur in such a small community, where strange patterns of behaviour would be instantly noticeable and any outsider would have stood out like a sore thumb.

He and his team interviewed every person over the age of sixteen during their exhaustive enquiry; the result was a zero. No one had been seen, nothing had been heard. At least, no one of consequence had been seen, he corrected himself, being of a literal turn of mind.

Now, with the trail cold and lack of evidence total, he had been recalled. It was his first true failure, and it rankled.

'This is a pretty unlucky village, Barbor,' he sniped, packing up his papers. 'More deaths here than in an Agatha Christie!'

'Yes, we've had a bad time. Unconnected deaths, mind you, but frightening for all that.'

'It began last year, didn't it?' continued the Superintendent, determined to ruffle the local man's calm. 'When that refuge burnt down. It wasn't until I went through the reports in your office that I realized how bad that fire really was. You kept it pretty quiet!'

'Hardly quiet! No one went round boasting about it, but the police were quite open over the entire matter. It did get a mention on local television.'

'Huh! The number of dead was played down. "Two or three", it said in one cutting I looked at. How the hell did you make it that low?'

'I wasn't here. I understand an estimate was given on

the night it happened. It was only later, when they found out precisely how over-crowded the place was, that the true figures became known.'

'And you never discovered who started it?'

'We think it was one of the husbands.'

'Think? What good's that?'

'No good at all; but even if we knew who started it, what would an arrest achieve?'

'Four women and eleven children dead and you don't care who caused it? You've got a funny attitude to death in Lower Ditton!'

Inspector Barbor's heart did an unpleasant leap. 'How many children did you say?'

Superintendent Parker was locking his briefcase. 'Eleven; four boys and seven girls, plus a small baby.'

'Eleven . . .' His voice trailed off.

'Incidentally, I've made a note of that Wright woman's sighting on the day Sara Gregory died, but I also spoke to the child and he definitely didn't see anything, Pity, he seemed a bright kid, could have helped a lot if there had been anyone around then.'

'Who did Mrs Wright see?'

'A young lad – Colin Masters – was apparently cycling down a lane to the woods at about the time the murder took place. I gather he was off to a bike scramble.'

'Yes, but . . .'

'What?'

No, thought Barbor, I'll keep this to myself. 'Nothing. I only wondered why she didn't tell me when I talked to her.'

'Thought it wasn't important, I imagine. It was only when I asked for every single detail, no matter how insignificant, that she told *me*.'

'I see.'

'Well, that's it. We're all off today. Somehow I don't think Mrs Gregory's murderer will ever be caught. He's probably miles away from here by now.'

'We did say that madmen are notoriously elusive when you got here!' said Barbor, enjoying the look of pain that crossed the Superintendent's face. He had arrived so full of confidence, making it plain that he expected village policemen to have straw coming out of their ears. Even the Inspector had been patronized. The failure was regrettable, but in its own way good for the Inspector's ego.

Only after Parker had gone did Sebastian Barbor make his way to the local library. He wanted to read through the accounts of the refuge fire, just to see for himself the details of that night; details that most village people had tried hard to erase from their minds.

At the same time as Inspector Barbor was reading through the back numbers of the local paper, Amy Rivero was facing her first confrontation with Carlo.

'Colin did wrong,' she stated firmly as they sat opposite each other in the kitchen. Lunch was the one weekday meal when they were alone together.

'Yes, that is true. I have told him so. He will not repeat his mistake.'

'Carlo, it isn't the first time he's taken money from my purse. There's no need for it, he gets far more pocket money than most children his age. I really think he should be punished.'

Carlo's eyes began to darken, a sure sign that he was annoyed. As his jaw clenched she could see a small muscle jumping beneath his left ear.

'Shut away in a cupboard perhaps? Or beaten? What would you suggest?'

'Don't be ridiculous! I only mean stopping his television for a couple of evenings, or his pocket money.'

'Then he would certainly steal again.'

'Why? He knows it's wrong and that it upsets us, why should he do anything so stupid?'

'He knows it upsets you, it is true.'

'*You* don't mind? You can't see anything wrong in stealing?'

When he was really angry Carlo became even more attractive than usual. His entire face tightened, emphasizing his excellent bone structure, and his eyes literally flashed with fury. At such a time there was no doubting his Spanish ancestry.

Amy wished that they had been married longer so that she could remain impervious to his physical attraction, but theirs was an intensely passionate relationship and even as she argued she knew she was going to capitulate and once again Colin would escape unpunished. She loved the boy dearly, and little Joanne as well, but both children were being spoilt because of Carlo's extraordinary reluctance to exercise any form of discipline stronger than a verbal rebuke. It was amazing that Colin was generally well-behaved, and presumably a sign of how much he valued Carlo's high esteem.

'It's ridiculous!' stated her husband in exasperation. 'So much fuss about such a paltry sum! I did not expect you to be small-minded, Amy.'

'I'm not!' she retorted furiously. 'I simply happen to think that stealing is a serious crime, which should be nipped in the bud quickly and effectively.'

'Why not report the loss of £2 to the police? They might take the matter with equal seriousness. As for me, it is over. He has been told off and apologized. There is nothing more to be done.'

'Your word is final?'

'Every household must have a leader, otherwise there is chaos. Have we a dessert?'

'*Listen to me!*' she shouted, getting up from her chair in a fury. 'You may think you can dominate our marriage, but I'm a mature woman with my own opinions, which I happen to believe in as strongly as you believe in yours. If we're going to go on increasing the number of children in this house then I insist on having some say in the way they're brought up. I'm not just a housekeeper and bedmate, I'm your wife, remember?'

'Very well! Amy, please don't let us quarrel over this. I promise you, Colin won't steal from you again.'

'But if he does?'

'He will not.'

To her fury tears of frustration began forming in her eyes. At once he was all concern. He came round the room and rocked her to and fro in the security of his arms, murmuring endearments that were his usual prelude to love.

As she had expected, and half-hoped, it ended in a passionate hour of love-making which left her slightly stunned by its intensity. All inclination to pursue the argument had vanished.

Carlo then went down to the shop, leaving his wife to take her time over dressing before she went to see how much progress was being made on the building of their new house.

She felt tired but desired, and reflected that she had probably been foolish to make quite such a fuss. After all, Colin had been through a terrible time, there were bound to be moments when his loss overwhelmed him. He most likely misbehaved in an attempt to draw attention to himself, needing the reassurance that despite Amy's presence he was still loved. She should have been more understanding.

It was most unlike her either to shout or cry, but then things were no longer normal for Amy because – though she hadn't as yet told her husband – she was pregnant. Tonight, she resolved, after the children were in bed, she would tell him. She could hardly wait for his reaction.

The children met in the woods. They were not supposed to go there after school now that the evenings were drawing in, but knowing that in reality there was nothing to fear they ignored the adults and went swiftly and silently about their business.

On this particular evening there were only ten of them. Richard's twin brother, Samuel, had not been told of the meeting. It was the first time that they had excluded one of their own kind. Samuel was being difficult. The children realized that quite soon difficult could become dangerous. They were meeting to talk over ways of protecting themselves: it was therefore an unusually solemn gathering.

'He didn't like it at Jody's house,' explained Richard in a shamefaced way, feeling diminished by his twin's faint-hearted behaviour. 'He can't sleep properly at night and says he won't take part in anything else. He thinks we were cruel.'

'Cruel?' chorused the children incredulously. 'Doesn't he remember.'

Richard shuffled his feet. 'Yes, but he says that Mrs Gregory never hurt anyone. He sometimes seems to forget who he is; I mean quite often he becomes the first Samuel again.'

'How often?' asked Colin sharply.

'Well, more and more recently. Why, he even wants us

to move away from here. Dad asked us ages ago if we'd like to go away and make a fresh start, but because we both said no he didn't mention it again. Now Samuel's dropping hints about the house having too many memories of Wendy.'

'Wendy?' asked Gillian.

'You know, the real twins' mother,' explained Richard.

'Oh, her! I wonder if she'll ever be found?'

They all laughed, remembering their hours of digging deep within these very woods.

'Never mind that,' retorted Colin. 'The question is, what are we going to do about Samuel?'

'Warn him?' put in Richard hopefully.

'Will he listen?'

'I don't know.'

Colin's face tightened. 'Nope, too dangerous. If we warn him and he panics, he might run to your father.'

The older children drew in their breath sharply. That, they knew, could never be allowed.

'I don't want anything bad to happen to him,' said Richard. 'He's my twin. We're the same person, one split cell.'

'You're not the same. Samuel's forgotten who he is, you haven't. You can't be the same person once one of you's reverted. I didn't realize it would be possible to go back. I hope it doesn't happen to any more of you.' He glared at the ring of bright young faces surrounding him. One by one they dropped their eyes, all shaking their head in an attempt to assure him of their continuing loyalty.

Fiona yawned. 'He'll have to be killed,' she said simply. 'Why should he be allowed to put us all at risk?'

Richard went pale. 'Please, don't! I'll talk to him, remind him who he really is. I'm sure . . .'

'She's right,' put in nine-year-old Gillian. 'I've never trusted Samuel, he's far too soft.'

Pretty little Sophie's large eyes were solemn. 'Bad boy!' she confirmed, before putting her thumb in her mouth.

'I'll give it some thought,' said Colin after a short pause. 'We'll meet at Fiona's house when I've come to a decision.'

The meeting was over. Quietly they turned, going their separate ways, but Richard's feet moved slowly and inside he felt sick and unhappy.

All the children had said was true, yet Samuel *was* his twin – past and present – and if the decision went against him it would be very hard for Richard to take any active part in the killing.

Later that evening, after Colin and Joanne were in bed, Amy was sorting through some albums that she had brought with her after a brief visit back to Leicester.

It was strange that Helena had never received one of her letters about work, but she put it down to the village postal system. Fortunately there hadn't been any crisis but it was possible that she would have returned had her letters received replies, in which case she might not have married Carlo, so she silently thanked the GPO.

Flicking through the photos, many of them portraits of small babies clasped in the arms of older siblings, reminded her of her own good fortune. She glanced up to see if Carlo was busy or could give her his full attention.

To her dismay he was sitting beneath the old-fashioned standard lamp, about to study her recent film of the village children. They must have got caught up with the albums and then fallen to the carpet without her realizing it, she thought, and wondered what on earth he would say when he saw what the camera had revealed.

Finally he was finished. As he put them down he noticed Amy watching him and smiled warmly at her. 'They're very good. We ought to frame a couple.'

'Good? They don't look a bit like the children! I've been wanting to show them to you for ages, but couldn't get up the nerve.'

'You need nerve to display your talent? Why so modest? They are truly excellent.'

Speechless with shock she could only stare at him, her mouth opening and shutting like a goldfish.

'May I see these?' he continued, reaching for one of the albums. She nodded dumbly, wondering if she was going completely mad. Surely he could see that the children looked completely different? If so, why wouldn't he tell her?

After a few moments she forced herself to speak. 'Carlo, the photos of the village children are terrible. They all look so pinched and . . . I don't know, vindictive somehow. There isn't a single smiling face. Why, I scarcely recognize Fiona.'

'It's a good likeness of Colin.'

'He's less altered than the others, I admit, but even he . . .'

'You are very strange to refute your talent. These too, here in the album, are excellent.'

'Carlo, stop it! Tell me the truth. They're dreadful photos and I need to know why. I meant to catch the children off their guard, and as a result I've turned them all into strangers. They look like a crowd of street urchins from the depression.'

It was peculiar, but with only the light from the standard lamp in the room Carlo's face, too, was that of a stranger. His eyebrows were raised in mild surprise, and his mouth twisted in a grimace of amusement or disbelief, but his eyes were dull. There was no animation, no spark of life in them. They stared unseeingly at her and his thoughts, if indeed he had any at that moment, were plainly miles away for when she moved towards him he didn't even notice.

She reached out and touched his arm. 'Carlo, is this how . . .?' She had no opportunity to finish her question for with a startled cry he jumped backwards, catching his leg on the side of the chair and nearly falling over.

Automatically she rushed forward to try and help him keep his balance, but he flung an arm protectively across his face, almost as though he expected a blow.

Completely disconcerted she stopped moving, looking down into the shadows as he struggled to stand upright again. His eyes were still blank, and as he looked up and saw her waiting he opened his mouth. Before he could speak, the most terrible cry rang through the house, a cry of such intense pain that Amy's stomach lurched with fear and she sped away and up the stairs, certain that Colin was in the grip of a nightmare.

Flinging open his door she rushed into the room, only to halt abruptly at the end of the bed. Colin was sleeping peacefully. His head was turned to one side and his bedclothes were undisturbed.

Remembering Joanne's distress over her mother's trial Amy immediately ran to the adjoining room, although for some reason the cry had sounded as though it came from a boy and not a girl.

Even so, she was stunned to find that Joanne too was sleeping deeply, her gentle mouth curved upwards in a half-smile as though her dreams were happy ones.

She stood on the landing, her heart banging behind her ribs, and waited in terrified silence for the sound to come again. She could still hear it in her mind, and the amount of despair contained in that one cry made her feel physically sick. She waited and waited, but it did not come again.

After a time she heard Carlo's feet on the stairs and stiffened in fright. Everything terrified her this evening. Her husband seemed a stranger, the house menacing.

'Amy, what are you doing up there?' he whispered.

'That cry – I thought it came from one of the children.'

'What cry?'

'You must have heard it!'

'I heard nothing. One minute I was looking at your photographs, the next you had vanished. Are the children all right?'

She stared at him. 'Yes, but you weren't looking at the photos, you were . . .'

She remembered the blankness of his gaze, the way in which he had backed away from her, and realized that for him there had been nothing after the photos.

'I was what?'

'Forget it; I'm confused. Let's go down again.'

As they descended the stairs she wondered if her husband had any history of blackouts, because if he did she needed to know, in view of the coming child.

Carlo sat her down in the most comfortable chair and went into the kitchen to make her a herbal drink.

'Here you are. It should be raspberry tea really, but you've plenty of time for that!'

'You know?'

'I am a reasonably intelligent man; I can count up to twenty-eight days and beyond! You're pregnant, is it not so?'

'Yes, but I wanted to surprise you!'

'You have. I hadn't expected to become a father.'

'Why not? We haven't been very careful!'

He shrugged. 'True, but somehow I imagined that it would not happen.'

'But you're glad it has?' All at once she was unsure.

He smiled warmly at her. 'I am very glad,' he whispered as he began to kiss her lips and throat, but inside he wasn't glad at all, he was terrified. If there was one thing Carlo Rivero knew very well it was the unpleasant habit history had of repeating itself.

Without realizing it both Amy and Carlo spent most of the night awake. Amy worrying about Carlo's lapse of memory and the terrible cry she had heard; Carlo remembering the past and realizing with mounting unease the limits of his own capabilities. Children he understood – indeed loved them with a complete disregard for their faults and occasional bad behaviour – but babies were a very different thing. He had always stayed well away from babies.

It was nearly midnight and Inspector Barbor was still at work. His wife had gone to bed at ten-thirty but his discoveries were so engrossing that it was impossible for him to stop. With mounting disbelief he continued, hoping against hope that he was wrong, for if he was right then there existed a terrifying twilight world peopled by thc unquiet dead.

According to the papers eleven children had died in the refuge fire, ten youngsters and a baby; also three adults, one of whom was a pregnant young girl of eighteen whose husband had already nearly killed her and their eleven-month-old son. The son had escaped because he was in care. Unprotected by the social services, his mother had died.

The Inspector made a list of the dead children, noting

their age beside them in brackets. It was a sad list, and also a frightening one. He looked at it again.

Felicity (8 years)
Lise (4 Years)
Mary (6 years)
Elaine (9 years)
Gary (10 years)
Twin boys: Chris and Wayne (10 years)
Karen (8 years)
Cheryl (9 years)
Sharon (8 years)
Craig (4 months)

He then made out a corresponding list, using the group of village children.

Fiona (8 years)
Sophie (4 years)
Georgina (6 years)
Gillian (9 years)
Mark (10 years)
Twin boys: Richard and Samuel (10 years)
Joanne (8 years)
Helen (9 years)
Jody (8 years)
No baby

With the exception of the baby there was only one child who did not correlate in age and sex and that was Colin. Try as he might the Inspector couldn't find any link between Colin and the refuge. No nine-year-old boys had died in the fire, and yet out of all the children the Inspector felt certain that Colin played the key role. He discounted the baby; at four months it was obviously unimportant.

Having matched every other child he then went through the list again, noting the tragedies in which these village children had been involved. To his mounting disquiet, the list of accidents was awesome.

The twins' mother had vanished, probably murdered; both of Jody's parents were dead, one a suicide, the other murder; Gillian Summer's parents, like Mark East's and Helen Blake's, were untouched. However, Joanne Harris's father had been murdered and her mother was being tried for the crime, leaving Joanne virtually orphaned. Fiona, Georgina and Sophie Burgess's mother had been murdered in the woods, and their father – now without the assistance of his sister-in-law – was rumoured to be going the same way as Sara Gregory and finding his consolation in drink.

Every single tragedy that had struck at the village had been concerned with one of these children. No one outside their circle had come to any harm, and that in the Inspector's opinion was rather too much of a coincidence. Somewhere there was a link.

He spent a long time puzzling over Colin. The boy was the undisputed leader of the group; bright, articulate and apparently guileless. However, his own parents had been killed in a car accident even before Kate Burgess was murdered, and to the Inspector's way of thinking the boy had coped too well with his bereavement. Come to that, so had the Burgess girls. People praised all four children for their courage and cheerfulness, but suppose that was because they didn't really care?

He shivered, then locked the sheets of paper in his desk drawer. He hadn't proved anything. It wasn't as though the children could have been responsible for any of the deaths; it was simply that in some way he sensed that they might be the source of the disasters.

It was as though everyone close to them was in danger. But why? How could the death of eleven deprived children a year earlier have any bearing on what was happening in the village now? Logically it couldn't, but the Inspector – normally a man of great logic – sensed that it had. The trouble was he didn't know in what way. Resolving to keep a careful eye on the children and their families in future, he finally made his way up to his sleeping wife.

Outside, face pressed to the lounge window but concealed by the shadow of a beech tree, Mark East stood silently watching. In the darkness his eyes glowed with a luminous red light, and his fists were clenched into tight balls which he kept firmly by his side.

'Interfering old fool!' he muttered. He hated the police, had always hated them, and knew very well that once they thought they were on to something they never gave up. Oh yes, he knew all about the fuzz; everything that the ten-year-old Gary had known, Mark knew.

Frowning, he returned home. Tomorrow he would tell Colin what he had learnt. Colin would know what to do, and it was always best to know your enemy.

Chapter 12

It was a cold January morning. Amy stood ankle-deep in mud, staring at the modern five-bedroom house she and Carlo were having built. It was intended to be ready for them by the end of April, and with her baby due in June this gave Amy plenty of time to get things in order.

Despite her thick wool coat and knee-length fur-lined boots, she shivered. The village was very quiet, probably because the children were back at school, but she wished that there were one or two people about. For some reason she never felt quite comfortable when she visited the site on her own.

It was ridiculous because she was in full view of a busy street with passing cars, and after Sara Gregory's death there hadn't been any more trouble in the village. Besides, she knew perfectly well that there wasn't anyone watching her, yet she always felt that she was being studied. Not when Carlo came with her, then it was all right. It was only when she came alone.

Slowly she moved closer to the shell of the building, peering in through the empty wooden window frames. The large kitchen was slowly taking shape, and in her mind she filled it up with fitted cupboards, a built-in hob and a large kitchen table surrounded by thickly cushioned, high-backed kitchen chairs. Yes, she would thoroughly enjoy the luxury of a large kitchen after her present small one.

She started to move round the side of the building, then stopped, aware of someone whimpering. It sounded more like a kitten than a person and she quickly glanced about, wondering if one had got trapped in some of the building materials.

She searched unsuccessfully for a few minutes, then froze in alarm as a high-pitched cry filled the air. Amazingly, after the one cry, there was silence again. Deciding that the sound must have come from a house at the back of the site she started to walk away. It was then that the screaming began.

It assailed her from all sides, terrible high-pitched sounds made up of numerous voices all shouting and screaming out in a jumbled cacophony of despair that made her clap her hands over her ears.

There was no relief. The screaming didn't abate, in fact, it increased in volume until she felt that her head would burst open it if didn't ease. There were no words, simply a ghastly collection of sounds composed of pain-filled cries and terror-ridden shrieks; sounds that were animal-like in their tone, yet horribly, horribly human.

She had never heard so much suffering before, and as the sounds swelled to unbelievable proportions her petrified legs suddenly found the power to move and she half-ran, half-stumbled round the side of the house and out into the safety of the front garden.

The sounds didn't vanish, but they diminished in quality, turning to soft, despairing sobs and unintelligible pleas that were heartbreaking in their terror.

Whimpering with fear she lurched towards the pavement, then screamed herself as she collided with a passer-by. Petrified, she backed away, only to find herself gripped firmly by the elbows as Carlo's soft brown eyes studied her face.

'Amy! Whatever is the matter?'

Her legs went weak with fright and relief at finding him there. 'Carlo! How long have you been here?'

'I have only just arrived. I wanted to see what was keeping you.'

'Someone was watching me, I'm sure of it.'

'From the road?'

'I don't know: whenever I come here without you I can feel eyes on me.'

'Then you must never come alone. Is that why you were running away?'

'No, it was the noise.'

'Noise?'

'I could hear people screaming. Lots of people. There were crying and shrieking; it was horrible.'

He looked at her with interest. 'Could you hear what they were saying?'

Shaken by his acceptance of her statement, she stared blankly at him for a moment.

'Amy, I said could you hear what they were saying?'

'I . . . that is, no, not really. It was horrible; like a lot of people in pain, or frightened for their lives. It went round and round in my head until I thought I was going mad.'

He put an arm round her waist and steered her back towards the house, pretending not to notice her resistance. 'You're not going mad,' he remarked, studying the back door thoughtfully, 'you heard things from the past, that is all.'

'All! Don't be ridiculous! How could I possibly . . .?'

'It is as I thought. You are a sensitive person and these things are well recorded. You are not the first to have such an experience.'

'But what was I hearing?'

He smiled gently at her. 'Why, the children, naturally.'

'The children?'

'Yes, Amy, the children from the refuge.'

'The ones who burnt to death?'

'Yes.'

She shivered. 'Why would I hear them near our new house?'

'Because this is where it happened.'

Amy felt the blood drain from her face. 'What do you mean?' she whispered.

'Here, on this piece of land, is where the refuge used to stand. That is why we got it cheaply; no one else wanted to build here. They thought it would bring them bad luck!' And he laughed.

'No!' She couldn't believe it. 'Carlo, how could you? Why didn't you tell me? I thought you loved children. Surely you don't want to live here, surrounded by such unhappy memories, spirits, ghosts or whatever? What if the villagers are right and it does bring bad luck. Have you thought about our baby?'

His eyes sparkled and he touched her lightly on the face. 'Poor Amy! I have upset you, but I assure you there is nothing to fear. The children wanted me to live here. They will be calm once I am near.'

'What on earth are you talking about?'

'I knew the children well, their spirits will not harm me.'

'You talk a though you're in touch with the dead children.'

'Yes.'

'That isn't possible.' She wished that he didn't look so cheerful.

'You heard them too, Amy.'

'I heard something, I don't know what.'

'What else could it have been?'

She licked her lips. 'The wind in the trees?'

'There is no wind, Amy. No, it was the children. However, they will be calm now that I am here. Come, we will look round inside.'

'No!' She backed away from him. 'I don't want to. I'm not going in there. I'm not ever going in there. You can live here if you like, but not with me. I'm staying where we are. I don't know if what you say is true or not, but I'm not taking the chance. You should have told me, Carlo. I was entitled to know.'

His face was solemn now. 'They need you too, Amy. They have no mothers, no women to help them. That is why we are together, to help the children find rest.'

'You're mad!'

'They're lost, Amy, and until they find peace again terrible things will happen. Believe me, it is true. I know them. I understand what is happening.'

'Stop it!' she shouted, heedless of an elderly woman walking by. 'Just stop talking about them like that, it makes me feel ill. You need some form of counselling, you're obsessed with those dead children. I'll help you find a doctor, and I'll willingly come with you, but I will not listen to another word about lost souls and haunted building sites. Do you understand?'

For answer he stepped forward, grasped her right wrist and dragged her through the open porch into the shell of the hall. Despite her struggles he held her tightly by the shoulders, pressing her against the brick wall.

'You shall see for yourself,' he told her contemptuously. 'I do not like your attitude towards this.'

'Let me go, Carlo! Let . . .'

All at once he began to sing, a gentle lullaby that she vaguely remembered from her own childhood. 'Golden Slumbers', she thought it was called, and his voice was deep and rich, wonderfully peaceful and soothing, so that even her taut nerves began to relax.

It was as she relaxed that they became visible to her. There were about a dozen of them, all crouched in the corners of the brickwork or huddled together in pairs, their pinched faces and sunken eyes staring at her with an almost tangible emotional hunger.

Amy whimpered with shock and moved closer to Carlo. At once the children jumped away, uttering small frightened sounds as they went. The light from the open windows went straight through their thin, transparent bodies but they tried to shield their eyes from it as though only content in the dark places.

Carlo was now humming the tune quietly, and slowly, step by step, they moved towards him, their bony hands outstretched as though pleading for nourishment, money, or simply comfort.

As they collected round him, trying to stroke his clothing or touch his hands, Amy recognized them. They were the children from the photographs. With one final high-pitched scream of fear she fainted. When she came round the apparitions had gone.

'You shouldn't have done that!' said Carlo, helping her up without any obvious concern for her momentary loss of consciousness.

'Where have they gone?'

'Where they always go when they are frightened. I do not want them to keep leaving. It is better that they stay here.'

'And where do they always go, Carlo?' she persisted. He gave her a brief glance of surprise.

'Why, to the children of course; the village children.'

And, with incredulous horror, she knew that he spoke the truth. It was the worst moment of her life.

The next morning she refused to get up for breakfast. She didn't say why, and Carlo didn't enquire. He simply ignored her and attended to the breakfast preparations and packed lunches with quiet competence. Prior to his marriage he had coped well alone, and it was no great hardship to return to his old ways.

Upon returning from their new house the previous day, Amy had become hysterical. Every time Carlo attempted further explanations she had started screaming at him, frightened out of her wits and unable to accept what she had seen.

Her terror and shock resulted in an immediate rejection of Carlo himself, whom she now saw as some kind of satanist dabbling with dark forces. His efforts to clarify the relationship between himself and the children fell on deaf ears. Amy was frightened, and neither he nor Colin were allowed near enough to help erase her fears.

As the boy got ready for school, he turned a troubled face to Carlo. 'She won't leave, will she? I mean, I like having her here with us. Don't let her run away, will you?'

Carlo ruffled his hair. 'Don't worry. She's had a shock. I thought she'd understand, but I was mistaken. However, I will make amends.'

'Oh, good! See you about four.'

'Sure.'

Once Colin had gone Carlo's sunny smile vanished. His expression was worried as he tried to work out how best to approach his wife. In truth he hadn't expected the children to show themselves in quite such an aggressive manner. It would have been better if she had first seen them at their most pitiful, instead of lurking malevolently in the shadows whispering to one another. Unfortunately the children were changing. Where once they had been pathetic victims, as lost in the second world as they had been abused in the first, they were now aggressive and spiteful. It was understandable; inhabiting bodies of children living in good homes, encompassed by family love, must be galling. As a result he sometimes wondered if anyone in the village was safe any more.

At ten A.M. Amy went into the bathroom, showered, put on her make-up and wondered what on earth she was going to do. The memory of the ghost children crouched in the corners of the new house was with her constantly. She had never believed in hauntings or evil spirits, laughing them off as hysterical sightings by unbalanced adults and pubescent teenagers. Now she knew better, but found it impossible to adjust her thoughts. Much worse than that, however, was the realization that Carlo was nothing like the man she had thought.

He had been so palpably relaxed and confident with the ghostly figures, had even talked about them as though they were a part of his daily life. She bit her bottom lip, wondering where she could go for advice. If only she was a little nearer Leicester, but here in Lower Ditton she was completely isolated from her friends. It was sobering to realize that apart from Carlo and the children she knew very few people well.

There had been Sara but she was dead, and Harriet was in prison. Then she remembered Christine Sumner, Gillian's mother and Kate's next-door neighbour. She had been friendly at Kate's funeral, and they frequently exchanged smiles and brief conversations when they met fetching or taking one of the children somewhere. Perhaps she could help.

After a moment she realized how ridiculous such a thought was. What would she say: 'Listen, Christine, my husband is having a new house built for us on a haunted site so that he can keep the souls of dead children company?' No, it was impossible. This was something she had to face alone.

At that moment there was a tap on the back door. Relieved at the thought of any visitor she opened it with a smile on her lips, a smile that faltered slightly when she found herself facing Inspector Barbor.

The Inspector noticed the change of expression his presence caused, and wondered what the new Mrs Rivero had to hide. In his experience only people with secrets looked alarmed by policemen: they were frequently small secrets, some petty piece of wrongdoing in their past that made them react in such a way, but Amy Rivero had previously greeted him with a cheerful smile and there had to be a reason for the change. Pretending not to notice her hesitation, he started to enter the kitchen, and she gave way without any fuss, stepping to one side with an almost fatalistic sigh.

Once in the living-room he realized that she was now fairly well into her pregnancy. Possibly it was that causing the change in her. Some women became uncomfortable with their bodies at this time. Perhaps Amy was one of them. He gave her his most fatherly smile as he sat down.

Amy remained standing. Thoughts were flashing through her head at great speed. Was it possible that she could talk to the policeman? If she did, would he think her unbalanced? No crime had been committed, as far as she knew, so there was very little point. It was only that he seemed a solid, reliable person. But what do you want him to say? she asked herself. What is it that you hope to gain by telling him?

She didn't know. She was frightened, confused, and insecure in a marriage that only twenty-four hours earlier had been perfect. It was natural that she should panic, but this man couldn't help her. No, she reflected sadly, her only choice was to allow Carlo to tell her more about the incident. Cutting herself off from him was self-defeating. She loved her husband, and whatever strange secrets he harboured she had no reason to doubt that this love was returned. It would be disloyal to talk to an outsider. The decision made, she relaxed.

'Coffee, Inspector? I was just going to make some.'

'That would be nice. Is your husband around?'

'No, he's in the shop, but I can get him for you.'

'That's all right. In fact, it was you I wanted to see.'

'Really? How intriguing!' And she smiled, the tension gone from her face, her eyes once again bright and shining.

They drank the coffee and chatted about various mundane matters before Inspector Barbor felt that the time had come to state the reason for his call.

'I wanted to speak to you about Colin,' he said casually. 'It's about Sara Gregory's murder.'

'Yes?'

'The man from Scotland Yard told me that Mrs Wright, who lives in a bungalow on the corner of Shipley Lane, just down the road from the Gregory house, saw young Colin on his bicycle on the morning of the murder. I wondered if he'd ever mentioned seeing anyone to you?'

'No. I understood that the children were all playing in the woods that morning.'

So did I, thought the Inspector, but he chose to remain silent.

Amy frowned. 'I wonder what he was doing that far away from the others?'

'He might have got bored, he is one of the oldest.'

'Yes, I suppose so.'

'It really doesn't matter *why* he was there, it's what he might have seen that interests me.'

'Of course.'

'Sometimes boys clam up with policemen. They expect a telling-off over some childish infringement of the law! Could you ask him about it, do you think?'

She laughed. 'Colin isn't the sort of boy to be afraid of the police! I'm sure it would be best if you talked to him yourself. After all, it won't be the first time, will it?'

'True, nor the last I'm afraid. His testimony is probably going to be needed at Mrs Harris's trial.'

Amy frowned. 'What do you mean, his testimony?'

'I keep forgetting it was before your marriage: young Colin told me all about a conversation he had with Mrs Harris concerning the benefits of peppermint tea.'

'Yes, I was there at the time.'

'So he said. Well, the peppermint tea isn't involved, since none was ever sent, but during the conversation Colin told her about a young mother getting her berries mixed up and nearly feeding poison to her baby, and it was the same berries that were used to kill Jonathan Harris.'

Amy stared at the Inspector. 'I don't remember any talk about berries.'

'No, Colin said that you were busy with Thomas. He needed feeding or some such thing.'

'That isn't true! I remember the talk about the peppermint, but then the children ran ahead and Harriet and I talked about Jonathan's condition. She was so worried.'

'I hardly think the boy would have made up such a story. After all, he didn't even know what killed Jonathan Harris, so what would be the point?'

Against her will a picture of Colin as he looked in her photographs came into Amy's mind. That boy would be capable of any amount of deceit and deviousness. Surely the children hadn't . . .?

'No, you're right,' she said quickly. 'I suppose I didn't take it in; it wouldn't have seemed important at the time.'

She knows something, thought the Inspector, knows but isn't going to tell me.

'Anyway, will you have a word with him?'

'What about?' asked Amy, still miles away with Harriet and Colin.

'The morning of Sara Gregory's death.'

'Yes, and I'll get Carlo to speak to him. Colin's more forthcoming with him.'

Inspector Barbor smiled. 'He's wonderful with the children – your husband, I mean. I expect he's longing for the baby to arrive!'

'Yes,' lied Amy, who was actually surprised at Carlo's lack of enthusiasm.

The policeman stood up. 'Right, I'll be on my way. You know, it's a most peculiar coincidence but when I was doing some research at the library the other day, I came across some articles about the refuge fire in this village last year.'

'Oh yes,' smiled Amy politely, her heart thumping.

'You wouldn't believe it, but there were eleven children killed, ten of whom correspond in sex *and* age to the group that your Colin goes around with. Strange that, don't you think?'

There was a buzzing in her ears and a rushing sound that threatened another fainting attack. Amy bit the inside of her lip and concentrated hard on the Inspector's face. She must not show any reaction.

'There are *eleven* children in Colin's group, Inspector.'

'True, but the eleventh victim in the fire was only a baby. Strangely, Colin is the odd one out. Everyone else matches up in terms of sex and age with a dead child. Now statistically that has to be pretty unlikely.'

'So what does it mean?' she asked quietly.

'Mean?' He gave a quick laugh. 'I don't suppose it means anything. I'm a mine of useless information. I just found it interesting, that's all.'

'What were you looking for?'

'Sorry?'

'When you "stumbled" on this piece of information, what were you really looking for?'

'I was researching the past, Mrs Rivero. Trying to find out if there were any clues in the past to help us solve our current problems.'

'And were there?'

'None at all.'

'You shouldn't have let the dead children sidetrack you.'

'I suppose not. You know, Colin keeps popping up in our enquiries.'

'Yet you say there wasn't anyone like Colin killed in the refuge fire?'

'No, and somehow I find that the strangest thing of all. I'll be off now, Mrs Rivero. Thank you for the coffee.'

As soon as he'd gone Amy found that she was trembling all over. The Inspector was on to something, or thought he was, and she knew that she should have been more helpful, but her fear of those strange children, and Carlo's possible reaction to any betrayal of trust of her part, had kept her silent. It was also highly unsettling to find that Colin hadn't been in the woods when he was meant to be. Why, he might have been murdered himself if he'd seen something.

No he wouldn't, said a quiet voice inside her head.

Colin was never in any danger. She wondered how she could be so certain.

At one o'clock Carlo wandered in with an uncertain air, obviously fully expecting to prepare his own lunch as well as breakfast. Amy, however, had decided that her refusal to face facts was pointless, and smiled at her husband's expression of relief.

'You feel better?' he enquired carefully, keeping his gaze on her.

'Yes, thank you. I had a visitor this morning, did you see?'

'No. Who come?'

She laughed. 'It's "came", Carlo. "Who came?"'

He shrugged. His mastery of English was sufficient for his requirements, minor grammatical errors never bothered him. He sensed that Amy's sudden concern was more a delaying tactic than anything else.

'OK. Who *came*?'

'Inspector Barbor.'

'Why did he come?'

'Because Mrs Wright saw Colin near Sara's house on the day she was murdered.'

'Mrs Wright has been murdered also?'

'No! All right, I admit it, my grammar wasn't perfect then either! Mrs Wright saw Colin near the Gregory house on the day Sara was murdered. There!'

'Is much better! So?'

'So, he wanted me to find out if Colin saw anyone suspicious.'

'He could ask the boy himself; he has before.'

'I know, but this time he wants me to do it – or you.'

'Me? There is no point. If Colin had seen anything he would have already said.'

'You told me he was playing in the woods that morning.'

'Correct.'

'So what was he doing along the lane on his own? It isn't even the way he'd go from here.'

'He will explain. Does the Inspector think Colin murdered Sara?'

'Don't be ridiculous! No, he's simply anxious for any clue, however insignificant.'

'You may ask him. I think the entire episode is ridiculous. A madman killed Sara Gregory and he has escaped; that is the end of the matter. Is there some cheese?'

Amy fetched a piece of Brie from the fridge. 'About yesterday, Carlo.'

'Yes?'

'I was frightened; I panicked and lost my head. Now that I'm feeling better I'd like to know more about what we saw. I promise not to scream again.'

He raised his eyebrows and shrugged. 'What are you talking about?'

'The children.'

'Which children? Joanne and Colin?'

'No! The children in the new house.'

Slowly Carlo tilted his chair backwards and hooked his feet beneath the leg of the table. 'You must have been having bad dreams. There were no children in the house yesterday. How could there be? School is back.'

If she had been afraid earlier, now she was petrified. 'But we both saw them. About a dozen children, all thin and cringing. You said they were the children who died in the fire. I was crying, when you arrived there, because of their noise. Don't play games with me, Carlo. I want to know about them. How long you've been able to communicate with them. Why they aren't at peace. How is it that they can flee to the village children. I need to know, Carlo.'

Now it was his turn to look frightened. 'Amy, what's wrong? Does your head hurt? Have you had a fall?'

'We talked about it yesterday, what's changed you? You were perfectly casual about them. Why, you made it sound positively mundane. Tell me what it is they want and why we have to go and live there. I have a right to know.'

'I'm going to ring for a doctor. Stay here, and try to relax.'

She leapt to her feet, grabbing at his arms in an attempt to keep him in the room with her. 'I don't need a doctor! Listen to me, Carlo, I want to understand what's going on. I'd like to help the children too, but I have to know more. I think Inspector Barbor is beginning to realize that those children are important, but I didn't tell him what I'd seen because I don't want them harmed any more than you do. Carlo, tell me, what *is* happening to the children in this village?'

His face was grave, his dark eyes unreadable as they searched her features.

'If you won't see a doctor then you must at least rest. There wasn't anyone in our new house yesterday. I have no idea what you're talking about, and if you're no better by tea-time then I shall call a doctor, with or without your permission. I am not willing to risk the health of our child.'

'Why not?' she shouted, infuriated by his lies. 'You don't care about our baby, you never show any interest in it. If you had your way all children would arrive in a brown paper package aged three years. Oh, yes, I'm not blind; I do see the expression on your face when you catch sight of my naked body these days. You don't care for it, do you? Fair enough, I don't like it much either, but that's Nature's way, so tough luck on both of us. And I've seen you flicking your eyes away when I'm trying to get you to choose a cot or pram. You don't like the baby pictures, they make you uneasy. Fine, lots of men don't like babies, but this one happens to be ours, and if you want children you've got to put up with the baby stage first.'

His face was tight with fury and he swallowed hard, trying to keep his temper under control.

'Go to bed,' he said softly. 'Go now, before I do something I regret.'

'Like what?' she challenged. 'Are you a secret wife-beater?'

'No, but unless you rest and keep silent I shall have you committed to a hospital.' Her mouth suddenly dry, she stared into the face of an impassive stranger.

'Carlo, don't! What is it? What have I done?'

'Begun to doubt Colin.'

'Doubt Colin?'

'Yes, I can see it in your eyes. You are unsure of him. You imagine that in some way he is not trustworthy. You link him with the past, a past which you, and you alone, have peopled with strange, unpleasant children. I don't know what the Inspector really said to you, and I don't think that I want to, but I tell you this: if you make one single attempt to harm that boy or get him into any trouble, then I will remove you from our lives without any hesitation at all.'

Amy swung her head from side to side. 'No! It isn't like that! I love Colin. It's true that Inspector Barbor seemed to think it strange that Colin was involved, albeit only marginally, in two of the local murders, but that was a meaningless conversation. I know him, and I know he's incapable of harming anyone. Besides . . .'

'Yes?'

'He's the only one who *doesn't* match up.'

The words were a mistake. Carlo's face darkened and he clenched his jaw in fury.

'Match? Match with what?'

'The dead children,' she whispered.

'The children you saw yesterday?' All at once his voice was light and pleasant, it was as though he were addressing a backward child.

'Yes, that is . . . no!'

'Oh, Amy, how bad you are at lying. So, you still insist you saw children yesterday. Poor Amy; perhaps I should make you some tea. An infusion from the shop might help.'

Amy remembered Jonathan Harris. 'NO!' Her scream echoed round the room and she saw the surprise on her husband's face; surprise followed by dawning comprehension.

'I see.'

She shivered. 'See what?'

'You are thinking that I might poison you.'

'Don't be stupid, I was only . . .'

'I am calling the doctor now. It would be better if you went to your room of your own accord.'

'I will not,' said Amy firmly. 'If you call a doctor I shall deny . . .'

'GO TO YOUR ROOM!' he screamed, his face twisted with rage. She had never heard him like that before, his voice shrill and ugly, breaking with emotion. She stared at him, hypnotized by the sparks of fury that danced in his eyes and the angry red patches standing out on his cheekbones.

'Do as I say or you'll regret it,' he ranted. 'Don't you remember last time? Do you want to go through all that again? You will, you know and this time it will be worse. Don't think anyone will help you. Who could? No one will hear you screaming. No one ever does. This time . . .'

Incredulously she stared at him, hearing the shrill, feminine pitch of his voice, and noting flecks of foam at the corners of his mouth as his tirade continued. Sobbing with fright, she tried to run for the kitchen but he blocked her way.

'Upstairs!' he screamed. 'Don't you ever do as you're told?'

She began to cry, then felt him give her a violent push in the back that forced her to the foot of the stairs.

'Don't!' she begged him. 'Please, Carlo, let me alone. I'm going up now, I promise.'

Slightly appeased he fell silent, but his furious eyes remained on her as she walked on shaking legs up the steep stairway. Then she heard him behind her, and was overwhelmed by such terror that her breath refused to come, and all at once she was gasping for air, clutching at her throat in an attempt to ease the constriction.

She felt Carlo's arms go round her and knew that she was about to be pushed down into the living-room. He intended her to lose their child, of that she was quite certain, and with a desperate cry she wrenched herself free only to feel her foot slip beneath her, and then there was nothing at all.

When she opened her eyes Dr Harris was standing at her bedside, his fingers gently testing her pulse.

'The baby?' she said, her voice weak and fearful.

'The baby's fine, Mrs Rivero.'

'Fine?' She couldn't believe what he was saying.

'Of course, you had a bad anxiety attack, that's all. It's fortunate that your husband heard you and got to you in time.'

Amy's eyes clouded in bewilderment. 'What do you mean?'

'You were half-way up the stairs, gasping for breath. He caught you just before you fell. Have you experienced similar attacks before this?'

'No! I thought . . .'

'What, Mrs Rivero?'

Over his shoulder she could see Carlo. He was pale and worried-looking and his eyes were gentle; full of love for her, love that she had never doubted until . . . until when? She tried to remember.

'Yesterday!' she whispered aloud.

'What happened yesterday?'

Again she glanced at her husband, but his face reflected only concern for her. There was no sign of the shrill-voiced, screaming stranger she recalled from earlier that day.

'There were children,' she said slowly. Carlo's face remained the same. He even gave her an encouraging smile.

'You've been having nightmares about children ever since I arrived. It's understandable. Most intelligent people worry about the responsibilities of parenthood, and I imagine you're always somewhat over-conscientious. We'd better try to keep you a little calm for the last few months. Nothing strong, only a very mild sedative. We don't want Junior harmed, do we?'

'Was it *all* a dream?' she asked.

'Of course. Try and rest. I'll leave a prescription with your husband for something to help you sleep tonight, and I'll look in tomorrow. Now, remember, stay in bed until I've called.'

'I'll see to that, doctor,' Carlo assured him, and with a final encouraging smile at his wife he led Dr Harris down the stairs.

'You're sure you can manage?' the doctor queried. 'It could prove difficult if she persists with her delusions. I've never heard anything quite like it before.'

'Her sister's death upset her. I think that perhaps this baby has come too soon, but maybe in the end it will distract her.'

Dr Harris liked and admired Carlo. 'Most probably,' he said with more confidence than he felt. Well, it was possible. He wished that he had Mrs Rivero's medical notes, but they hadn't been passed on from her previous GP yet.

Carlo went slowly back to the bedroom and tiptoed over to Amy's side. 'All right now, darling?'

Amy looked at him carefully. He had such a kind face. She remembered thinking that the very first time they met, and his eyes were always laughing. Even now, there was the suggestion of a smile in them, but a kind smile, not the taunting, sneering travesty of amusement that her mind had conjured up during her blackout.

'I suppose so,' she said slowly. 'I had such terrible dreams.'

'I know: the doctor and I heard them!'

'Did Inspector Barbor call here this morning?'

'He may have done. I was busy in the shop.'

'Didn't I tell you over lunch?'

'I was coming for lunch when I found you unwell.'

'Oh! I thought . . . How peculiar. What's the time now?'

'Four o'clock.'

'The children will soon be home.'

'Don't worry, we will manage splendidly!'

'Did we go out to look at our new house yesterday?'

'No, little one, not yesterday. Last Saturday we all went.'

'But I can remember it so well.'

'You must try to forget. Dr Harris wants you more tranquil.'

'Yes. It was a horrible dream, Carlo.'

'But now it's over.'

'Yes, now it's over,' she repeated obediently, and closed her eyes to prevent further discussion.

All that they were telling her might be true, and it might not. One thing was quite certain: she would never mention the ghost-children to her husband again. If she was right, and the doctor wrong, then those creatures threatened not only the children of the village but also Amy herself and, ultimately, the entire structure of her marriage to Carlo, because within her husband – the man she knew and loved – there dwelt another Carlo, a person of frightening instability, capable of both violence and cruelty.

Until she knew the truth she intended to go very carefully indeed, and if she ever wanted to talk to someone again it wouldn't be her husband, it would be Inspector Barbor. Comforted by that thought she finally fell into the dreamless sleep Dr Harris had prescribed.

Chapter 13

Mrs Down, who taught the top class of the junior school, looked along the room at the rows of bent heads and immediately her attention was caught by the sight of Samuel Beckett's pale face as he gazed about him, looking at everything except the maths test that was on his desk.

She coughed gently, but he didn't hear. For over a week now the boy had been inattentive. It wasn't only in his work. He had started to play alone during the breaks, and no longer spent his time at the side of his twin.

'Samuel!' she called quietly. He looked at her with a startled expression on his face.

'Get on with your work, please,' she chided him, but kindly because both he and Richard were nice children who normally caused her no trouble at all.

When the class went out for mid-morning break she kept Samuel back, ostensibly over his maths but really because she felt that he was in need of someone to confide in, and hoped that he might find it possible to speak freely to her.

'What's the matter, Samuel!'

He blinked nervously and shook his head. 'Nothing.'

'Oh, come now! I know better than that. You haven't even done your homework this week, and that isn't like you. Is there something wrong at home?'

He began to fidget and glanced anxiously out of the window to where the children were playing. 'No, nothing.'

'There is something troubling you, isn't there?'

He swallowed hard. 'Suppose so.'

'It often helps to tell someone when you're worried. A trouble shared is a trouble halved they say!'

'Not this one,' he muttered.

'Have you talked to Richard about it?'

He looked down at the floor. 'I can't.'

'Why ever not?'

'Just because.'

Mrs Down realized that she wasn't going to make any progress. He was obviously a troubled child, but until he felt free to open up to her there was nothing further to be achieved. She gave him a smile.

'Run out and play then; but remember, I'm here if you need me.'

'Yes, Mrs Down.'

He walked slowly out of the classroom, and when she glanced out at the playground five minutes later he was mooching aimlessly about, ignoring all the games going on around him. If it continued much longer, she thought, then his father would have to be told.

After school, Samuel tried to slip out of the cloakroom and down to the school gates alone. Once with Amy Rivero he would be safe enough, the group wouldn't dare talk to him in her presence. Colin, however, was too quick to allow that to happen. He was waiting right in the cloakroom doorway.

'Richard's going to talk to you tonight,' he said sternly, 'then he'll let me know what you said. You're going to cause trouble if you keep mooching around with a face as long as a fiddle. Don't you know how important it is that we don't draw attention to ourselves?'

'Shut up!' muttered Samuel. 'Mind your own business.'

'This *is* my business, and don't forget it.'

'Fat chance, lard-face!'

Colin sighed and stepped to one side. 'You're terribly

immature,' he remarked. 'I don't think you're properly one of us.'

'Good!'

Frowning, Colin watched the older boy walk away. This could prove difficult to deal with. They had never anticipated having a rebel in their own camp, and he wondered how it had come about.

The truth was that Samuel had always possessed great strength of character. Wayne – his particular alter ego – had not. The result was that Wayne's influence under normal circumstances was slight. It was only during retaliatory exercises that Wayne was able to dominate. Once the adrenalin had stopped flowing and life returned to normal, Samuel came to the fore. Richard understood this, but if the group was threatened then he too would do whatever was necessary to protect them.

At tea that evening Colin asked Carlo if he could go and play with the twins for an hour. His guardian frowned.

'What about your homework?'

'I did it as soon as I got in, didn't I, Amy?'

'Yes, for once you did!'

'So, may I go?'

'I want you back by eight.'

'Sure. Do you want to come, Joanne?'

Joanne knew that it was really Richard that Colin was going to see, and she knew who they would discuss. She shook her head, not wanting to be asked to pass judgement on one of her own friends.

'I've still got my homework to do. Besides, I ought to help Amy with the washing up.'

Amy smiled. 'You are a helpful girl, Joanne.'

Joanne smiled back at her, and Amy studied her features carefully. She had a rounded, cheerful face with an air of calm inner strength that made you certain she would one day be an excellent wife and mother. Yet none of this was apparent on any of the photos.

Why not? she asked herself, and again the memory of the children in the half-built house returned. She was certain that her mental image of them was far too vivid to have stemmed merely from a dream, but kept her doubts from Carlo.

A few minutes later Colin hurried in through the back door of the twins' house. Their father was working late tonight, and because of this the meeting had, of necessity, to be conclusive. Such a chance might not come their way again.

Richard was sitting at the kitchen table, his face resting on his cupped hands. When Colin entered he failed to look up.

'No good, Richard?'

'No, he wants to go to the police.'

'About Mrs Gregory?'

'Yep.'

'That's daft. They'd never believe him.'

'No.'

'No, but it would cause a lot of trouble. Old nosey-parker Mrs Wright saw me on my way back to the woods that day, and according to Mark, Inspector Barbor is suspicious of us as it is. He keeps asking me questions about lots of things; he'd certainly be interested in Samuel's story. Well, I guess that's it.'

'I guess so.'

The boys looked at one another, half-excited, half-scared. For a few minutes they remained silent, until at last Colin took the initiative.

'We'll go out, but only after we've told him it's OK and not to worry because we understand. Right?'

Richard blinked hard, trying not to show any emotion. 'Right.'

Together they went upstairs and found Samuel lying on his bed reading a comic. He looked at them with thinly veiled hostility.

'What do *you* want?'

'We're going to the bridge to time some trains with Richard's new stopwatch,' said Colin. 'Are you coming with us?'

'No.'

'OK. By the way, it doesn't matter if you do go to the police. They'll think you're barmy, but that doesn't bother the rest of us. If it will make you feel better, run along and tell.'

'They will listen. How would I know the things that were done to her if I hadn't been there?'

'You could have read them in a paper.'

Samuel wasn't convinced. 'They put all that in the papers?'

'Yep, in the scandal rags. We're off now. The high-speed train is due through soon and I want to time it passing under the bridge.'

Samuel looked suspiciously at his twin. 'Is Colin telling the truth?'

Richard knew that this was the most important moment. If he failed to convince Samuel then Colin would lay the blame for what followed squarely on his shoulders. He summoned up every ounce of will-power and grinned straight into his brother's eyes.

'Yes! Come on, let's go and enjoy ourselves before Dad gets back. You know what he's like about us going out in the evening!' Minutes later they left the house, arms linked, laughing and joking as they went.

Samuel felt better than he had in weeks. Now that the

other children accepted his feelings about Sara Gregory, he didn't think that he would go to the police. After all, he had taken part himself, and would probably be sent away along with the rest of them. He didn't want that. No, all he had really wanted to do was make the others realize that things were getting out of hand; that there was a limit to what he was prepared to do.

With that aim achieved he could once again enjoy himself. He was especially grateful to Richard, for he knew that if his twin hadn't spoken up for him then he would have been in grave danger.

Once on the bridge the boys peered down the track. Colin consulted his wrist watch. 'Only a couple more minutes. Let's time it from the moment its engine appears your side until the whole train's clear of the tunnel. I'll stand here and warn you when it's approaching. You and Samuel stand over there, Richard, then you can keep a check on each other.'

The boys separated, and the twins stood alone together on the far side of the bridge. Richard glanced at his brother and gave an involuntary shiver.

'It's a bit cold,' he muttered, trying to hold Samuel's attention.

'Yep. Thanks for not telling on me, Richard.'

His brother didn't answer.

'I know what Colin's like. I was quite frightened when I heard him arrive.'

Richard tried to moisten his lips. His throat was suddenly thick and he wished the train would hurry.

'Here it comes!' shouted Colin, and in the distance the twins could hear the train's approach.

'Ready?' checked Colin.

'Ready!' agreed Samuel enthusiastically.

'Start looking . . . NOW!'

Concentrating furiously on the stopwatch and the imminent emergence of the engine from beneath the bridge, Samuel never even heard Colin crossing over to his side. He leant over the bridge to get a better view and at once both his legs were seized and he was hurled bodily over the edge on to the track beneath. He gave one terrible, ear-splitting scream of terror, then nothing was heard but the roar of the high-speed train as it hurtled over the track.

The driver, aware that he had hit something, applied his brakes, and further along the line the train began to slow. White-faced, Colin and Richard stared down below them. There was virtually nothing left of Samuel except for a terrible mess of mangled flesh and – grotesquely – the bottom half of an arm, severed and thrown to the side of the line where it lay palm uppermost, as though in supplication.

With a cry of horror Richard ran off the bridge and down to the shredded remains of his twin. His shock and distress were not lessened because he had been the cause of the death. Pale and incoherent he stumbled through his speech about the timing game, and Samuel's poor sense of balance.

When Dean Beckett arrived home from work his house was full of neighbours and policemen. Numb with grief he held his remaining child tightly to him and vowed silently to get away from the village as soon as possible. The whole place had something wrong with it; something almost tangible, a sense of corruption and evil that had never been there before.

He was not an imaginative man, nor a superstitious one, but he knew when something felt wrong, and the entire village was rapidly coming alive with something – he had no name for it – that he sensed could only be avoided by moving right away. As soon as possible he and Richard would go; he clung to the thought as a panacea, to help him through the next few weeks.

On the day of the funeral, Amy was late dressing. She was just hurrying into the living-room when the sound of Carlo and Colin talking stopped her. There was something about their tone that told her this was no normal discussion. It was secret; and, because of this, she did something that prior to her experience at the new house would never have entered her head. She stood outside the door and listened.

'I still don't understand how it happened,' Carlo was saying.

'He just fell. I wasn't looking. I was on the other side.'

'Colin, I don't believe you. Mrs Down told the twins' father that Samuel hadn't been himself for some time.'

'So?'

'So, did he fall?'

'Or?'

'Did he jump?' pressed Carlo. The speed with which Colin grasped at this alternative gave him away.

'Yes, perhaps he did! He missed his mother a lot, you know.'

'You didn't mention this to the coroner.'

'No point; dead's dead, ain't it?'

Amy gave a small gasp. Quite apart from the atrocious grammar the voice itself didn't belong to Colin. It had a London whine to it, and was weary beyond nine years of age.

'Yes, Colin, dead is dead. It also occurs to me that he could have been – how shall I say – assisted off the bridge.'

'He could have been.'

'By whom?'

'Richard, of course. Brothers have been killing each other ever since Cain and Abel.'

'Colin, kindly do not be flippant with me. Was he pushed?'

In terrified silence Amy waited for the reply, then jumped as a hand touched her gently on the back.

'Isn't it time we went, Amy?'

She turned to look at Joanne's grave features.

'Yes, it is. I thought that Colin and Carlo were having a private discussion, so I didn't like to go in.'

'Really?' There was a wealth of meaning in the way the child said it, suggesting disbelief, contempt and even a hint of patronage. 'Well, I don't mind interrupting. We mustn't be late for poor Samuel's funeral.'

Amy watched as Joanne marched into the room and immediately the other two came out, Colin with his eyes averted and his head down. Carlo took hold of his wife's hand.

'You're sure you want to come, darling?'

'Of course.'

'It's good of the school to give his friends time off to attend his funeral.'

'Yes.'

'A child dying is always tragic.'

'I know, but don't you think the children are coping awfully well?'

Carlo nodded. 'But, of course. They're getting so much practice.'

'That's not very funny.'

'No, Amy, neither was it intended to be.'

She could see that he was tense and angry as well as distressed. If only Joanne hadn't come along she would have heard Colin's answer. Now – although fairly positive that it had been in the affirmative – she would never know for sure, unless Carlo took her into his confidence. Somehow she thought that highly unlikely.

Dean Beckett had decided that he wanted more than a brief cremation service for his dead son. As a result there was an initial church service, followed by the cremation itself. Amy hoped that Colin and Joanne managed to sit through it all without getting too distressed.

When she and Carlo walked into St Matthew's church the front pews were already full. They hesitated for a moment, looking for a space to sit, and suddenly Amy became aware that people were staring at them.

All around the church heads turned, and she heard the soft whisper of conversation as people murmured to their neighbours, exchanging low confidences. Carlo didn't appear to notice, but the children did. They moved closer together, linking hands and lifting their heads slightly in unconscious defiance.

Feeling instinctively protective, Amy put her arms round them and shepherded them into an empty pew. She bent her head in silent prayer, but when she opened her eyes found that many of the villagers were still staring openly at the family, their gaze hostile.

Carlo sat completely motionless. His hands rested on his thighs and he looked straight ahead of him; he gave no indication that he knew he was being studied, not once did he even look about him. He simply sat and waited for the service to begin.

Outside it was a cold March day, but inside the church was stiflingly hot. The previous winter new heating had been installed, and it was working so well that Amy wished she had worn a lighter coat. As she started to undo her top button she saw Mark East's parents across the aisle, and they were glaring at Colin, their patent dislike mingled with fear. She recalled the overheard scraps of conversation between Colin and Carlo, and wondered what the other people knew that had set them so strongly against the boy.

Logic dictated that it was probably no more than a magnification of her own unease concerning the number of times he had been involved in tragedies over the past months. In olden days he might have been accused of being in league with the devil. In the nineteen-eighties such a statement would only have provoked laughter but the years didn't change people's ideas, merely their willingness to express them openly.

If Colin and Joanne were aware of what was happening they, like Carlo, ignored it. They too sat like statues, hymn books at the ready, their faces guileless but pale, as was to be expected considering they were attending the funeral of one of their closest friends.

The vicar's arrival put an end to the silent scrutiny. After the opening hymn he went into the pulpit and spoke about the tragedy of a young life prematurely ended before it had properly begun. Amy scarcely listened, until her attention was caught by a change in his voice.

'There are people,' he intoned, 'who feel that we – in this village – have suffered more disasters than is natural for such a small community. Indeed, I myself find that as each disaster strikes my faith is sorely tested, but I appeal to you . . .'

'Not to me!' sniggered Joanne. Shocked faces swivelled round to glare at the girl. Carlo shot her a look of such fury that she flushed and bent her head.

'. . . not to let yourselves be carried away by superstitious fears,' continued the minister. 'We live in an enlightened age, and we know that whilst we may not understand the reasons for life's misfortunes, it is all part of a far wider plan devised by God for . . .'

'It's him!' screamed a dark-haired woman, leaping to her feet and pointing accusingly at Colin. 'He's the one! Ask him how it happened. Ask him about his parents. He's always around. It's that boy!'

Amy gasped and looked over the children's heads at Carlo. He was listening carefully, spots of colour standing out on his cheekbones, but when Amy rose to leave he shook his head. All around them people were muttering, nodding their heads and voicing agreement.

The vicar, caught unawares, hesitated too long. Before he could think of what to say the dead boy's father stood, tears falling from his eyes as he faced the packed congregation.

'It's true!' he cried. 'Colin's always there. He found Kate Burgess *and* Pete Gregory. He told Harriet Harris about poisons. He destroys everything he touches. As long as he continues to live here this village won't be safe! I . . .'

'This is a house of God!' thundered the vicar. 'Whilst grief is only to be expected, such . . .'

Dean Beckett was still on his feet, his mouth open as he continued pointing at Colin. Amy moved closer to the boy only to retreat in shock from the freezing air that was surrounding both children. They seemed protected by it and sat together in apparent indifference while their gleaming eyes flickered round the church, almost daring people to say more.

Amy shook as she felt the surge of hostility that the two speakers had released. Everywhere there were sounds of agreement, and the vicar was completely ignored as he tried to continue his pacifying litany.

Just as one or two more adults began to rise to their

feet in apparent support of Dean Beckett, Richard jumped up on to his pew. He stood looking down at his father, then raised his clear young voice so that it rang stridently through the church.

'My brother is dead,' he reminded everyone present. '*I* was there when he died, but my father doesn't accuse me of being involved. Samuel loved Colin, he was like another brother to us both. Please, stop all this quarrelling and remember why we're really here – to say goodbye to my twin.'

A shamed silence fell upon the congregation. Slowly they all sat down, their eyes now averted from where Colin and his family sat. Only Amy failed to be moved by the plea, for to her mind it was a calculated and emotionless one. What they had heard wasn't the heartbroken voice of a bereaved twin, it was a cool, logical speech designed to stop the swiftly spreading hysteria and also, posibly even most importantly, to divert attention away from Colin.

The vicar called the number of the final hymn, and as Carlo leant in front of the children to speak to Amy she was hypnotized by the cloud of steam that his breath created in the overheated church. Steam caused by the freezing air surrounding both Colin and Joanne.

When everyone left church to move on to the crematorium, Amy hung back.

'Let's go home,' she begged Carlo. 'I don't want to . . .'

'We go to the crematorium,' replied her husband crisply. 'If not, people will believe there is truth in what has been said.'

'But . . .'

'We are going, Amy.'

'I want to go,' added Colin. 'Stupid old windbags! What do they know?'

'Colin!' Amy couldn't believe her ears. The child should have been shocked, and certainly distressed, but not abusive. Joanne laughed.

'They should be careful what they say! If you're so wicked then they ought to be frightened of you.'

'They are,' said Colin smugly. 'I could tell that.'

'Carlo, don't they realize . . .' began Amy.

'Into the car!' he ordered, ushering his wife ahead of them. 'I'm sure Samuel wouldn't want you to miss his cremation.'

'I'm quite sure he would!' Colin whispered to Joanne, and she shot him a winning smile. Amy, who both saw and heard it all, shuddered.

At the crematorium there were further prayers, but this time everyone remained silent, and it was only when the curtains closed round the coffin that muted crying could be heard from the front pew. Dean Beckett was mourning his son, but beside him Samuel's twin sat upright, composed and calm and when he breathed gentle wisps of steam formed in the cold air around him too.

At the end, when everyone filed out to look at the floral tributes, the children – without any apparent directive – detached themselves from their relatives and moved silently together until they formed a circle round one large wreath bearing the inscription: '*For Samuel, with love from all his friends.*'

'Clever, that,' murmured Fiona. 'I mean, it doesn't actually commit any of us, does it? No names at all.'

'Precisely!' enthused Jody. 'It was Colin's idea.'

As they stood there, unsmiling but plainly absorbed in their conversation, Inspector Barbor stood well back from the mourners and studied the children carefully.

He had been at the back of the church and had heard the disturbance, just as he had noted the lack of reaction by Colin and the remarkably composed speech by young Richard Beckett. The two boys who had been closest to the tragedy had displayed no emotion at all during the final day of mourning, and this interested the policeman. He too was uncomfortable about the role of Colin in the various village tragedies, but being unable to pin down one specific way in which the boy had contributed to any trouble, he – like other adults in the village – had to confine himself to a general feeling of unease. Unlike the others, however, he could have the child followed, and this he intended to do immediately he returned to the station.

For Amy those final few minutes were like a nightmare. She clung tightly to Carlo's arm, trying not to show how much she was hurt by the manner in which people whom she had previously known and liked now ignored her. Even Christine Sumner refused to acknowledge her presence. In her heart she could understand it, for she too was beginning to fear Colin, and not only him; she feared the entire group of children, and as she saw them all standing together, their voices muted and their expressions impassive, she knew that she was right to feel fear.

To her relief Carlo didn't suggest that they went to the Becketts' after the service. Instead he took them all for a drive into the countryside, finally stopping in a small wooded area where they got out and the two children raced off down a muddy path, chattering excitedly to one another.

Amy and Carlo followed slowly, neither speaking for some time until Amy had managed to assemble her thoughts into some sort of order.

'He wasn't the same, was he?' she queried at last.

'Sorry?'

'Samuel – I don't think he was as possessed as the

others, and so they decided to kill him. It's all there in their faces. I don't think they have any regard for human life. If someone gets in their way they remove them. That's their idea of law – jungle law.'

'The survival of the fittest, you mean?'

'In a way. Poor little Samuel.'

'That is nonsense!'

'It is not. Carlo, I want to talk to you.'

'We are already talking!'

'It's about the other day. I didn't dream up those ghost-children in our new house. You know perfectly well that they exist; in fact, you probably try to help them when you can.'

'Is this a joke?'

'No! It's very serious. Just think, one of those children murdered Samuel.'

'Indeed? In that case you only have a choice of two.'

'Yes, I . . .'

'Amy!' he interrupted quickly. 'Amy, do you love me?'

She didn't hesitate. 'Yes, I love you.'

'And will you always love me?'

'Yes, always.'

'Then I will be truthful with you. You are correct, our new house *is* a meeting place for the children who died. You call them ghost-children but this is not so. They are simply the unquiet dead.'

Amy shivered at the soft, calm way he was talking to her and trembled with fear at what he was saying; yet she knew that such honesty was vital if she and Carlo were ever to be happy and free themselves, for gradually these children were taking him further into their world. It was up to her to save him.

'Why?' she asked. 'Why can't they rest?'

He shrugged. 'Who knows? The terrible way they died perhaps? The violence they encountered during their short lives? There could be many reasons.'

'And what do they want? Peace? Are they looking to you for peace? Is there some way in which you can set them free?'

'Of course; they will be free once they have had the revenge which is their right.'

'Revenge? What harm have the people here ever done to them?'

'Someone started the fire.'

'I was told it was one of their fathers.'

'Not so, it was a villager; this much they have told me.'

'Who?'

'That they keep secret.'

'Carlo, were the children involved in my sister's death?'

He stopped and caught hold of her arm. 'Do not get this out of proportion. How could they have been responsible for such a thing? No, they may be malicious and spiteful but to suggest that they killed Kate is nonsense. Why should they?'

'I don't know, but if they didn't kill her then what have they actually done?'

'Possibly they did kill Samuel, that is all.'

'You're lying to me.'

He gave her his most boyish, endearing grin. 'No, I am telling you the truth. These children do exist, and they have occasionally manifested themselves through children from the village, but that is all. The rest is untrue.'

'So the fact that people are dying like flies in Lower Ditton isn't connected with the presence of ten malevolent spirits hell-bent on revenge upon unsuspecting adults?'

'Precisely!'

'And Colin? Where does he fit in?' He failed to answer.

Amy closed her eyes and felt the child within her move restlessly.

'I want to go away,' she said at last. 'I want to leave this village.'

'I cannot, not yet.'

'Why?'

'The children need me.'

'*I* need you; our child needs you. Why do these ghosts have to come first? You asked if I loved you – well, if you truly love me then do as I ask and leave here now, before things get even worse.'

'Amy, there is nothing for you to fear. You are my wife. No one will harm you.'

'I don't want to live somewhere where there are walking dead masquerading as normal children! I've seen what they're really like, my camera showed that only too clearly, and I know that such children are capable of anything. They may like you now, but what if you too annoy them? Will you fall under a train, or will I be the one to end up with my throat cut?'

'Amy, please! If you continue like this I shall wish I'd never told you.'

'Call in a priest!' she cried. 'Get him to exorcize them. If they want peace a priest will be able to give them it. If you won't leave until they're peaceful then call in the church. Call in anyone you like, but get those children out of our house before we move in.'

'You lack compassion: I am disappointed.'

'I don't lack compassion! Comprehension, yes – not many wives expect to take on a family of wandering spirits – but not compassion. I want them to be at peace as much as you. That's why I suggest the church.'

'Peace!' He almost spat the word out as his mouth

curled with contempt. 'Revenge is more important than peace. I don't expect you to understand for you were raised with love and kindness, but I was not and I realize that revenge is necessary. If you had memories such as these children have then you would not settle for peace. Why shouldn't adults suffer the fear and indignities they inflict so casually on their children?

'Why is murder so wrong now, when it was treated as a mere misfortune before? If eleven children could be killed without the law taking any action, are not these same children entitled to mete out the punishment themselves? There is no justice here on earth for anyone unless they attend to it personally. Children are weak and vulnerable, therefore abuse them. That is reality! Childhood is not Little Grey Rabbit and marmite sandwiches for everyone, Amy.'

She had never heard him so impassioned before. His eyes blazed as he spoke and she knew that most of the time she was forgotten, he was talking to the entire world, not his wife, and his message was one of unremitting hatred and resentment. She was shocked, yes, but also filled with an overwhelming tenderness for the terrified boy he must once have been. Despite her shock and fear it was compassion and love that took over without any conscious decision being made, and it was quite probably this that saved her life.

She caught hold of his hand and drew him closer to her. 'Carlo, the past is over. You have me now, and soon we will have a child of our own. Please, don't keep looking back. I love you, I don't want to see you destroyed.'

'Destroyed?' His forehead creased in bewilderment.

'Yes. If you don't destroy yourself with such bitterness then these children will do it for you the moment you cease to champion them. Can't you see that?'

'It is not so.'

She sighed. 'Let's go home. I don't want to talk about it any more today.'

'But you do understand?'

Amy literally ached for his pain and the futile hatred for his past. 'Yes,' she assured him, 'I understand.'

'These children are not bad.'

'No, I accept that.'

'They have been brutalized.'

'Yes. Please, Carlo, let's go home now.'

'They hate the dark. I can't stop their fear at night-time. I hear them crying out and I can't help.'

She tightened her grip on his hand. 'We'll talk further tomorrow. Colin! Joanne! Come on, we're going back home.'

'*You* do not think they are responsible for . . . anything?'

'No, as you said, why should they be?'

'It is possible to lose control of so much hatred.'

'Yes. Colin! Come along.'

Slowly the children emerged along the path. They were carrying posies of wild flowers and laughing together.

'When the baby comes . . .' began Carlo. Amy watched her stepchildren and wondered what they were finding amusing.

'Yes?'

'You will not stop loving . . .?'

'Colin and Joanne? Of course not.'

'No, I meant . . . me.'

'You?' She stared in amazement seeing the doubt and confusion on his face.

'But, Carlo, you're my husband! Of course I won't stop . . .'

'We collected some more flowers for Samuel!'

announced Joanne. 'Can we leave them outside the crematorium with the others?'

'Why?' asked Amy sharply. 'You all sent a wreath.'

'These are especially from me,' said Colin. 'Wild flowers, growing free, I thought he'd like that. After all, he's free now, isn't he?'

'I hope so,' said Amy flatly, and Colin blinked in surprise.

'It's OK, then?'

'Yes, if it's what you want to do.'

She felt considerable satisfaction during the ride back to the crematorium because she had obviously taken all the pleasure from Colin's symbolic gesture. From now on she would fight these children with every facility at her command, for she was fighting to save her husband and it was a war she had no intention of losing.

Only at night, in the dark that Carlo had said they feared, did Amy too feel afraid. In the day she was strong. This was fortunate for the children too were strong, and growing stronger. They also had the advantage of numbers and were prepared to bide their time, for their beloved Carlo loved Amy and so for the present she would be allowed to live.

Chapter 14

'I know we've got a nice house here,' remarked Carol Blake to her husband Tony over breakfast, 'but I really think I'd be happier if we were to move away. Not far away, say Stroud. You'd still be able to commute to work easily, and I wouldn't be forever wondering who was going to be next.'

Their nine-year-old daughter Helen spooned sugar over her toast without thinking, but fortunately her parents didn't notice. Quickly she brushed it on to the floor and reached for the butter. Her face was calm, and she had an abstracted air about her, but every word was being memorized for relaying to the group.

'I wanted to move ages ago,' answered Tony. 'I told you the place would go downhill once that bloody refuge centre was set up, but you wouldn't listen. "The poor creatures must have somewhere to go," you kept saying. Well, this is what comes of woolly-minded liberalism.'

'Darling, I really don't think you can blame those unfortunate families for everything that's happened recently. Besides, it isn't right to talk about them like that. Think of what happened in the end.'

'Serve them right. What did they expect, living ten to a room? It's like re-housing people from the slums, it never works. They simply take their disgusting habits to perfectly decent areas and lower the price of property.'

'I wasn't asking for a party political broadcast, Tony.'

'Well, you know how strongly I feel about these things. I've got every sympathy for the National Front.'

'Tony!'

'What's the matter? It's a legal party, you know!'

'You can't be serious!'

'No, actually I'm not, but I hope you're serious about the move.'

'Yes, I am. I'd quite like to remove a certain person from the influence of "you-know-who" as well.'

Helen kept her eyes fixed on her plate.

'That boy, you mean?'

Carol nodded.

'Couldn't agree more. I always knew that Jackie and George were mad to adopt him. Bad blood comes out in the end.'

'Sshh! I don't think he knows that he was . . .'

'Surely he must? He was four before he left the foster home; children of that age have memories. It isn't like adopting a baby, though God knows that's risky enough.'

Carol glanced at their daughter. 'Helen, hurry up with your toast and then go and plait your hair; it's terribly untidy.'

'Sorry!' She quickly ate the last remaining piece and then walked casually from the room.

'You shouldn't discuss Colin in front of her,' said Carol angrily. 'I'm quite sure she repeats every word. He seems to have the children completely under his spell.'

'Apparently the adults aren't so besotted. That was quite a scene Dean threw in church yesterday.'

'It's understandable, he's lost . . .'

'I do know the extent of his loss. Just the same, he should have kept his opinion to himself. Mind you, it was interesting to see how many people agreed with him. Only to be expected in a village this size. I'm surprised they haven't retained a ducking-stool!'

'You've always patronized the people here, Tony, but I can't think why. What's so special about you?'

'Not a lot, but I think I'm a trifle too intelligent to blame a nine-year-old boy for a series of deaths among the adult population!'

'Perhaps that isn't quite as intelligent as you think. After all . . .'

'One thing's certain, if I'd been as intelligent as I thought I'd never have married you. You've got a village mentality. I only hope you can cope with life in a decent-sized town.'

Carol ignored his sniping, just as she had been ignoring it for the twelve years of their marriage.

'I'll cope. So are we moving?'

'Definitely. Ring up Justin and Peach and get this place valued. We'll put it on the market straight away. Now I'm off, or I'll be late for work.'

Within minutes Helen too had left the house. With a sigh Carol loaded the dishwasher. She had embarked on her marriage with such high hopes, flattered that someone as educated and dynamic as Tony Blake should want her for his wife, only to discover that he was a man who liked to shine in company, and his choice of wife was largely influenced by the fact that Carol could never compete with him at any level. There were times when she wondered whether Helen realized how much discontent there was in the home. On the whole she thought not; both she and Tony attempted to maintain a united front for their daughter's benefit.

In the school playground Helen ran straight past her classmates and headed for the bike shed where Colin and his group congregated. She was so out of breath when she found him that for a moment she couldn't speak.

'Sorry!' she gasped at last. 'I ran all the way; something urgent's come up.'

'We'll meet after school, up in my bedroom,' responded Colin. 'You tell the girls and I'll do the boys.'

'Right,' responded Helen. She was content. Colin would know what to do.

At four-fifteen Amy was surprised to find ten children trooping into her house. She caught hold of Colin's arm. 'What's this? An Annual General Meeting?'

'Sort of! We won't be long. You don't mind, do you?'

'As long as it doesn't last more than half an hour.'

'It won't. Thanks!' He smiled his pleasure and then led everyone up the stairs. Amy didn't smile back, for she was no longer fooled by the gentle exterior that had once made her open her heart to him.

In the bedroom the children's faces began to change. Their sharp features contrasted strangely with the affluence of their clothes, and when they spoke their voices were harsh with London vowel sounds that echoed as a disturbing whine.

'Mr and Mrs Blake are going to move,' Helen announced at once. 'Mrs Blake is frightened and Mr Blake despises everyone here anyway.'

'We know that,' said Fiona. 'He's a stuck-up snob.'

'A snotty snob!' laughed pretty Sophie.

'A potty, snotty snob!' giggled Georgina.

'A grotty, spotty, potty snob!' shrieked Jody.

'SHUT UP!' bawled Colin. 'Don't you realize what this means? If we're not quick Tony Blake is going to get away.'

They shook their heads in unison. Tony Blake was one adult who most certainly wouldn't be allowed to escape retribution.

* * *

On the morning of 20 May, three weeks before the baby was due, Amy woke with a start. She looked at the alarm clock, but the hands showed it was only 6.30 A.M. She didn't have to get up for another hour, yet still her heart continued to pound and there was a churning sensation in her stomach. Rigidly she remained beneath the covers, trying to control her mounting panic, but it was useless. She was terrified, and the persistent ticking of the clock only increased her fear.

'He'll be furious,' she thought to herself, glancing across the bed to where Carlo lay sleeping. Of course, that was it – she had to get up for her husband. He went to work early, and when she overslept his rages were almost inhuman.

With an effort she dragged her heavy body from the safety of the bed and slid her feet into her slippers. For some reason their warmth surprised her. She had expected them to feel thin and cold.

Shivering, she pulled on a dressing gown and tiptoed gently down to the kitchen. If she made too much noise he would be angry again. Fear made her clumsy, and as she filled the teapot some water splashed on to her right hand. Instinctively, she muffled her cry of pain. Her husband's sleep must not be disturbed.

As she laid the table and fried the eggs and bacon she kept glancing at the clock. It all had to be done by seven A.M. She knew that. If it wasn't then he would hit her again, and at the thought her entire body flinched, memories of his beatings flashing through her brain. No, she couldn't stand that. This morning everything would go well.

'What on earth are you doing?' asked Carlo, standing half-asleep in the doorway. 'Why are you up this early?

And who wants a fried breakfast? You know you're meant to be resting.'

He sounded as though he were truly concerned, but Amy knew better. She had been tricked and baited too often to fall into the trap of false consideration.

'Nonsense,' she said, keeping her voice cheerful but also placating. 'I'm only pregnant; it isn't an illness. You know that. As you rightly say, your mother raised six children under ten single-handed; there weren't any lazy lie-ins for her, and she never came to any harm.'

Carlo blinked. 'Six children? My mother didn't have six children! You've had a dream, darling. Come back to bed.'

She began to tremble. He was at his worst when he pretended to be kind. How often she'd relaxed at such times, grateful for any gesture of affection, and then he had pounced, yet still with the mock-smile on his face as he hit and kicked her. No, this time she wouldn't raise false hopes.

'Do eat,' she cajoled him. 'You know how much you hate the eggs if they're over-done.'

'Amy, I never eat a cooked breakfast!'

She frowned. Despite her terror of him she couldn't let such an obvious mistake pass unnoticed, otherwise he'd start reminding her about her own mother who'd become senile in her sixties and died hopelessly adrift in a world of her own imagination.

'My name isn't Amy!'

'What?'

She had never realized what a good actor he was.

'I said my name isn't Amy.'

He frowned. 'What is it then?'

'Julia! Is this Amy a girlfriend?' She wished she hadn't

said that, he might not laugh, but a retraction now would be useless. Nervously she awaited his reaction.

For fully a minute he continued to stare at her, apparently bewildered and not advancing into the room. That was some consolation. Physically she preferred him at a distance. Then, as though someone had thrown a switch, his expression changed. He nodded to himself and walked quietly towards her.

'Of course, how silly of me. You're Julia, Julia Ritchie.'

'Yes!' She gave a nervous giggle, then tried to cover her mouth with her hand. He hated her to giggle.

'Well, thank you for my breakfast, Julia.' As he sat down at the table and began to eat, her taut nerves relaxed. It was going to be all right. For once she had safely negotiated the ghastly early-morning period when almost anything could trigger one of his rages.

She didn't watch her husband eat, but instead sat on a chair by the gas stove and drank some of the hot, sweet tea that she enjoyed so much. Its warmth spread through her. Her eyelids drooped. She was so tired; if only Keith would let her sleep more. A mist began to swirl about her, blotting out the kitchen, the man at the table and everything else that made up her small, fear-filled world.

'Amy! Can we have a cooked breakfast too?' Colin's loud demand preceded him through the door. Carlo jumped to his feet, a finger to his lips, but he was too late. The woman by the stove jumped and stared at them, her eyes completely blank.

'AMY! AMY! Aaam . . .' The sound reverberated through Amy's brain, dying away at last to leave complete silence. She opened her eyes, astounded to find herself in the kitchen. She couldn't remember getting up or setting the table; couldn't even recall waking the children, but there they were. Quickly she drank some tea, then spat it out in disgust. It was strong and sweet, the exact opposite of the way she liked it.

'Yuck! who made that?' she demanded, but nobody replied. Carlo was looking at her with a curiously detached air of appraisal whilst the children stood side by side seeming, for one brief moment, emotionally closer to Amy than ever before. However she realized this couldn't be true because Joanne and Colin only had time for one adult, and that was Carlo. No, the children were the same as usual and the only query that Amy had now concerned her own movements. What had she been doing before she woke up virtually in the middle of breakfast? Confused and disoriented she frowned, feeling the beginning of a headache at her temples.

'What's happened?' she asked her husband.

'Happened?' His eyebrows rose a fraction, indicating a slightly amused lack of understanding.

'Yes. What am I doing here? Why are you eating a fried breakfast when you only like rolls and jam in the morning? I can't even remember getting out of bed!'

'You were up with the lark!' he said lightly. 'All eager to play the little housewife, right down to conventional bacon and eggs. I didn't have the heart to stop you!'

It wasn't true and she knew it. The children knew it as well for they kept their faces expressionless as they looked from one adult to the other.

'Why the sweet tea?' she queried urgently, desperate to make some sense of the situation.

'I made it,' volunteered Joanne. 'You felt a bit faint so I put some sugar in. Sorry!'

'You made it?'

'Yes.'

'Oh!' There was nothing more she could say about that.

Joanne had never made tea before, but there always had to be a first time. If only she didn't feel so peculiar, she thought, as perspiration broke out on her forehead. The figures in the room started to blur, and at the same time a fresh wave of panic swept over her. Her fingers curled round the discarded mug of tea again. She needed the tea, needed the strong sweetness of the liquid if she was to get through another day of Keith's ill humour. If only the child would be born, she thought wearily, then life might become bearable again.

Colin watched as Amy swayed slightly before sinking down on the kitchen chair again. He knew her at once. He remembered Julia Ritchie, a gaunt, pale-faced young woman heavy with pregnancy and living in dread of a sudden visit from her husband. Full of compassion he took steps towards the slumped young woman who was usually lively, resilient Amy.

'Come away!' commanded Carlo. The boy jumped in surprise, but obeyed instantly.

'She's frightened,' he protested.

'Yes. Unfortunately there's nothing we can do about that. It will pass.'

'How did it happen?' asked Joanne, deeply unsettled at seeing Amy reduced to the level of women she had known in her other life; known, despised and yet sympathized with because she had recognized that her future – if indeed she had any future, and even at eight she had doubted that fact – would be exactly the same.

'She must be at the same stage of her pregnancy as Julia was when she died. I suppose that just as you were all drawn to me so is Julia, but until today she had nowhere to live, no body to inhabit. Now she has Amy's. It's fascinating.'

'For how long?' asked Colin.

'God knows. Hopefully only until the child is born. We'll have to keep her indoors for now. Help me get her back to bed.'

In the maternity wing of the cottage hospital the consultant obstetrician looked down at the young woman as she twisted and turned on the narrow high-sided cot. She had been admitted twenty-four hours earlier with high blood pressure and the situation was getting worse. She was only semi-conscious and the few sentences that he could understand were garbled cries for help that made no sense. Neither did her general physical condition which had altered dramatically from her last hospital visit, when everything had been going perfectly.

Now, despite no obvious weight loss, she appeared pale and under-nourished and there were dark rings beneath her eyes. Puffy fingers and ankles indicated toxaemia, previously undetected, and her distressed condition made control of the blood pressure impossible. It was inexplicable, but if he was to be sure of the prospective mother's safety he had to perform an induction and hope that the baby was able to survive such an abrupt and premature arrival in the world.

Three hours later Carlo Manuel Rivero junior was hurried from the delivery room into the premature baby unit. He weighed 4lbs 3ozs, was able to breathe of his own volition, and the only obvious thing wrong with him was a touch of jaundice which quickly cleared. The light covering of hair on his head was jet black and his skin the same deep olive shade as his father's. Everyone who saw him fell in love with him because he was so beautiful.

As soon as he was born Amy's blood pressure returned to normal and she became fully conscious again. She felt slightly cheated that she'd missed the birth, but one look at her son more than made up for this. She had no recollection of the three days leading up to the induction, and no one attempted to tell her what her condition had been. It was over. Mother and child were fit and well, and all was right with the world – or so most people thought.

Chapter 15

'What's the baby's name?' asked Gillian as a contented gurgle carried into Colin's bedroom from the adjoining nursery.

'Carlo, but he's called Pepé, so that he isn't confused with our Carlo.'

'Is he nice? I like babies.'

"He's all right. Amy's potty about him.'

'Carlo isn't!' laughed Joanne. 'He gets tired of Amy fussing round the cot all the time!'

'I think he almost dislikes the baby sometimes,' added Colin. 'It brings back memories he'd rather forget.' The children nodded wisely. They too suffered from memories they would rather have forgotten.

'About the Blakes,' said Helen Blake forcefully, and at once little Pepé was banished from their minds.

'Yes?' queried Colin.

'They've got a buyer for the house. He's paying cash, too, which means that everything will happen very quickly, especially as they're buying a new property.'

Colin frowned. 'In other words, no chain? No possible breakdown along the line?'

Helen sighed. 'Not a chance. Mr Blake hopes to be gone within eight weeks.'

A rare smile flickered over Colin's features. 'Well, I think we can promise he won't be disappointed in that respect. He should definitely be gone within eight weeks, we'll all see to that!'

They laughed, but the laughter was harsh and chilling.

It was completely unchildlike and Amy, passing the door on her way to check the baby, felt the hairs on the back of her neck prickle with fear. She hurried on towards the nursery, knowing that as yet she wasn't strong enough to become involved with the children sitting huddled together in Colin's bedroom. As yet she wasn't strong enough, but she would be – given a little time.

It never occurred to her that the children might not allow her that time. Content in her ignorance, she picked up her beautiful, dark-haired child and took him downstairs to be fed, kissed and cuddled before it was time to get the evening meal.

Almost as soon as she had finished there was a tap on the back door. The woman standing outside was a stranger to Amy. She was in her early sixties with permed blue-grey hair and wore a tight tweed skirt and jacket that only emphasized the excess weight she carried. Her face, however, was cheerful and kind. Amy instinctively liked her.

'Mrs Rivero?'

'Yes.'

'My name is Madge Hutton. I knew your husband many years ago, when he was a small boy.'

'You knew Carlo as a child?'

'Certainly, quite well in fact. I've always felt . . . I don't know, a little guilty I suppose, and when I read about the birth of your son in the *Telegraph* I made some discreet enquiries. Once I'd confirmed it was the same Carlo I vowed to come and see you for myself, as a belated penance really. I'm afraid it's only to put my own mind at rest; selfish, but when one gets old . . .'

'Look, do come in. I've never met anyone who knew Carlo as a child. I'm really pleased you made the effort. Come through into the living-room. I'll put the kettle on.'

The woman glanced quickly about her. 'Where is your husband?'

'He's gone into Cirencester. He owns the health shop here, but every so often he goes to the warehouse to stock up. He should be back in an hour or so. I'm sure he'll be pleased . . .'

'I doubt it,' interrupted Madge Hutton. 'I imagine that he would like to forget the past completely. I'm so pleased to see that you're a nice girl, not at all like . . .'

Amy picked up Pepé and jiggled him about on her knee. He laughed, his dark eyes shining. 'Like who, Mrs Hutton?'

'His mother.'

'Ah. He never discusses his mother. He seems to think that she's still alive, but that's really all I know about her.'

'I'm afraid that she died a year or so ago.'

'You'd kept in touch with her, had you?'

Hrs Hutton shook her head. 'Certainly not! No, her death was in our local paper, that's the only reason I know. She was strangled by a drunken lover. Much the way one might have expected her to finish up, given her history.'

Amy put the baby against her shoulder as his eyelids began to droop. 'I'd like to hear about Carlo's childhood. You see, occasionally I feel that I really don't know him at all. He's such a kind, gentle man and yet – sometimes – it's very hard to explain this but he can seem almost a stranger. As though there are parts of him that he keeps to himself, areas where I'm never allowed to trespass, and his childhood is one of them.'

'He was a gentle little boy as well. His mother was Spanish, as you no doubt know, and his father was some sort of gypsy from a travelling fair. A big, handsome man with a terrible temper, and completely feckless. As soon as he learnt that young Carlo was on the way he vanished and Consuela – Carlo's mother – was turned out of her parents' home, literally on to the streets. She rented a couple of rooms in the house next door to mine and I could see at once that she wasn't going to cope on her own.

'She came from quite a good family, I think, and having to deal with ordinary, everyday things like washing and cleaning was beyond her. Once the baby arrived everything got completely out of hand. For a time there were visits from friends and welfare workers, but then she got a new boyfriend and people stopped calling.

'The baby was scarcely ever taken out. Weeks would go by without my seeing his pram and I got worried. I asked Consuela if I could see the child. She didn't seem to mind and took me into a tiny, dark, damp little room where Carlo lay soaking wet on filthy sheets. I don't think at that stage she was deliberately harming her son, she simply didn't know any better.

'For a few months I popped in and out once or twice a day and saw to the baby myself. Consuela was more than happy for someone else to cope, and the boyfriend made it plain that as long as she was free for his pleasure nothing else mattered.

'Of course the situation didn't stay like that. The boyfriend drifted away; I became busier with my dressmaking, and Consuela found herself a new man. He was another heavy drinker, and didn't want anyone interfering in his life. I stopped visiting.

'I'm ashamed to admit that I was afraid of the man. His name was John, and he had those dead, grey eyes that look straight through people. I used to hear them quarrelling at nights, and sometimes little Carlo would cry for hours at a time, but I couldn't do anything.

'Now and again I would see him in the back garden. He was very thin and pale, but with the most beautiful eyes. Unfortunately he was too timid, too cowed by his experiences, to make friends with me. He used to accept chocolate biscuits or cakes when I offered them, but he wouldn't speak. By the time he was three he wouldn't even take the food. His fear was greater than his hunger.'

Amy held Pepé closer to her, nauseated by what she was hearing. She moistened her lips. 'Go on,' she whispered. Madge Hutton hesitated.

'This is difficult for me. There came the time when Carlo stopped going into the garden. I occasionally heard him crying, but only faintly, and that was all. I knew his mother left him alone in the house, and I noticed too that he cried only when she and this John were at home, never when he was alone, but I didn't do anything. I simply looked the other way.

'One day I was gardening in the front of my house when Consuela came screaming out of her front door, shouting at me to get an ambulance because Carlo had had an accident. They arrived very quickly, and I caught a brief glimpse of the little boy as they carried him out in their arms. He was just a pathetic bundle of bones, with skin like wax. The ambulance man looked as though he were about to be sick, and afterwards, when I went into the house and saw the state of Carlo's room, I understood why.'

'What happened to his mother?' asked Amy in horror. Mrs Hutton gave a bitter laugh.

'Virtually nothing! She was pregnant again, you see, and said to have been hopelessly under the influence of her boyfriend. He went to prison for two years, but Consuela was put on probation and came back to her old lodgings. The baby was born, a little girl, and after a year Carlo was returned to his "loving" mother.'

'What possible justification could there have been for that?'

'I've no idea. No one seemed to grasp the fact that for Consuela mother-love was an unknown emotion. At first Carlo was all right. He was a beautiful little boy by this time, and for several months he stayed clean, alert and cheerful. Then his mother found a new lover and this time . . .' She stopped

'Yes?' pressed Amy. The older woman shook her head.

'I can't . . . It was too . . . I should have . . .'

'What happened to him?' Amy's voice was urgent, compelling.

'I didn't know about it,' said Mrs Hutton. 'If I had, well then of course . . .'

'WHAT HAPPENED?' Pepé stirred in her arms and she quickly hushed him.

'Consuela took him to the local hospital herself one evening that summer. She left him in the Casualty department and ran off. It was in all the papers, he'd been . . . They'd tortured him, you see. Systematically tortured a three-year-old child simply for the pleasure of watching him suffer. They caught her of course, and this time she did go to prison – but not for long enough. Her lover fled abroad. They never did catch him. If only I'd been braver . . .'

'What about the baby?'

The woman blinked. 'Oh, the baby was fine. Clean, well-fed and cheerful. A little girl, Laura she was called. She was adopted. Most couples want little girls, but it was too late for Carlo. He was so suspicious of adults that he was unable to settle down with any family. I believe he was fostered by numerous people, but I'm afraid I don't know how he got on. Perhaps he's told you that part of his story?'

Amy shook her head. 'No, he never talks about when he was a child.'

'My dear, I'm sorry if I've upset you but I suppose I wanted to see for myself that everything had turned out well for him in the end despite my . . . my weakness, really. And it has, hasn't it? You're a pretty little thing, and now he's got his own family and no doubt the past is all well and truly behind him. How resilient the human mind is, thank God!'

'Yes, he's got his own family now,' agreed Amy; but she wasn't thinking of little Pepé, she was thinking of the children who surrounded him, ghost-children who had shared his experiences and now turned to him for help and comfort. No, the past wasn't behind him. However, she had no intention of telling the flustered woman in front of her any of this. Her burden was already heavy.

'Well, then, I'll be on my way. What's your baby's name?'

'He's called . . .'

'Amy? Whose car is that by the back gate?'

Both women jumped at the sound of Carlo's voice, and then he was in the room with them, his dark eyes sparkling as he flashed his devastating smile at the elderly woman sitting opposite his wife. Amy stood up and kissed him. He put an arm around her waist and waited. No one spoke.

'Aren't you going to introduce me to your friend?' he asked at last. Amy cleared her throat.

'Darling, this is Mrs Hutton. She's . . .'

The smile vanished as though a switch had been thrown. The eyes became darker, harsher, without any vestige of life in them. Amy had never seen his face so cold. A muscle jumped at the tip of his jaw and he took slow, deep breaths as though trying to control his emotions.

'I remember you,' he stated flatly. 'You lived next door when I was small.'

Madge Hutton smiled with relief. 'That's right, and I gave you chocolate biscuits.'

'I'm sure they made my life easier.'

The two women exchanged a brief glance.

'I must leave now,' said Mrs Hutton, rising with some difficulty from the armchair. Carlo watched her struggle but made no attempt to help.

'Why did you come?' he queried.

'I was in the area, I'm staying with some friends on the outskirts of Cheltenham, and I saw the announcement about your little boy in the *Telegraph*, so I decided to look you up.'

'You went to much trouble.'

'I wanted to make sure that you were . . .'

'Happy?'

'Yes, happy! I was so relieved that . . .'

'What a pity you didn't trouble yourself over my welfare when I was small. Surely now is a little late for such concern? Or perhaps you thought that I was still being abused? Imagined that people were burning my feet on the electric fire, or plunging me into cold water?'

His face was dark with fury. His hands clenched and unclenched convulsively as he stood trembling from head to foot. Mrs Hutton was ashen-faced, her voice faltering.

'My dear boy, of course not. I felt guilty, you see, and . . .'

'Guilty! So you should, you stupid, ineffectual old woman! *You* could have saved me. You knew what was happening. You must often have heard me crying. I tried also to tell you, but you were always too busy to let me finish, too impatient with my stumbling efforts at communication. You let it happen, and today, when you finally think it's safe, you come sneaking into my home purely to ease your own conscience. I despise you. Now get out of my house before I throw you out.'

Madge Hutton wilted beneath such hatred. Murmuring pathetically to herself, she collected her coat and bag then tried to edge her way past the seething Carlo.

'If it's any consolation,' she told him quietly, 'I've scarcely had one unbroken night since I last set eyes on you.'

'It is no consolation!' he spat at her. 'Go now, and don't ever come back.'

Without another word she left, closing the front door quietly behind her. Husband and wife looked at each other. Amy's tension communicated itself to the baby, who began to cry.

'Shut that child up!' Carlo said flatly, and his very lack of vehemence chilled Amy more than any amount of shouting. She cuddled Pepé closer, crooning gently to him, but although he did respond the look of hatred that Carlo cast at the now docile baby made Amy realize she had made matters worse and she left the room.

Once she had gone, her husband sank down on to the settee and buried his head in his hands. His whole life was coming apart with terrifying speed, and there was no one who could help him. He was alone, just as alone as when he had been a small, frightened child.

Only the children understood. His very special children.

Chapter 16

'In three weeks time we'll be gone!' stated Tony Blake with satisfaction. Carol nodded. 'I wish it were sooner. Helen's in a terrible mood these days. She simply will not accept that she has to leave her friends.'

'She'll be all right once she makes new ones. Are you going shopping today?'

'Yes, I wanted to take the car.'

'Suits me. I'm going to give the garden one last tidy up. It isn't too bad, but I don't want the Callows inheriting a wilderness. I'll do some weeding and edge the lawns. Once we move I'm going to employ a gardener.'

'Fine. I expect Helen will want to stay here. She hates shopping on a Saturday.'

'As long as she doesn't get in my way, that's OK.'

'I'm sure she won't,' Carol called as she left to find the car keys. 'She's at Fiona's house for the morning.'

Thirty minutes later Tony was down on his hands and knees, pulling up the weeds from the borders. There had been a light shower of rain during breakfast and they came out easily. He whistled to himself as he worked, deeply satisfied with the forthcoming move.

It wasn't until her shadow fell across his line of vision that he realized his daughter had returned. He looked up in surprise. 'Forgotten something?'

She looked different in the sunlight. Her eyes reflected the rays and glittered strangely. It altered her appearance completely. The cheekbones stood out far more than usual and her face was drained of all colour. He squinted up with narrowed eyes.

'I said, did you forget something?'

'No.'

'Well, if you want your mother you'll have to wait. She's gone shopping.'

'Good.'

'Good?' He frowned and started to stand up, but Helen dropped a hand on his shoulder and accidentally leant too hard. He lost his balance and fell awkwardly on the grass.

'Stay where you are,' commanded a boy's voice. Tony froze as he felt something hard and sharp pressing into the nape of his neck. His ever-ready temper started to flare.

'Stop playing about,' he ordered harshly. 'I'm busy.'

'We're not playing,' the voice responded. 'We've come to kill you.'

Tony wasn't afraid, he was furious. 'I'll give you ten seconds to pack up this stupid game and after that I'll personally clip any child still here round the ear, understand?'

The sharp instrument dug more painfully into his neck.

'Violence,' said another child's voice. 'That's all you understand.'

With a hiss of indrawn breath Tony began to rise. Immediately something hit him hard on the side of his head. He felt the garden tilt crazily and bright lights flashed before his eyes. Now he did begin to feel fear.

'Pack it in, you lot,' he coaxed more quietly. 'Enough is enough.'

'He doesn't believe us!' cried Helen, and she laughed lightly.

'Helen! Will you please take your friends out of here at once.'

'Oh, I can't do that; not until you're dead.'

For the first time ever Tony Blake cursed the isolation of his house, and the tall brick wall he had erected round the garden. He was beginning to remember all the other deaths in the village, and what had been said at Samuel Beckett's funeral.

'Now why would you children want to murder me?' he queried, with a pathetic attempt at jocularity.

There was no answer, but all at once he was surrounded by them. They were children he knew, friends of his daughter, but – like her – they were subtly altered. He blinked to clear his blurred vision, then recognized Joanne and Jody, despite the fact that both of them had shrunk and looked gaunt and tired. The boy called Colin was holding the large garden spade in his hands, and when Tony attempted to stand he lifted it threateningly in the air.

'Look, what's the matter with you lot? Is this some kind of sick joke or something?'

'Yes,' said Colin with a sneer, 'that's right. It's a joke. A very funny joke. We know you like a good laugh. That's why you set light to the refuge, wasn't it? For a laugh?'

'Set light to . . . You're talking nonsense!' He was blustering now, his face turning red. 'Don't you know there's a law against saying things like that, it's called the law of slander.'

'No it isn't,' retorted Jody pertly. 'Not when the statement's true. And it *is* true, isn't it?'

'No, it bloody well isn't, and if you don't . . .'

Something sharp pricked him in the small of his back. He twisted his head and saw Richard Beckett, the surviving twin, holding the garden fork aggressively.

'Don't lie,' commanded Richard, 'you'll only make things worse.'

'We saw you,' continued Fiona Burgess. 'We weren't asleep and we saw you creeping round the side of the house.'

'You couldn't have done, your house is nowhere near where that damned refuge stood.'

'We did,' repeated Fiona in a high, sing-song voice. 'We all saw you, didn't we?'

'YES!' they chorused, and then they closed in further.

'You're all mad!' he cried. 'What's it got to do with any of you? None of you was hurt. They were nothing, riff-raff, slum children, with no idea of right and wrong.'

'So you killed them?' queried Colin politely.

'NO! I . . .'

The fork pressed harder against his skin and trickles of blood edged their way down his back. The pain startled him into telling the truth.

'All right, YES! I killed them, but I didn't mean to. I only wanted to show everyone in authority how over-crowded it was there. I wanted them moved out of my village, that was all. I didn't think . . .'

'Precisely! Your kind never do,' said Helen with contempt.

'My kind? I'm your father! I . . .'

She merely laughed. He looked up at her and gave a scream of horror as he stared into a face horribly scorched and charred, with wisps of blackened hair hanging like string around her disfigured face.

Petrified he glanced around him, and everywhere he looked it was the same. Twisted limbs deformed by heat; gaping mouths trying desperately to find air, but instead sucking in searing smoke that scalded and burnt their throats. They were hideous in their terror.

Then their crying began. Thin wails of pain and fear beyond the point of sanity. Shivering, he had to listen to their choking, despairing cries and their pleas for help that he knew only too well had gone unanswered.

With a groan he opened his eyes again, willing the nightmare to have passed. Now only Colin stood close. He was the same as usual, there were no marks of fire on Colin, for some reason Colin was not involved, yet his features were full of hatred and malice, and there was no doubt that he suffered for the other children as surely as if he were one of them.

'I didn't mean it to be like that,' whispered Tony.

Colin shrugged. 'You didn't seem devastated afterwards. We all watched you, waited for a sign that you felt some remorse, but it never came. Why not? Because they were lower class? Was that the reason?'

'No, of course not. It was because . . .' But that had been the reason. He knew it, the children knew it, and now they were here to kill him. He began to whimper himself, pleading for his life just as the children had pleaded. There had been no one to help them, and no one would help him. Justice would be served, the children's idea of justice, and Tony Blake understood the futility of his pleas even as he uttered them.

As though watching a film in slow motion he saw Colin lift the sharp metal spade high in the air, and his eyes widened in a brief moment of horror before the sharp cutting edge severed his spinal cord.

They waited a few seconds, surveying their handiwork, then – without a word – they trooped towards the side entrance and began to make their way out of the back gate. Just as they did so, Amy passed in front of the house pushing Pepé in his pram and she turned, smiling, to give them a wave.

The children stood quite still, faces frozen in shock, and gradually the smile died away from her face as she noticed the flecks of red on Colin's clothes, and the bloody spade clutched in his hands.

'What in God's name have you done?' she whispered. No one answered her, and slowly, almost against her will, she turned the pram and began to wheel it up the path towards them.

At the tall, wrought-iron gate leading to the side entrance of the Blakes' house, Amy's progress was halted by Colin, Joanne and Jody.

'Don't go in there,' said Colin quickly. 'There's been a . . .'

'A what? An accident? Is someone hurt? Has one of you been injured?'

Joanne trembled slightly. 'We're all fine, Mrs Rivero. It's Mr Blake, he's . . .'

'What? Let me see for myself,' and she tried to push the children aside.

'You won't like it,' Colin cautioned her. 'He's dead.'

'Dead?'

'Yep,' confirmed Helen coolly, 'quite dead.'

It couldn't be true, Amy reasoned frantically. Helen would never speak so calmly about it if it were. They were all playing some kind of a game. But there was the blood, and the spade. Something had happened.

'Move out of my way,' she said more firmly. 'I want to see for myself.' The children glanced at each other. Suddenly the three who had been blocking Amy's path scattered, running away from the house at top speed and all taking different routes. For a moment the others hesitated, then they too dispersed swiftly and silently, leaving Amy alone with only Pepé for company.

The gate creaked slightly as she pushed on it. She jumped in fright, then laughed at herself for allowing the children to unnerve her. At first sight the garden looked peaceful and deserted. Then, out of the corner of her eye, she glimpsed a figure lying on the grass at the far end of the lawn.

Her heart was hammering violently but she pulled the pram inside the gate, left it by the side of the house and walked purposefully towards whoever it was who lay so still beneath the warm June sun. As she got nearer she recognized Tony's green linen slacks and black sweater, but she didn't remember it having a red polo neck before, it seemed a peculiar design for a man.

Finally she stood looking down on him, and at first she didn't realize what was wrong. Certainly he shouldn't have been lying so crumpled and still, and the dye from the red polo neck had started to run causing small spots of colour to stain the grass beneath him. How unusual, she thought, wondering if Carol would be able to get it exchanged.

Her mind continued to dwell upon ridiculous thoughts because it was incapable of assimilating the full horror of what lay before her. For several more minutes she continued to look at the sweater until, almost as an afterthought, she wondered why she couldn't see Tony's face. He was lying on his back so she should have seen it, but she hadn't.

She gave a small giggle. 'Tony, where are you? Come on, stop playing games! Where's your face?'

The silence irritated her.

'Tony, don't be childish, let me see your face!'

Still the silence, followed by the appearance of a small sparrow that hopped on to the flower border and then stopped short at the sight of the round object in its path.

Amy smiled at the bird. 'What have you found?' she queried. Startled, it flew away. She wandered to the edge of the lawn and looked for herself. The shock and terror that hit her when she found herself staring down into Tony Blake's sightless eyes jolted her wandering mind back to unwelcome sanity, and at last she began to scream.

She screamed at the top of her voice. High, shrill and almost sub-human, the sound reached the ears of Inspector Barbor as he stepped from the police car which had sped to the house following an anonymous telephone call. He ran to the back gate and down the path, followed by his Sergeant and two police constables. All three of them stopped short at the sight of Amy, still screaming and standing over something that looked horribly like a severed head.

'Mrs Rivero!' the Inspector said softly. 'Come away. Leave it where it is.'

Amy turned to him in bewilderment. 'But it's Tony's. It belongs over there.' She nodded towards the corpse crumpled on the grass, and as one of the constables began to sway on his feet it was left to Barbor and the other constable to catch Amy, who staggered briefly before collapsing into unconsciousness.

'Call an ambulance at once, she's in deep shock,' commanded the Inspector. 'You, Constable, pull yourself together. We've got a hell of a lot of work to do.'

Eventually Amy was safe in hospital, Carlo had been contacted, and it only remained for the forensic men to start their work while the Inspector waited for Carol Blake to return so that he could break the news to her.

He dreaded that. He also dreaded facing the indisputable fact that somewhere in the village there lived a homicidal maniac who killed at random for the sheer pleasure of the act. Madmen were always the most difficult to catch, and since he – or she – lived here then they were certainly someone Barbor knew, and possibly even liked. He was furious with himself for allowing yet another murder, and vowed that from now on he wouldn't rest until the killer had been caught.

The very first thing he intended to do was find out exactly where Carlo Rivero had been that morning, because he had a feeling about the friendly Spaniard, a sense that he wasn't quite what he seemed, and from now on he would follow his instinct, since if this murder was anything like the others that would be all he had to go on.

'Mrs Blake's here, sir,' called the still pale constable. Barbor braced himself for what lay ahead. He was beginning to wish he'd never heard of Lower Ditton.

Chapter 17

To the Inspector's annoyance Amy Rivero was so deeply in shock that the specialist at the hospital flatly refused to allow her to be questioned.

'Not for at least another twenty-four hours,' he stated, 'and even then I'm not promising you anything.'

'But she was the first one on the scene. It's vital that we talk to her. You can be present, stop us if she starts getting distressed. Surely you want this madman caught?'

The doctor was annoyed. 'Yes, I do. However, my primary concern is for the patient, and by the time you've "distressed her", as you so delicately put it, the damage will have been done. She is not to be questioned and that's final.'

Sebastian Barbor knew when to accept defeat. He shrugged helplessly, left a policewoman at the bedside – for protection purposes, he told the doctor – and returned to the police station.

The desk sergeant looked as though he had some good news, but Barbor couldn't imagine what it was. 'Yes?' he snapped.

'It appears that Mrs Rivero wasn't the first witness on the scene after the murder, sir.'

'She wasn't?'

'No.'

'You mean we've got our anonymous caller here?'

'Yes, sir. It was one of the children.'

The children. Always the children. Inspector Barbor gave a slight shudder.

'What children?'

'Colin Masters and his friends. They found the corpse. Mrs Rivero arrived later.'

'In that case I must talk to them at once.'

'They're in the interview room, sir.'

'Sergeant?'

'Yes, sir?'

'How many children?' Even as he asked the question he had the terrible suspicion that he knew the answer. He remembered the report of the fire, the number of children who had lost their lives in it.

'Ten, sir.'

'Oh, God,' he muttered, 'let me be wrong.'

'Sir?'

'Ten, you said?'

'That's right, sir.'

'Including the boy called Colin?'

'Yes, sir.'

It was always the same, nine plus Colin; almost as though Colin were the catalyst.

'I'll go straight in.'

In the interview room the children were sitting upright on the hard-backed chairs. They showed none of the nerves that most witnesses displayed. They were a composed, alert little group with bright, brilliant faces and pleasant smiles but they terrified him.

By the door a policewoman rose from her seat, notebook in hand.

'Have they had a drink?' he asked her, despising himself for trying to postpone the moment of questioning.

'Yes, sir. They've all had squash and biscuits.'

'Fine. Right, let's get started, shall we? Who is going to speak first?'

They all looked towards Colin and Barbor decided to

try and confuse them. He glanced at Helen Blake; red-eyed, it was true, but still incredibly composed.

'Helen, do you think you're well enough to answer a few questions?'

She swallowed hard and bit at her bottom lip. 'Yes,' she whispered, before lowering her head. The Inspector knew that he'd probably gone down in the policewoman's estimation, but he had watched the child's eyes carefully and the only thing he had seen had been a spark of contempt before her gaze was averted.

'Good. Now, take your time and tell me in your own words exactly what happened.'

As she hesitated, apparently assembling her thoughts, he looked across the room at Colin hoping to see some annoyance or malice in the boy's face but the lad smiled helpfully back at him. He was the epitome of a well-brought up boy who wants to help the police in any way he can.

'Well,' began Helen, 'it was like this.' The Inspector noticed how all the children were watching the young girl intently. He suddenly held up his hand. 'I've had an idea: why don't you come into my office, Helen? The others can wait here with Policewoman Dawson. That way each one of you will tell your story exactly as *you* remember it, not as you've heard it told by your friends.'

'That sounds very sensible,' said Colin cheerfully. 'I'm surprised you didn't think of it straight away. They always separate witnesses on the television!'

The children laughed, but Barbor didn't. He was furious. The boy was right, but because of their ages and the trauma of what they had all endured over the past months he had been willing to let them take courage from each other. Not any more. In his mind they were now ten hostile witnesses, and that was how they would be treated.

Oh, he would be polite and pleasant, but mentally he had them marked as hostile. He would be on his guard.

'What a clever lad you are!' he laughed, and Colin actually blushed as though overcome by the compliment. Barbor had put up with enough. He held out a hand to Helen Blake and led her from the room, leaving the children alone with the policewoman who would take down anything they said to each other while they waited their turn.

The little girl was completely dwarfed by the large leather chair opposite the Inspector's but she didn't seem to mind and aimlessly swung her thin legs in front of her while she waited to begin.

'Right, let's hear all about it, young lady,' he urged.

Helen gave a flicker of a smile. 'That's what my daddy calls – sorry called – me.'

'What?'

'Young lady, but he said it in a cross voice whenever he thought I was getting too full of myself!'

'I see. Did you get on well with your father?'

Her face crumpled. 'Yes, but now I won't ever see him again.' The constable by the window cleared his throat.

'Sorry,' the Inspector apologized abruptly. 'Please, tell me about this morning.'

'I went to Fiona Burgess's house to play. Mummy was going shopping and Daddy had to tidy the garden. I wasn't going to go home until lunch-time because Daddy doesn't – didn't – like children around when he was working.'

'I see.'

'Yes, but then we joined up with the others and decided to play rounders so I had to go home for my rounders bat and trainers. I'm not allowed to get my sandals scuffed. They're rather expensive, you know.'

'Isn't Sophie a trifle young for rounders?'

'She wasn't going to play, but we always keep her with us.'

'Why?'

Helen frowned. 'Because she's a member.'

'A member of what?'

'Our gang!'

'Yes and how was this gang formed?'

'I don't know what you mean.'

'I mean, who decided which children should belong and which shouldn't?'

She shrugged. 'No one; we just found out who fitted in. It's like grown-ups deciding what people they want to have as friends. I mean, you don't know why you like some people and not others, do you?'

'I suppose not.'

'It's the same for us.'

She looked pleased with herself, and Inspector Barbor was forced to abandon the subject.

'Go on. What happened when you got home?'

'Well, the front door wasn't open so we went round the back.'

'All of you?'

'I'm not sure, perhaps not Georgina and Sophie at first.'

'I see.'

'And then I saw Daddy lying on the grass. I thought he must be ill and so I ran up to him calling out, but he didn't answer me.'

'And then?'

Helen kept her head lowered and her face was concealed by a curtain of hair.

'When I got right up to him I saw that . . . he didn't have . . .'

'Yes?'

Behind him the constable caught his breath and immediately Helen stiffened. Her legs went rigid and she began to scream.

'*I don't want to talk about it!* I don't want to think of it! I want my Mummy! I want Mummy!'

Barbor cursed the young man. If he had kept silent the girl would have talked on, he was certain of that. She had forgotten her role of bereaved daughter and would have continued without undue emotion, but the constable had ruined it.

'All right,' he said irritably, 'I'll get a car to take you home.'

Still sobbing profusely, Helen was helped away.

The Inspector rounded on his subordinate. 'You bloody fool! Don't you ever make a noise like that again, whatever you may think of my line of questioning. Is that clear?'

'But, sir, I . . .'

'Is that clear?'

'Yes, sir.'

'I'll see Fiona Burgess next.'

Fiona was quieter than usual when she came into the room, but since she had undoubtedly passed the sobbing Helen Blake this would have reminded her of how to behave, reasoned Barbor.

'Right, Fiona, tell me about this morning.'

Her story tallied exactly with Helen's right up to the moment they went into the garden, but at this point she said that her sisters *were* still with the group.

'Helen had been calling her father and when she got to him she suddenly saw that . . .'

'Yes?'

'He didn't have a head.'

'Did you realize that as well?'

'Not really; not until I saw it in the flower border, then I realized it couldn't be on his neck as well.'

'You what!'

She looked at him with surprise. 'I realized it couldn't be on his neck as well. People only have one head, don't they? If you see it lying on its own somewhere then obviously it's been cut off.'

Barbor swallowed hard, feeling his stomach turn at her lack of emotion.

'How did you feel when you saw it lying there in the border?'

'Surprised! After all, it isn't exactly what you'd expect, is it?'

Now she was being pert, which suggested over-confidence.He smiled gently.

'No, it isn't. Did you like Mr Blake?'

'Not much. He didn't like children and was always trying to spoil Helen's fun. He was a bit of a pain.'

'So you weren't sorry to find him dead?'

'He's not *my* father.'

'Quite. Did you notice anything else in the garden?'

'Yes.'

'What?'

'The rest of him.'

The Inspector couldn't keep the disgust from his face. 'Don't try to be amusing, Fiona.'

She glared. 'I'm telling you the truth. That's what I saw.'

'I see. Apart from the other children, did you see anyone else?'

'Nope.'

'No weapon that the murderer might have used?'

'Oh yes.'

'Yes?'

'Sure, the garden spade. It was lying on the grass covered with bits of skin and things. Ugh!' And she shivered daintily.

'Where is it now?'

'What?'

'The spade!'

'Back in the shed.'

'Who moved it?'

'Jody did. It was upsetting Helen so Jody washed it under the garden tap and put it away again. There was a fork there, too, that had blood on it.'

'And Jody cleaned that?'

'No, Richard did.'

'WHY?' he shouted. 'You're intelligent children, why on earth destroy valuable clues?'

'Clues?' She looked blank.

'There might have been fingerprints on the handles; traces of fibre from the killer's clothes.'

'Oh!' She was round-eyed now, both innocent and apologetic.

'You mean you didn't think of that?'

'I'm not allowed to watch that sort of thing on television.'

'I see,' he said with heavy irony.

'Colin does though,' she volunteered.

'But he didn't stop you?'

'He didn't realize what we'd done at first, but when he found out he really yelled at us all. He watches more TV than the rest of us.'

And he's a clever little sod, thought Barbor as he signalled for Fiona to go. He would carry on with the questioning, but already he knew that it was hopeless. He would get nothing from the children.

* * *

'You may talk to her but for ten minutes only,' stressed the doctor twenty-four hours later.

Inspector Barbor nodded curtly as he pushed his way through the curtains that were drawn round Amy's bed. Her eyes looked enormous in her pinched face, and her long chestnut hair was spread out over the pillow, making her appear more like another child than a married woman with a baby son.

'How are you feeling, Mrs Rivero?!

'Not too bad, thank you.'

'I only want to ask you a very few questions.'

She nodded, her eyes panic-sticken.

'What made you go into the Blake's back garden?'

'I . . . Tony had promised me some cuttings from his heather before he left. He often gardened on Saturday mornings and I decided to find out if I could have them for that afternoon.'

'Did you see any of the children?'

'Children?'

'Colin and his friends: did you see any of them?'

'No, why? Did they see me?'

'No, but they had already found the body and run off to ring the police station.'

'Oh, God! The poor children. Are they all right?'

'They're fine.' Much better than you, he thought silently to himself. 'Did you see anything that could have been used as a murder weapon in the garden?' he continued.

'No! Once I found the . . . once I realized what had happened I just . . . I went to pieces. I don't suppose I'd have noticed even if the murderer had still been there. I'm sorry, I . . . It's horrible!' she finished, and began to cry, tears streaming from her eyes as she tried to muffle her sobs with the back of her left hand.

'That's enough!' said the doctor's voice from behind the Inspector. 'I said I didn't want her upset.'

'Yes, I'm sorry. How much longer will Mrs Rivero be in here?'

Amy lifted her head from the pillow. The doctor smiled encouragingly at her.

'Not much longer. The sooner she's home with her family the better.'

'Naturally.'

Just before he stepped through the curtains the Inspector turned to smile at Amy Rivero, and the look of fear in her eyes made his heart quicken in sympathy. She didn't even notice his quiet goodbye, she was staring past him, into some area of horror beyond his comprehension.

He was quiet all the way back to the police station. It was interesting to find that Amy Rivero, far from being delighted at the thought of returning home to her family, was almost frightened out of her senses.

The standard procedures for a murder enquiry were already under way: house to house checks, a twenty-four hour a day incident room, stringent investigations into the victim's background, but even as his men carried out their tasks Barbor knew in his heart that nothing would come of it. No, the answer to all the horror that was engulfing Lower Ditton was to be found in the children. He knew it, and he was convinced that Amy Rivero knew it. What he didn't know was in what way they were involved, and whether Carlo Rivero was behind everything.

He could be patient. From now on he would watch and wait. Sooner or later something would show itself. Something tangible. And when it did, he would be there.

'She's still very unwell,' the doctor cautioned Carlo when he arrived at the hospital to take Amy home.

'I understand.'

'But we feel that in familiar surroundings, where she can relax, she'll recover more quickly. However, she must avoid all stress.'

'Naturally.'

The husband seemed an intelligent and caring type, the doctor thought, more sensitive than a lot of men. He was certain he had made the right decision.

Amy remained silent all the way home. Once or twice Carlo would make some comment about the children or the house, but she failed to respond. She was lost in a world of her own.

It was the baby who forced her back to reality. He needed her so badly. Carlo had done his best, but the nappy hung loose round Pepé's ankles and he was in urgent need of a bath. Slowly, immersed in routine baby care, she began to unwind.

Colin and Joanne spent the day with the Burgess girls. They didn't return until supper-time, and by then Amy had herself sufficiently under control to hug and kiss them and see them settled in their rooms for the night.

Finally, when all the children were asleep, she turned to her husband. He was making a model ship on a small table by the window, apparently deeply immersed in the work, but as soon as she spoke his name he crossed the room to her, as if he had been waiting for the summons.

'Carlo, about Tony Blake's murder . . .'

He put out a hand and softly smoothed her hair. 'Don't think about it. Put it out of your mind.'

'No, I can't. Carlo, the children did it.'

He frowned. 'Which children?'

'All of them.'

'All?'

'Yes, all of Colin's friends.'

'You're talking nonsense.'

'I am not. I saw them coming out of the garden. They had blood on their clothes and were carrying gardening tools which were also covered with blood. They did it, Carlo.'

He smiled sweetly. 'Amy, you've over-tired yourself running about after Pepé. Go and lie down for a while.'

'Don't patronize me!' she snapped. 'You know perfectly well what I'm trying to say. Tony Blake was murdered by the children of this village when they weren't themselves. They were possessed, they had no choice, I know that, but it doesn't alter the horrible truth, which is that they're murderers. Furthermore, this obviously isn't the first time they've killed, and we've got to stop them.'

He rubbed at his temples as though trying to ease some tension. 'Possessed? By what?'

'By whom, you mean. By those horrible children from the refuge, of course.'

'They weren't horrible children, Amy. They'd suffered all their lives. They were pitiful, not horrible.'

'Perhaps that was true when they lived, but it certainly isn't true any more. They're evil and malicious and they've got to be destroyed.'

Carlo shrugged and pulled a semi-humorous grimace. 'I think you've been reading the wrong kind of books!'

Amy was furious, and her temper drove away the last of her fear.

'Stop it! We both know what I'm talking about so don't try and pretend otherwise. I've protected them from the police, lying about what I saw and why I was there, but I'm not going to pretend to you as well. These spirits, ghosts, whatever they are – they listen to you, and for everyone's sake you've got to put an end to the killing. If you don't . . .'

'Yes?' He was still smiling, but there was no warmth behind his eyes.

'Then I'll tell the police the truth.'

'And they'll believe you?' He gave a deprecating laugh. 'Somehow I rather doubt that.'

'Inspector Barbor will. He's already got his suspicions.'

'Has he said so?'

'No, but . . .'

'Huh!' He dismissed her words with a contemptuous gesture of his hand and went to stare out of their front window on to the high street.

'Carlo, why Tony Blake?'

He didn't turn round. 'Ask the children,' he said coldly. As he spoke Colin and Joanne came quietly into the room, and Amy knew by their faces that they had been listening outside the door.

'Why Tony Blake?' she repeated.

'He set fire to the refuge,' said Joanne.

'No! I can't believe . . .'

'Why not?' queried Carlo, but still without turning to face her. 'You believe in the children's guilt quickly enough, why not his?'

'Because no normal adult would . . .'

'But they would,' her husband responded. 'Normal adults will do terrible things to children without thinking twice. They will inflict pain, cold and hunger on them and yes, they'll even let them burn to death, because they know they're bigger and more powerful and the law won't touch them for it since the law is upheld by adults as well. Isn't that so?'

And now he did turn to face her, but he didn't look the same. He looked far younger, yet at the same time older. His eyes were old; wary and hunted, eyes that had seen too much so that the soul behind them had been sickened and twisted by the experiences. His voice was lighter, too. He sounded like a young boy, younger even than Colin. The last of the sun's light shone through the window on to him, reflecting the red glow from within his pupils. Amy was afraid.

'He's right,' said Colin, and she turned to look at the boy.

'Right?'

'About the law.'

'What do you know about the law protecting children? You've never suffered, never been abused.' She stared into his face but, unlike Carlo's and Joanne's, it wasn't changing. 'Why you?' she asked in bewilderment.

'My parents were never married. My father left when I was two,' recited Colin without expression. 'My "uncle" didn't like having me around. He broke my arms. He bit a piece off one of my ear lobes. He tied me up like a chicken and left me for four days. He even tried to drown me but my mother stopped him. I lived with him for nearly a year before I was taken away and finally put up for adoption. Don't ask me what I know about the law. I know from experience that it's totally corrupt and biased in favour of the powerful. Adults have abused it for years, now it's the turn of the children.'

She shook her head. 'I didn't know.'

'How could you have done?' said Carlo. 'We kept it a secret. I'm the only adult Colin's ever told. It was safer that way.'

'Safer?'

'Yes. It means that people will always say, "But why Colin?" should he come under suspicion; and there is no reason, no reason at all that they will ever know the truth.'

'You killed your adoptive parents, didn't you?' whispered Amy. 'You began all this yourself by killing them.'

The boy nodded, smiling pleasantly. 'They were beginning to argue a lot, always shouting and banging doors. I didn't want that again, so I killed them.'

'And Kate? What happened to Kate? She wouldn't ever have hurt a child. She loved children.'

'She loved Thomas best,' whined Joanne. 'Just because he was a boy. She stopped loving the girls once he came along, so they decided to get rid of her.'

'NO!' shouted Amy. 'That's wrong. Don't you see, you're all so eaten up with jealousy, hatred and fear that you twist everything, even ordinary healthy emotions, and turn them into imaginary threats to yourselves? You distort things all the time.'

'We don't,' said Colin. 'I can see why it looks that way to you, but you're wrong.'

'And Samuel? Why did Samuel have to die?'

'Because he was going to tell. He stayed Samuel, you see. No one enjoyed killing him, but we had to protect ourselves.'

Amy felt so cold that she wondered whether she would ever be warm again. Her teeth were chattering, her fingers numb and swollen. It was an unnatural cold, and as more children came slowly into the room she knew that they were bringing the chill with them, just as they had in church after Samuel died.

They were all there now, the children from the past. These pathetic, abused refugees from London, who had come to Lower Ditton to find peace, and instead discovered only more hate and finally death.

She wrapped her arms around her body, trying to force some warmth into her bones but it was useless. Upstairs Pepé started to cry, and immediately ten pairs of eyes swivelled up towards the ceiling, assessing the sound and pondering on what action to take.

'Leave him alone!' screamed Amy. 'He's innocent; he hasn't done anything to you. Let him alone.'

They shrugged and nodded, murmuring amongst themselves. Their voices were thin and reed-like, their bodies transparent and fluid. She prayed that Pepé would keep quiet.

'But he has,' piped up a light, hesitant voice with the faintest suggestion of a stammer. 'He's stopped you loving me.'

It was Carlo. He was standing in the middle of the massed children with his arms crossed over his chest and a look of pained bewilderment on his handsome face. 'Why?' he asked plaintively. 'Why is the baby good and Carlo bad?'

Amy remembered Madge Hutton speaking of a baby sister who had been cherished even while little Carlo was being abused. 'Carlo is good too,' she said, trying to stop her voice from shaking. 'Carlo is very good.'

For a moment he considered her remark, but then he pouted and shook his head. 'No! Baby bad. Kill baby,' he added casually.

The children huddled closer to him, then they all moved purposefully towards the hall and Amy heard their footsteps on the stairs.

'DON'T! she screamed at them. 'LET HIM ALONE. FOR GOD'S SAKE, DON'T HURT MY BABY!'

They ignored her; it was doubtful if they even heard. Frantic with terror she stumbled after them, but she was so cold that every movement was agony and took far longer than usual. By the time she reached the top of the stairs Pepé's cries had stopped. She burst into the nursery and saw them all gathered round the cot. They looked at her in gloating triumph as she pushed them aside and lifted her beautiful child in her arms.

He was still warm, and soft to hold. He looked peaceful and content and at first she thought she was in time, but then she saw the thin trickle of vomit from the corner of his mouth and realized that he wasn't breathing. Swiftly she lowered the side of the cot and placed Pepé back on his mattress, then she put her mouth over his minute nose and mouth and began to blow.

It was Carlo who stopped her, Carlo who pulled her away and held her beside him for endless minutes until she knew that it was far too late for anyone to help her son. Then, and only then, as she screamed in despair, did he release her.

She slumped against the cot, realizing that at some point in time the ghostly travesties of children had left, slipping away back to their normal lives with their unsuspecting families, leaving her with Carlo, Colin and Joanne.

'And now,' said Carlo with a beautiful smile, 'we must decide what we're going to do with you.'

Chapter 18

Inspector Barbor shuffled the report sheets together and placed them in an already over-full clip file. Rubbing his eyes he glanced across at the Sergeant.

'You've got children, haven't you, Ian?'

'Two, sir.'

'Then think about this. If they went into a friend's garden and found a decapitated corpse, what do you think they'd do?'

'Hard to say, sir. They're only three and eighteen months.'

The Inspector felt like screaming at his subordinate, but with a superhuman effort maintained his self-control. 'Then let me put it another way. Do you have any nieces or nephews aged between, let's say, four and ten?'

'Twin nephews – they're nine.'

'Right. Picture if you can a warm summer day. Your two nephews wander round to a neighbour to collect a friend and stumble across the headless body of the friend's father lying in the back garden. Now, what would they do?'

The Sergeant chewed thoughtfully on the end of his pencil. He wasn't a highly imaginative man and it took him some time to visualize the scene. 'Run screaming home for their mother,' he announced at last.

'Quite! But what do the children of this village do? Including, I would remind you, the daughter of the dead man. They walk quietly home, without attracting any attention to themselves, and one of their number makes an anonymous call to the station reporting what they've seen. How about that for keeping their cool?'

'Put like that it does seem odd.'

'Odd! It's absolutely unbelievable, Sergeant! Nevertheless, that's what they did. I'm not happy about the children. They bother me.'

'You're not suggesting they killed Tony Blake?'

'Don't be bloody stupid! No, I don't think they crept up behind him, whacked him over the head and then proceeded to sever his spinal cord just for fun – they're not that odd! All I'm saying is their behaviour isn't normal. In my opinion they're covering up for someone.'

'Who's that?'

'Work it out for yourself. Who is there that the children of this village would do anything for? Who is the one person they follow as though he were a modern Pied Piper?'

'Carlo Rivero.'

'Precisely, and I think it's time I had a little chat with the ever-charming, handsome, self-assured Mr Rivero.'

'I've always thought he seemed a decent kind of bloke. He's never seemed like a . . .'

'Murderer? They don't necessarily go round with a sneer on their lips and a furtive look in their eyes. This is life, not a cheap thriller.'

The Sergeant was annoyed. Inspector Barbor wasn't a local man. He hadn't been there the night Carlo had nearly lost his own life trying to pull children from the burning refuge. His annoyance couldn't be hidden.

'Why should Mr Rivero want to kill Tony Blake?'

'I've no idea.'

'And the other murders? Do you think he's involved with those as well?'

'Possibly.'

'But why? He had no motive for killing any of them, and he certainly didn't kill Sara Gregory, he was in his shop at the time.'

'But the children were around. Remember, they were seen.'

'The boy, Colin, was seen, but so what? You've already said you don't suspect the children of murder, in which case sighting the boy means nothing.'

'I don't know!' shouted the Inspector in frustration. 'I can't work it out, and I do realize that it sounds like rubbish, but all the killings in Lower Ditton over the past year have, at some point, touched the lives of these children.'

'Mostly by leaving them orphaned or in one-parent families. I'd call that sad and unlucky, but hardly suspicious!'

'Yes, I take your point, but I still feel . . . There's something I'm missing, damn it and I can't think what.'

'One of the children died too,' added the Sergeant remorselessly.

'That's another thing – the children were most peculiar at his funeral. They collected in their little group and ignored everyone else; not one of them cried either. It was weird, unnatural. The atmosphere at that crematorium was all wrong.'

The Sergeant stood up. 'I'm off home. If kids can't take comfort from each other any more, and self-control has become a crime, then I don't think I want to be a policeman. I'm sorry, but considering what a terrible time the local children have had recently I think they've behaved incredibly well, and I don't like hearing them criticized. Good night . . . sir.'

'Blast!' muttered Barbor in frustration. He hadn't meant to alienate the man, he'd only wanted to use him as a sounding board for his own ideas. He glanced at the clock. It was late, and his wife would be annoyed again, but somehow he couldn't let things drift any longer. He was going to visit Carlo Rivero on his way home. He'd make it informal, more of a friendly discussion, he might even ask the man if he had any theories about the latest murder. It didn't matter what excuse he used, he wanted to hear him talk, and watch the expressions on his face as he did. Somehow, in some way, he might let slip a vital clue and give the Inspector a lead. He certainly needed one.

While Inspector Barbor was coming to this decision, Amy was attempting to placate her husband and the two children sufficiently for them to let her escape with her life.

After Carlo's matter-of-fact query about her future she had remained quiet, sobbing silently every time she glanced at her dead child but forcing herself not to show her hatred for the rest of her so-called family.

'I think she'll have to die,' said Colin after a long silence. 'She knows too much and she won't keep it to herself, not after that.' And he pointed to the cot.

'It's a pity we killed him,' added Joanne. 'I think Amy would have stayed on our side if we hadn't.'

Carlo chewed on his fingernails. 'I wanted him dead,' he said sulkily. 'He took her away from me. I trusted her and she let me down, all because of him.'

'No!' protested Amy. 'It isn't true, Carlo. I loved you just as much after Pepé was born. Perhaps even a little more, because he was *ours*, yours and mine, and I knew how much you loved children. I was proud to have given you a son of your own.'

He shook his head. 'I loved you, Amy. I thought you

understood. You were kind and pretty, and you were affectionate. We had good times at the beginning, didn't we?'

'Yes, and we will again, we . . .'

'No we won't. You were fantastic in bed, did I ever tell you?' She flushed at the look of interest in the children's eyes.

'Carlo, please!'

'You really were. It meant so much to me. To have someone who wanted me like you did, to be able to show my love and never have it rejected. I was happy then.'

'Why should it have changed? What made you think . . .?'

'You haven't let me near you since that . . . that thing was born.'

'But the doctor explained. I've got an infection. It won't last long. A couple more weeks and . . .'

'No! You're different now. You don't want me to touch you. All you want to do in bed is sleep. I lie there watching you, listening to your breathing, and then the minute the baby cries you're awake. Oh, it's different for the baby. You've got plenty of affection for him. Hugs and kisses, constant endearments. That tiny scrap of humanity took it all away from me, everything I most treasured he took. Just as she did. It was exactly the same then.'

He looked totally lost and betrayed, the pain on his face so stark that Amy automatically reached out to him.

'Carlo, I never stopped loving you. I was tired and yes, I suppose I was off-hand, but I didn't mean it personally. I love you, Carlo, you know that.'

The pain and vulnerability vanished from his features. 'It's too late, Amy. You've rejected me once, you won't have a second chance. Besides, how could you ever want me near you again after that?' And he jerked his head towards the cot.

Amy tried to blank the thought of Pepé from her mind. Her husband mustn't see the desolation that she was feeling or he would know that he was right. After this she would never want him near her again, but until she was out of the house and safe she would keep her grief hidden, show only the genuine love she had once felt for him and the pity that she was truly experiencing for the tortured, neglected child that lay within the handsome, confident exterior Carlo Rivero displayed to the world.

'You've got to die,' Colin told her brusquely. 'I'm sure you know that already. You're very bright.'

'And what of you?' she asked softly. 'How long are you going to carry on like this? Do you intend to spend your life punishing adults for the fact that your own mother ill-treated you? And you, Joanne – or whoever you are at the moment – do you and your friends intend to wipe out the entire village as retribution? If so, what then?'

'Why then,' said Joanne slowly, 'it will be over. We can all rest.'

'Really? For how long? Until some unsuspecting parent gives their child a smack on the bottom or shouts at them to pick up their clothes? Will that trigger it all off again?'

'Oh no!' said Joanne, her large blue eyes shocked and innocent. 'Very soon we will be finished. Once we've dealt with Gillian's mother – she's having an affair with her solicitor, you see – I think that's the end.'

'Christine? You're going to murder Christine?'

'It's her own fault. If she'd remembered her marriage vows and concentrated on creating a happy home she wouldn't be in any danger.'

'But . . .'

'As I was saying, after Mrs Cross it will be finished. We

can all rest then. We won't come back. We don't like coming back. It's lonely and frightening living as we do. We'll be pleased when our job is complete.'

'And you?' pressed Amy, turning again to Colin. 'What about you?'

He stared at her, his jaw set and his eyes cold. She wondered how she had ever considered him lovable.

'I shall do what I think right,' he said defiantly. 'I'm real, I'm not possessed like the others, I can go on having revenge for the rest of my life.'

'But, Colin, it's wrong. You've got to start looking for the good in people. Try to see things from a different perspective.'

'No thanks! Carlo tried that with you, and look what happened to him!'

'*Nothing happened to him!*' she yelled furiously. 'He thinks that it did but he's wrong.'

'Carlo's never wrong,' replied the boy firmly.

'In heaven's name stop looking up to him like you do,' she whispered urgently. 'He's unbalanced, can't you see that? He's insane.'

'She says you're insane!' Colin repeated loudly to Carlo, who had been staring out of the bedroom window. The man's face darkened.

'Thank you, little Amy. At last you're telling the truth. I rather think that settles the matter. It's a great shame, but we're going to have to kill you.'

'NO!' With a desperate lunge she grabbed the door handle and began to turn it but Carlo threw his body against it, slamming it shut and tearing her fingernails in the process.

She had nothing to lose any more. The situation had gone beyond words, so she raked his face with the jagged nails, missing his eyes by a fraction of an inch as he jerked his head away at the last second. He hit her a stinging blow round the ear, but she continued to fight him, kicking out wildly and screaming at the top of her voice.

Dragging herself away from him she reached blindly for the jars of cream and jelly that stood on the shelf by Pepé's changing mat and as her fingers closed round a glass container she hurled it with all her force at her husband.

It struck him squarely on the forehead. He staggered backwards, shaking his head and brushing his hand over his eyes, which were watering profusely. Still screaming, Amy's hand encountered the safety pins and she fumbled frantically with the clips until a few sprung open, piercing her fingers in the process. As Carlo moved towards her she jabbed them at his face and throat. He gave a yell of shock, and then stood still in disbelief as small beads of blood trickled slowly down his shirt front.

He remained quite still, his mind dazed and retreating into the past where pain and blood could only be stopped by silence and his ability to make adults forget his presence. Therefore he didn't move.

Unaware of the reason for his stillness Amy, too, waited, but after a few seconds sensed that for a brief moment she was safe. She looked towards the children. They were hypnotized by Carlo's immobility, feeling his pain and humiliation, suffering with him and moving to his side to offer the love and comfort they knew he needed.

Amy opened the door and sped down the stairs. The hall was small, only a few feet remained between her and the front door. Sobbing with relief she jumped from the last step, and then felt something hard hit her in the stomach, stopping her progress and making her gasp with pain.

All at once the air became stale and oppressive. There was a smell of sweat and suffering that made her gag. She reached for the light switch, but small, bony fingers grabbed her wrist and prevented her. They were all around her, and knowing who they were she shuddered, remembering how grotesque and malevolent they looked. Her refusal to move into their new house had not helped her. The children had moved instead.

They were pinching and poking at her now; pulling at her clothes, twisting her fingers, nipping at her ankles and calves with sharp little teeth. Not one of them spoke, but they filled the air with sounds. Whimpers of excitement, hisses of delight when she cried in pain, grunts of effort as they tried to pull her to the ground. There was no chance of screaming, for whenever she opened her mouth one of the bodies clinging to her clothes would poke fingers or even a tiny hand down into her throat, making her retch violently. Then they would croon their pleasure with mindless chuckles of glee.

They were all spiteful, vicious and obsessed. They had no purpose other than to punish; no object except to inflict pain and degradation. As she sank down beneath their weight, overcome by the futility of trying to injure them when they were already dead, she knew that they would never be satisfied. Even if they destroyed the entire village it wouldn't be enough. They would go on forever. Happy in death as they had never been in life, and drawn eternally to Carlo and Colin's side, they would continue their reign of misguided destruction.

She felt one of them bite the side of her neck and screamed as moist lips sucked voraciously at the wound. 'Help me!' she screamed, but knew that there was no one to hear.

With a superhuman effort she struggled to her feet,

throwing the skeletal bodies to one side and hearing their wails of frustration as they fell to the floor. They missed the physical bodies they usually inhabited and moved clumsily on their own. She sped through the living-room and into the kitchen. Once there she opened the oven door and turned on the gas jets; then, as stealthily as possible, she moved to the foot of the stairs to turn on the gas heater that helped keep the bedrooms warm in winter. Again she didn't ignite the pilot light.

The kitchen was quickly full of gas, the smell sickening. Holding her breath she reached for the box of matches, praying that it would be on the usual shelf.

It was.

She made her way to the side door and slid back the bolt. As she did so there was the sound of footsteps upstairs and she knew that Carlo and the two children would be down any minute. Standing as far from the stove as possible she lit a match, then opened the door a crack before throwing it in the direction of the stove, hurling the box of matches after it.

The blast catapulted her out on to the side path, and immediately flames leapt from the stove and out into the kitchen, catching the tea towel lying on top of the grill and spreading from there with incredible speed out into the hall.

Amy was across the road when the heater in the hall ignited. She heard the boom of the explosion and suddenly the entire house was aflame. She could hear cries. Many cries. Shivering she remained with her eyes fixed on the windows, and at last she saw them. Carlo and the children stood outlined in the top window, looking down at her but making no attempt to escape. Then she realized that there was no point, for the curtains were already blazing and in any case the drop to the pavement would have killed them. Suddenly Colin lunged towards the glass, beating frantically on it, his mouth open in terror as the flames within the room advanced remorselessly towards him. Amy pressed a clenched hand to her mouth as she saw his clothing catch alight and Carlo began to beat frantically at the terrified child's burning body.

At that moment a police car drew up beside her. Inspector Barbor jumped out and saw her crouched by the hedge. He pulled her to her feet.

'Where's your husband?'

She pointed to the upstairs window, but he was no longer in view. Barbor dashed back to the car and called for a fire engine and ambulance before returning to her side. Then he put a rug round her shoulders and propelled her towards the back seat of the car. 'Sit there. Help won't be long.'

'Dear God, let them die!' she prayed earnestly. 'Don't let them escape.' She tried not to think of the pain and the suffering she had inflicted and concentrated all her thoughts on what would happen if they escaped. There was no doubt in her mind that what she had done was right. Carlo and Colin had to die. There was no alternative.

Her prayers were answered. By the time the fire engine arrived it was too late. A silent gathering of villagers watched as the firemen brought out three bodies covered by blankets and one tiny, pathetic bundle. Amy shivered with mingled horror and relief while all around attempts were made to comfort and console her.

She stayed in hospital for forty-eight hours, weeping copiously for little Pepé and the husband she had loved but never really known. No tears were shed for Colin and Joanne. She could still feel the hands and teeth of the children from the refuge as they attacked her like small rodents with their relentless ferocity. Joanne was one of them, and Colin little better. No, she could not weep for the children.

On her final afternoon as a patient, Inspector Barbor came to see her. She had been expecting his visit and waited to hear what he had to say. He was patently uncomfortable in his official role, fidgeting nervously as he uttered the usual conventional phrases of regret.

'You're going back home to your studio, once they discharge you, Mrs Rivero? Is that right?'

She nodded. 'There's nothing left for me here; it seems the sensible solution. Fortunately I never got round to selling it. I kept meaning to but somehow . . .'

'Fortuitous, it would appear!'

'I'd rather have my baby back.'

'Of course. I didn't mean . . .' No mention of the husband, he noticed, but perhaps that pain was too deep even to mention.

'You don't happen to know how the fire started?' he queried with deceptive disinterest.

'I've no idea. I'd gone to the kitchen to fetch a glass of water for Colin. He had a tickly cough and couldn't settle. All at once there was an explosion and I was thrown against the back door. The far end of the room went up at once, I could only get out. There was nothing I could do to save the others.'

'A paraffin heater, was it?'

'We didn't have any. I think it must have been the oven. There had been a slight smell of gas from it, but as we were due to move we didn't take too much notice. Sometimes the pilot light blew out, we always blamed that. Maybe we were wrong.'

'Maybe.'

'Why did the fire engine take so long?'

'There was a bad accident on the main road: five people dead, three critically ill.'

Silently Amy thanked the unknown motorists.

'Mrs Rivero.'

'Yes.?'

'I have to ask you this, it's been on my mind for a long time. Did you ever wonder if your husband was in any way connected with the murder of Tony Blake?'

'My husband?'

'Yes.'

'No, Inspector. I'm quite sure that my husband didn't have anything to do with that. He was . . .'

The Inspector waited.

'A very gentle man,' she continued at last. 'Almost childlike at times. I'm quite sure he wasn't involved.'

'And the children?'

This time he did get a response. Something stirred at the back of her eyes, a flicker of fear, possibly even dislike, it was hard to pin it down, but there was definitely something.

'Which children?' she asked him.

'Colin's crowd.'

'Ah, yes, Colin's crowd. In what way do you mean connected? Helen was Tony's daughter, that's presumably a connection.'

Barbor nodded. He had been right. The children had been involved, and this woman knew it. She knew more than he did, but she would never tell, and presumably with the boy dead it wasn't important any more. Colin had always been their ring-leader.

'It doesn't matter,' he responded slowly. 'We'll go on searching for the killer and if nothing comes up, well, it's just another unsolved crime to add to the somewhat extensive list connected with Lower Ditton.'

'Yes.'

'When I checked my records,' he added, almost as an afterthought, 'I couldn't help noticing that everything started to go wrong here after that terrible fire, when the battered wives' refuge was burnt down.'

Amy looked at him in silence for a moment. 'How well do you know *Macbeth*?' she asked.

'*Macbeth?* Reasonably well. It's one of my favourites.'

'Mine too. I particularly recall one of the early lines.'

He frowned. 'Which one?'

'"Were such things here as we do speak about?"'

Their glances locked. They were two intelligent adults trying to come to terms with something beyond the normal scope of human experience and reluctant to commit themselves to any statement of fact, yet they each knew at least some part of the truth.

'Perhaps it will all go right after this second fire,' she added.

'Is that what you think?'

'Yes.'

He gave her the briefest of smiles. 'I hope you're right.'

'I am. Believe me, I am.'

'But we won't ever catch ourselves a murderer?'

'No, Inspector, I don't think you will.'

'Then I'll say goodbye, Mrs Rivero. I wish you well for the future.'

She rested one small hand in his. 'Pray for me,' she whispered, her eyes suddenly sad and haunted. He tightened his grip.

'I will,' he said gently, 'and . . . thank you.'

Utterly exhausted by his visit she lay back on her pillows and closed her eyes.

Epilogue

Amy arrived at the Registry Office accompanied by Christopher's brother. The morning was slightly overcast, but sun had been forecast for later on and even rain wouldn't have diminished her happiness.

It was almost exactly two years since Carlo had been burnt to death in Lower Ditton, and they had not been easy years. For months she had found herself remembering her husband as he had been prior to Pepé's birth. She would recall the feel of his hands on her breasts, the texture of his skin beneath her lips and, above all, the way he used to smile. How she missed his smile. It had been so frank and open, so full of joy and pleasure. She would never forget his smile.

Eventually the other memories grew faint. She busied herself in photography, took up badminton, went to pottery classes, anything at all that kept her busy and allowed her to fall exhausted into bed at night. That way she didn't have time to think.

She hadn't anticipated marrying again. Carlo needed to die, she knew that, otherwise the ghost-children's orgy of death would have continued, but whilst not regretting what she had done she felt guilty and, her original overwhelming love for him lingered intrusively.

Friends introduced her to plenty of men, and she went out with most of them at least once, but they always failed to come up to her expectations; expectations that were governed by how she had felt when she first met Carlo. The magical chemistry was never there for anyone else.

Then, six months earlier, she met Christopher at a dinner party. He was tall and slim with straight fair hair and blue eyes which were generally grave but always kind. He was the antithesis of Carlo, comparison was virtually impossible, and this enabled her feelings to progress from friendship to attraction and finally to love. At least, it was a kind of love. Not the stomach-turning, obsessive longing that she had felt for Carlo, but a peaceful, relaxed relationship that was – she assured herself – another kind of love, and possibly more likely to endure.

Surely this time things would go well, she thought as she joined Christopher in the ante-room. She wanted a home and family, and the years were passing. Nothing must jeopardize this union. He took her hand and squeezed it lightly.

'Nervous?'

'A little.'

'Happy?'

'Very.'

'Good. I promise I'll do my best to keep it that way!' She smiled, and then it was time for the ceremony itself.

The registrar looked faintly bored and she was grateful for the flowers that filled the room and for Christopher's numerous relations who compensated for her own solitary state.

'. . . in sickness and in health,' she repeated obediently.

'For as long as we both shall live,' concluded the registrar.

'For as long as we both shall live,' she endorsed, lifting her head to smile at Christopher. He looked down at her with happiness and pride and she smiled slowly back at him.

All at once a cool breeze drifted in through the registry office window. The flowers in front of it stirred briefly.

Amy shivered slightly, her cotton dress seeming suddenly flimsy. Now Christopher was repeating his vows.

'For as long as we both shall live,' he finished firmly.

'With this ring . . .' intoned the registrar.

Amy wished that it was over. She was so cold.

'With this ring . . .' repeated Christopher.

'I thee wed.'

'I thee wed.' It was possible to hear the pride in his voice and Amy blushed, looking up at him from beneath lowered lashes. Immediately she wished that she hadn't. He no longer looked like Christopher at all. His eyes were darker, the irises virtually black, and deep within the pupils a small red light danced fleetingly before vanishing from her gaze.

She blinked and glanced at her husband again. Once again Christopher looked reassuringly normal. His eyes were still blue, his face slender if a trifle over-long. It had been an illusion. An understandable one. A final remembrance of Carlo before she began her new life. Yes, that was what it had been. An illusion.

Just the same she was pleased when it was over and they could walk outside to pose together for the photographs, and Christopher's arm was round her, promising love and protection for the rest of her life.

'A bit chilly out here!' he remarked casually.

'I felt colder inside,' she told him. 'There was a terrible draught from the window.'

'Really? You must have been protecting me, I didn't notice it.'

The reception was at a nearby hotel. Amy and Christopher made sure that they spoke to everyone and thanked them for their gifts. The speeches were brief but good, the food excellent. When it was time to set off for the honeymoon Christopher's mother slipped away after

Amy, following her to the small room where she was changing into a silk two-piece for the journey.

'My dear, I can't tell you how happy you've made me,' she enthused, while Amy brushed her long hair in front of the mirror. 'It's taken Christopher such a long time to settle down; I'd quite given up the hope of any grandchildren.'

'Let's hope I won't disappoint you!' she said gently.

'You could never do that. When I think back and remember how Christopher was two years ago, I can't help but believe in miracles.'

'Miracles? Why? What happened two years ago?'

'Why, hasn't he told you? How strange! He nearly died in a terrible car crash. I was told that the ambulance men thought he was dead when they arrived on the scene, but by the time the surgeon saw him he was regaining consciousness. He was on life-support for weeks. We were warned that even if he lived he'd be a vegetable, but as you know very well he's one hundred per cent fit. Why, if anything he's better than before! More lively somehow. I suppose that a close brush with death has that effect. It's made him appreciate everyday things; the things that most of us take for granted.'

Amy put down the brush and tried to repair her make-up. She was surprised that Christopher hadn't told her, but then she hadn't given him details of Carlo's death. He knew that she was a widow; nothing more had seemed necessary.

'Where did it happen?' she asked casually.

'In the Cotswolds, on the outskirts of some little village called Lower Ditton.'

Amy froze. The blood drained from her face and she went chalky-white.

'How long ago did you say?' she murmured.

'Two years almost to the day. When we went to the hospital to see him they said there had been a fire in the village at the same time, and four people had burnt to death because the engine had been out at the accident. I felt terrible, but grateful as well. It could so easily have been the other way round. Still, these things happen, and we must thank our lucky stars that Christopher was saved. Perhaps you were destined for each other. I'm a great believer in fate myself!'

Destined for each other. The words were like a sentence of death.

She moved automatically through the final part of the celebrations. She kissed people, hugged them, smiled her thanks at their good wishes and waited for the time when she and Christopher were alone.

'You're very quiet, darling,' he remarked after half an hour. 'Feeling all right?'

She licked her lips. 'Fine. Perhaps a little too much champagne!'

'I hope you like our honeymoon hotel. I've checked it out myself. It's got a lot of atmosphere.'

Amy tried to force some interest in the subject. 'I'm sure it will be wonderful. Where is it?'

'In the Cotswolds.'

Yes, she might have expected that.

It was a nice hotel. Low ceilings and genuine wood beams made Christopher stoop all the time, but apart from that it was perfect. Their room was large, the bed a king-size four-poster, and the manager had sent champagne and flowers up to them with the compliments of the staff.

They were already lovers but suddenly Amy felt shy. Christopher had to take her slowly through the initial stages of love-making, but put it down to the tensions of the day. He was a patient man, and after a time she relaxed.

Amy could feel her husband's hands on her, experienced the familiar build-up of tension that was the prelude to a climax, but her mind wasn't there, it was still back at the reception listening to her mother-in-law.

'Darling, I can't wait much longer,' said Christopher gently. She wound her arms round his shoulders and moved slightly to make entry easier for him. He sighed with contentment and quickly found his rhythm. They moved well together, it was always good for them, and she scarcely had to think about what she was doing.

His head was on her neck now, his tongue flicking inside her left ear and she knew by his quickened breathing that he was almost there but she wasn't; she was still some way behind.

Then, unusually for him, he moved, twisting round until his mouth was on her left breast and he sucked hard on it, nibbling lightly at the nipple and tugging insistently at the breast, almost like a child feeding.

The breast felt swollen and began to ache. The ache sent flickers through her entire body and she arched up against him. He was hurting her breast now, but she liked it. He had never been so aggressive. One of his hands tightened on the other breast, squeezing it almost brutally, making her cry out with desire and unbearable tension.

His rhythm changed, no longer familiar and relaxed. He pounded into her, every stroke jerking her body back towards the head of the bed, but the pleasure was there, waiting for her, and when she finally climaxed she gave a scream of ecstasy and relief that made Christopher muffle her mouth with his hand.

Utterly exhausted she lay passively until he had finished

and then closed her eyes, trying to keep the sensations for a little longer, but already they were gone and only the memory was left.

It had never been like that with Christopher before. Only Carlo had taken her to such heights. He had been an expert at knowing how to please. He had studied her reactions so carefully that with him she had always been utterly sated. It was amazing, but if she hadn't known differently she could have sworn that it had been Carlo making love to her on this her wedding day. Even the hands had felt like Carlo's hands; and the mouth, so desperately nuzzling at her breast, that had been Carlo's mouth. That had . . .

'I make it good for you?' queried a voice. Her eyes flew open. The phrasing of the question was so distinctive. She could have wept with relief when she saw Christopher's familiar face looking down at her.

'Yes,' she agreed with a sigh. 'Very good.'

'It was always good with us.'

'I . . .' The face above her was changing. The hair was wavy, the face seemed squarer, and there was dark shadow round the jaw; but most of all it was the eyes that were different. They gleamed blackly at her; soft, compelling, intelligent eyes. It was a face that she had never expected to see again. Shock, fear and – amazingly – a sense of pure relief all coursed through her as she looked into her dead husband's eyes.

'Where's Christopher?' she whispered, reaching out to touch the satiny skin of his cheeks.

'Still here, but he's a marvellous host – very easy to banish when necessary.'

'You made him live again, didn't you? After the crash.'

'That is so. He died at exactly the right moment. I was free, without a body but not dead. It was a most peculiar experience. All at once I found myself above him and willed myself into his body. It was a risk, but one I willingly took for it was my only chance of remaining near you. Perhaps it happens often; it would be an explanation for the "changes in character" that occur after close encounters with death. It is interesting, yes?'

'How did you find me?' she asked, for she had no interest in theories at that moment.

'It was easy. The villagers used to come visiting me – or rather Christopher – and eventually they recounted the tragic tale of your terrible loss. They told me – us – that you had gone back home to Leicester. I waited a long time to approach you, but that did not matter. Time is meaningless to me now.'

She was terribly cold. He had brought the chill with him and she shivered. Reaching out he cupped her chin in his hand.

'How could you kill me, little Amy?'

'I had to, because of the children. They were always going to be drawn back to you for as long as you lived.'

'Is that the only reason?'

'Yes.'

'Well, the children are gone now. There is only me.'

'What about Colin?'

His expression was anguished. 'I cannot find him; perhaps he is truly dead.'

The face was beginning to blur. The eyes were fading back to blue, the skin texture altering.

'What do you want?' she asked.

'You, of course!'

'Me?'

'I've come back for my wife.'

'I'm married to Christopher.'

'Only until death you do part!' And he laughed softly.

'You mean . . .?'

'It won't be long,' he promised her. 'We will soon be together, as before. I have missed you so much. Death will set you free, Amy. You love me still, I know you do. It will not be long, I promise. Soon, little Amy, very soon . . .'

'NO!' she screamed, jumping from the bed in terror. 'No! I don't want to die. I want to live. I want a home and children. *Leave me alone!*'

Christopher rubbed at his eyes and sat up. He felt strangely light-headed, and was amazed to discover his wife cowering by the window, screaming that she didn't want to die. Quickly he crossed the room and wrapped her in his arms, trying to warm her icy body with his own.

'What's the matter? Don't cry, Amy, it was only a dream. Come back to bed. That's better. Let me warm you up. I must have taken all the covers. God, you're going to catch pneumonia if you're not careful.'

She lay beside him, shivering with shock and fear.

'Want to tell me about it?'

She studied his face intently. He looked perfectly normal. He was acting normally. Perhaps he was right. She could have dozed off and had a nightmare. Probably it was because her mother-in-law had mentioned Lower Ditton. She had brought back the memories with her talk of the village. Yes, that was the reason. Her breathing began to slow.

'It's all right,' she said at last. 'Sorry! I'm probably over-tired.'

'You musn't worry about anything,' he said gently. 'I'm here now, and I'm going to look after you very, very carefully, little Amy.'

As she watched him he looked down at her and smiled a slow and beautiful smile of incredibly piercing sweetness.

The true nightmare was only just beginning.